THE SINNER

Stuart MacGregor

THE SINNER
by Stuart MacGregor

Pierpoint Press Edinburgh 2021

First published in 1973 by Calder and Boyars Limited

ISBN 9781914090103
Set in Garamond No 8
Digital scan and prepartion by Lesley Storm

Pierpoint Press is an imprint of
Leamington Books
32 Leamington Terrace
Edinburgh

The author Stuart MacGregor previously acknowledged with gratitude the assistance given to him personally by the Scottish Arts Council during the writing of this book.

The publisher wishes to acknowledege the support and assistance offered by the author's literary executor, John Herdman. We would also like to express our gratitude for the continuing kindness and encouragement offered by Jane and Andrew MacGregor, Richie McCaffery, Craig Gibson, Gordon Wright and Lesley Storm.

A version of the essay "The Sinner by Stuart MacGregor" by Richie McCaffery previously appeared in *Bella Caledonia*.

A Word to the Wise

The character of The Sinner is destructive and self-destructive in rapid turns. At war with brutal impulses of an id that has never forgotten a single instance of abuse, Denis Sellars was a character who shocked with his mysogyny, even in 1973. In this novel the worst excesses of this young man's journey are its darkest parts; and the book contains several suicide attempts, racial slurs and scenes of domestic abuse.

The Sinner by Stuart MacGregor

An introduction by Richie McCaffery

Stuart MacGregor (1935-1973) was a Scottish novelist, poet, occasional playwright and songwriter who worked as a medical doctor and a lecturer in social and preventative medicine. As John Herdman, his literary executor, notes, MacGregor's heart was never entirely in his day-job and much of his energy was expended on his literary and musical endeavours. MacGregor lived nearly all of his life in Edinburgh but he died in a crash in Jamaica when a tyre on his car blew out as he was returning from a Burns Night supper. He was 37 and had been working as a visiting lecturer at the University of the West Indies. Far from dying in reluctant exile, MacGregor had previously longed to spend some time outside of Scotland, for all of his intense immersion in Scottish culture. In a 1971 letter to fellow medic Dr. Raymond Mills, MacGregor confided that 'I am very anxious to spend some time out of the country before we have to settle down for my childrens' senior schooling in two to three years time'. MacGregor was granted this wish, but at a terrible cost.

MacGregor's first novel *The Myrtle and Ivy* (M. Macdonald, 1967) comes directly out of his extracurricular experience of the folk-music and pub scene in Edinburgh while he was a medical student. The novel is arguably rather hamstrung by some florid overwriting but it is of value today for vividly capturing a sense of its time and place. *The Sinner* (Calder & Boyars, 1973) is a more complex prospect of a novel, although it shares with *The Myrtle and Ivy* the same problem of occasionally wooden dialogue, considering that MacGregor's real talent was for writing songs to be performed aloud. *The Sinner* was published hastily after MacGregor's death and is a more ambitious and well-executed work but not without some unsavoury baggage from its time, to which I'll return soon.

It's worth bearing in mind the main details of MacGregor's life when reading The Sinner, because it is strongly autobiographical – at times bordering on *roman-à-clef*. The Edinburgh folk-pub-institution Sandy Bell's becomes 'Connor's' and Denis Sellars (the folksinger protagonist who refuses to sell out to a hot-shot London producer) bears some resemblance to MacGregor himself. Ronald Johnstone seems a lot like Norman MacCaig and Hugh MacDiarmid remains himself as the ne plus ultra of Scottish poets. Rollo Wilson Craig and his 'Spontaneous Fluid' poets seem to be a cruel caricature of Ian Hamilton Finlay and other concrete poets. Sellars' mentor, the 'genius' older novelist Nichol Ross is highly evocative of Hamish Henderson. Ross served in the Intelligence Corps during the war, travelled across Europe and Scotland in search of folksong and wisdom and he is not beyond getting pugilistic over something that really matters, such as the future of folk-music. We know that Henderson himself wasn't above raising his fists to certain figures who crossed him intellectually or ideologically. He did punch Norman MacCaig for sneering at the working-class. Throughout the book it's suggested that Ross might in fact be Sellars' father and this in itself brings to mind the disputed paternity of Hamish Henderson himself.

By anchoring his story in a recognisable historical reality MacGregor brings his novel to life. In addition to this, what distinguishes *The Sinner* is that it takes conflicts of many kinds – religious, ideological, personal, intellectual – and plants them firmly in the Edinburgh of Knox and Montrose and of the 'Caledonian anti-syzygy'. Although the idea of duality in Scottish literature is an extremely tired one, it is employed with good effect in this novel to intensify Sellars' 'sinning'. The novel draws on the 'folksong flytings' that dominated the Scottish newspapers in the 1950s and 1960s; between factions espousing essentialist and nationalist ideas on poetry and song and others who advocated populism or the avant-garde in the form of concrete poetry or beatnik and Black Mountain poetry coming from the States. Here, the fight is between the slick and poppy folk-music that is earning London producers (like the ruthless Len Hackett) a fortune and preserving the purity of the folk-music of the travelling communities of Scotland for future generations. Sellars makes it clear that this is the sort of music people have bled over and the living owe a debt to their ancestors to ensure only the song is passed on in its purest form, not the celebrity of the singer. The battleground is the bodies, ears and minds of those involved, so naturally the novel shows how fealty to a cause or person can be tested to breaking point.

Although the novel begins proleptically with a rather garbled and frantic attempted suicide and note by Denis, the rest of the novel unfolds chronologically and works its way up to the show-down, between two rival performances: Len Hackett's popular televised variety show and Nichol Ross' revue of poetry, drama and folksong. The novel opens and closes in a rather Hoggian fashion; with that of metatexts (from struggling novelists) and found texts (the letters they left behind). Thus Ross dies and bequeaths all of his work and knowledge to Denis in the form of manuscripts and letters. Ultimately, the theme of conflict is addressed, not via Knox and duality, but via the work done by figures such as Nichol Ross to glimpse something greater beyond all the fighting and the egos.

One of the uglier aspects of the novel is its shocking attitudes towards women. Even for the era of its publication, the 1970s, *The Sinner* was controversial for its scenes of domestic abuse. There are unpleasant moments of objectification and the Madonna/whore complex rears its unsightly head more than a few times. At his worst Denis treats Kate Fraser abominably – at one point he nearly throttles her – but Nichol Ross intervenes to thrash Denis with his walking stick. While Denis' misogyny is not tackled head-on, it is challenged at times like these. Much of the talent and creative power in the novel actually lies with the women – Lisa Kendall, the brilliant singer who is used and dumped by Denis, and

Kate who writes an outstanding new folksong on an old theme of the '45 and who offers acute feedback on Denis' work, which he violently rejects. Denis' misogyny could arguably be seen as part of his sinning, and this most egregious sin leading in the end to his salvation. At Denis' nadir, he loses nearly everything including his sanity, yet Kate remains and it is his love for her, and her love for him, that prevents him from committing suicide. The closing pages of the book are in Kate's hand, and it is Kate who calls for a reconciliation between Denis and Murdo (his closest friend). Denis realises Kate's talent, worth and love very late on but the reader is often stunned into disbelief by Kate's continued forgiveness, which only runs out briefly on one occasion.

The lesser themes of the novel are supernaturalism and mysticism, which are also present in *The Myrtle and Ivy*. Denis has premonitions about his own death - he feels doomed and Nichol Ross actually possesses physic foreknowledge about things that are going to happen, such as his own death. While it is perhaps easy to dismiss this thread, it makes the novel a charged and poignant read to those who know that MacGregor himself had 'a superstitious belief in his own ill destiny' (Herdman). Before leaving for Jamaica, MacGregor appointed John Herdman as his literary executor 'in case anything happens' though he stressed that it wouldn't come to that. Tragically, he was to die shortly after, just before his second novel saw print. Herdman put together a selection of MacGregor's numerous poems and songs and these were published in 1974 (Macdonald Publishers) simply as *Poems and Songs*. This volume follows up on MacGregor's appearance as a poet in *Four Points of a Saltire* which was published by Gordon Wright's Reprographia in 1970. This four-poet anthology was of signal importance in bringing back into critical circulation the largely neglected work of two pre-eminent Gaelic poets: Sorley MacLean and George Campbell Hay as well as the trilingual (Gaelic, Scots and English) poet William Neill, but the book opens with a selection of MacGregor's poems as an exciting newcomer. MacGregor was at the time over two decades younger than the other poets in the book and there was much expected of him as an inheritor of the mantle of the Scottish Renaissance. His early death prevented him from really expanding on his initial promise as a poet, songwriter and novelist but *The Sinner* gives us some insight into his direction and progress as an artist.

The opening poem of *Poems and Songs* is titled 'O My Love' and it seems much concerned with the main themes of *The Sinner* and the conflicted mind of the (self and societally) tortured artist:

> Yet there was wisdom
> In my cruelty.
> Even as my mind whispered
> The marvellous cliché
> That my hate and love were
> Twins of the same great mother,
> I saw that you were looking
> Through the murk
> Into the deep mirror
> Of your soul.

THE SINNER

To
Alex Reid
Norman McCaig
with gratitude,
and
to
Jane
with much love

I wonder now why I was born dismayed
What was the shape that gibbered through the room?
Who told me that all good men were afraid?
I think I lay and trembled in the womb,
As mindlessly as rags flap in the wind
My soul knew guilt before my body sinned.

John Wain *Time Was*

The positive psychic as defined by us is a person who has done more than develop or make conscious an extra sense. He must have acquired some degree of wisdom, and have direct experience of reality. This shows him that there is a better way of extending his knowledge of life than by scurrying from place to place in search of experience at secondhand. He will look at things for himself, and accept as valid only that which he himself knows to be true, either because he has undergone it personally, or, because what he learns from others strikes up a note and taps some level of himself where true knowledge is no longer personal but vicarious and available to all who can function at that level. It does not matter what name we give to it: universal mind, cosmic consciousness, illumination or the spiritual vision. It is the level of direct contact and at that level he will know that people, whether living or dead, and objects, thoughts or feelings, whether concealed or accessible at the material level, are always within his reach, so to him there is no such thing as death or painful separation. There is only change and progression, and that along the orderly lines of a plan formulated by some Intelligence beyond his understanding. He is thus brought back to a religious attitude: that of the only religion worth while, which is the sense of order and mystery and of wonder, which grows unceasingly as his wisdom grows.

Payne and Bendit *This World and That*

CHAPTER ONE

Two minutes to hell. And my City is listening, in at the death. My City, and the City of Mad John Knox of Haddington. Stop laughing, you bitch!

It's the sound of your poor pretentious thoughts, Denis. Ha ha! Who told you that you were a wordmaker?

My poor pretentious thoughts. Like everything else of me. Except that I still believe I'm some sort of God-forsaken wordmaker, and even now I'm damned if I'll think any other way. Somebody. Somebody please listen. Hear my splendid thoughts, somebody, always creative... There isn't much time ...

Before me a window, and a pool of night beyond it, haunted by swimming shapes of stone. Below me the cobbles septic with muttering lamplight, a two-headed shadow of Lover swaying into it, furtive parody of unsanctified passion. Kin of my own fear-shagged soul, I love you down there. Right from the sea through a serpent-twist of Canongate a thrust of milder east slicing into brew-stink and acid smoke, an unhappy meeting beneath my window-sill. To my right new hope (a lie) to my left a stale hopelessness (smell of my destroyer) and in the middle Sellars. I have chosen what I once feared; I no longer trust the springsmelling wares of the North Sea wind. For salvation is within the grasp of my hand.

Salvation comes in twenty-odd bullet-parts, each three yellow grains, smooth on the whorls of my fingers. Courage? Better the de'il ye dinna ken than the one that stalks our streets. Damn that adrenaline and do it, Denis. Cherish this voice that whispers bloody well nothing beyond. Sweat and trembling and Nembutal in spite of them all.

I came from a country as old as the tears of children.

My bed-mate and tutor the pitiless honesty shown only to the helpless. Turning in my narrow cot from weals to empty gut I called Promise a liar: I knew, Tristran, why you were a fool to drink gold, and why your deep fat colours would bring you madness, Vincent. Lying under the fragrance of April I foretold its sodden winter pyre.

I have written a lesser story than I have lived. Forgive me, empty white sheaf, but who would have loved you filled? I might have scorched this paper crucible with every retch of my tortured soul—but in such unforgivable terms. Calvinism in the context of John's City—a cliché already. When Scotland is dying for an outward-looking eye, how dare I ravage this City with an inward-thrusting pen? Southward a critic would write—Once again we are presented with a type-novel from Scotland, Calvinism an' a'; when will the poor ghost of Scottish literature learn that we are sick of its rattling chains and the parochial voice that cries in the metre of psalmody?' Shallow heart, don't you think that we are just as sick of the Black Gown as you are of your peers and pouffes and patriotism? The world is certainly our country, well though we've been shuttered from it behind the purple cloak of imperial bigotry. We are now ready to scan and love an entire globe, but what can honest men learn from a voice that speaks without first understanding the passions of its body's heart? We must exorcise our demons before our talents can be truly exercised. I-about-to-die assert it. With nobility.

And my other talent, six nylon strings on stained wood, over there by Kate's dressing-gown in the corner. Symbol of our age and need, psycho-therapist of adolescent sickness. I haven't been a bad folksinger, either, but in an era when the City cats are considered ethnic artists I seem to lack a gimmick. *O tempora!* O City of failed writers and successful folksingers - Great Whore of Babble-on, if only Mad John could see you now!

Do it, Denis. Courage at last. It's in the family, after all. Hell's teeth, but I'm so frightened!

It is warm in this old house: outside the City is sprawled like a great predator on her rocky couch, purring complacently under the chill singing stars. Bitch-goddess of the North, who-with-eyes wouldn't love your face, nor wish to kindle passion behind your plump grassy breasts? Yet the heart of icy courage that cracked Nichol Ross and Denis Sellars together has split never a fibre for either.

Those thoughts of yours, Denis! Ha ha, those thoughts!

You have spoken to me so long in your dark voices, City-of-pride, I know you as well as my succulent Kate. You have sung me the kind hearts and cruelty of your cobbled closes, the time-qualified bravado of your grubby taverns, you have boasted your rows of polished cars and trim lawns and solid heads. Were you ever in Morningside, John? Or Ravelston? They'd soon have sorted you there, they don't go for this ill-bred working-class language in the pulpit. If only the City had possessed suburbs in your day, we'd have had you in the Royal Scottish Nut-House before you did your damage.

Speak to me for the last time. City—convince me that I dreamed the worst—

The dark-toned wind leaping to my windows: *No hope, Sellars, duplicity has been my sole survival. I live on, grey and beautiful, you die. I was too old for you to change, or Nichol Ross.*

You bitch, you've turned your coat again!

Why should I care? For years I was faithful, the first loyal woman ravished by the South. My rewards were scandal smeared across me by beasts who fashioned harlotry from innocence, and the enduring lunacy of a Madman. All this beneath the most wicked seasons of God's spleen. A woman has her pride, Sellars—where is your cynical sense of humour? And the Empire calls me Royal so gently: compromise, progress, compromise. Inevitable. A little kindness and warmth from the South.

We promised him so much. I dreamed it all, surely?

We both crucified him, and rightly so.

No, surely not me? I worshipped him—comfort me for the last time, for God's sake!

No comfort, Denis. Die quietly, for I fear your restlessness. Life is so peaceful now. Bowler-hats and pin-stripes in Queen Street. Gentle gardens blooming in South Side.

I didn't do it!
We both did it. Both of us, Denis.

Nichol Ross. Rasputin. Your cradle the winds, we were told, your destiny the stars.

Four years of pale streets and clean light ago, and a hand trembling on my shoulder at the Writers' Conference: 'Sellars? Rob's brother? I've read your poems. Lot to learn, but you've got what it takes. Come and have a drink.' The strange compelling timbre that ranged from bass to baritone, wrapped in a thin suspicion of Argyllshire.

And the long walks and the brittle paths of Midlothian in autumn and the mysterious sadness that almost made your fierce eyes lamblike beyond a drift of pipe-smoke: 'An orphan, laddie? Suicide? Well, dinna worry, we're all orphans in this country one way or another,' but the words were so pale against that look.

Frost-lit winter, the two of us skidding a street with Murdo, our cold flesh enlivened by a surfeit of the barley, and the Black Crow who said noo luik here ye cannae dance like that in the middle o' the road ye're holdin' up the traffic ye hairy-faced Hieland nutter, and you shook the water globules from your mottled beard, Nichol, and looked at him hard, and that bobby reeled away with a look on his face I'll never forget though I've seen it on others again and again.

'—This deep irrational fear is in most of us, Denis, but it can be conquered. We've lost the antidote for centuries, but we can find it again', and those awful eyes so obviously thought they knew it, but the questions were deftly turned: 'Not yet, Denis, not yet, but I'm convinced there is a quicker path to Truth than logic.'

The rumours, particularly in Connor's: a ruined aristocrat, the bottle. A fisherman's son, left home because of a woman, said Joe the Rat. Really an Englishman, said Starkey Shearer, there are Oxford undertones in thet eccent. An unfrocked priest, from Ollie the Bull, the Harlem schizophrenic. Deals in black magic, queer noises from his house at night. Best novelist we had fifteen years ago, hasn't written much since.

We talked about you, Nichol, how could we help it? Even Kate, least curious of animals, used to ponder your mystery. But then she loved you, for even in her you first saw what I missed right from the beginning.

Were you a fragment of God? But it's too late now. The Powers of Darkness, the two Mad Johns, still rule this City.

Do it, Denis. Rattle of yellow lifetaker in cardboard. What else to lose? Kate. Much?

A thing that was so simple. And now seas roar over my head and strange agonies chant in the deepest cell of what I call my heart. Woman of Scotland, plump and pretty, one of a thousand in a city—that it should have turned out like this. Strange, Kate. Strange and terrible. I can still hear your song in every pore of me, one of the few things left that is defiant of desolation.

The spine of the Crags was sunwarmed under cobalt above your shoulder; approaching scent of autumn but so warm last early September round the damp-footed sheep, the shaggy plunge of rough to the hollow; the crumbling City wall opposite, the twinkling spires and spiky black churchstone rigid and razorsharp, out against us they stood like serried pikemen. Misty your blue eyes in that gulf of brightness, Kate, your nostril moistened by freshness that lifted from the steelshiny dagger-blade of Firth; and you I turned to me by the copper cliff and you felt queer, you thought you'd been here before, and funnily enough so had I—

Wind and dreams that parted that moment from perception, I was deceived by you. I didn't see it. A start like that points away from all simplicity. You carried a scar between your womb and your womanhood; I was fool enough to think it made you cheap at the price.

Kate. Much. Too much.

And Murdo. Vulpine-lean. Pride of a race dying in the narrows of your cheeks, in the lean line of hair above your lips. The minims and crotchets of your Lewis voice rising and falling more predictably than light and darkness—we sat, Nichol and I, bereft of will, hypnotised through time to the noonday of your civilisation, a woman on battlements, a galley spewing green sea beyond her hopeless lament.

Your exile from home and poverty, Murdo, how have you borne it? How you hate the City, but you're far too full of ideals to stay away from limelight and comfort. I have seen you pluck a girl from the dance floor, rat-nimble, sleek and polished, heard the swift banter and the glasses echo with laughter. And yet you were an incongruity, you belonged five hundred years away from soda siphons and suspender belts, in a cool chamber of the Old West with music in your soul and a stone on your belly.

There were those who laughed at your language.

'I didn't mean to be rude, Denis, but he was so damned contemptuous. God, if only I were rid of it! '

You struck me last week, my brother, here on the scar where scalding water once ripped the skin off a child. 'You've thrown him to the wolves, you Lowland bastard!' I shattered a bit, I healed a bit less, I believe I'm glad it came because of Nichol, and not because you were bound to say it anyway, in the charming idiom whereby we've always kept ourselves divided in this bloody wasteland.

The Tragedy of Scotland, Murdo. You and me. Those nights of poetry and philosophy, the fag-ends high in the fireplace, and the fiddling in pockets in Connor's to see whose silver was heavier.

All nothing. For behind the smiles and gallantry we were thinking in different languages, and one of them was dying.

Your fine freckled face, my old friend, and those lecherous brown eyes that smelled of pain.

A great loss, Murdo. But inevitable.

Connor's. No need for the sad farewell I might once have taken.

Connor's, home of talent and debauch, Prince-Bar of the campus, you have been struck by the abomination of desolation well-loved by Jeremiah and Mad John. Haven of the incredible, to you my passing is no longer important. For the old Connor's men are few.

Starkey Shearer is still there and all his Morningside accent, scrawny and lying like silk. Wangled a job this summer, guide out at Kincamus Castle, sold five hundred-weight of the East staircase to tourists, stone by stone. They say the Marquis broke his ankle.

And Joe the Rat, evil and undersized belligerent, you've lost eight fights this winter. We forgave your incompetence for the ninth you won was a pawnbroker's wife.

Ollie the bull, negro-saint-the-afflicted, our naturalised deserter from the U.S. navy, what a part you played in our bitter battle! But they didn't approve of it. It's the jug for you this summer.

Ricky Slater still leads his folksong group by the oaken arch, but the whoops have lost their soul. Folksinging now belongs to the public platform, and the dollar dictates the ditties that sweeten the spotlight. Smooth imitations slide between teeth that sparkle like shillings, and where the Connor's élite used to lurch we smell the lotions of sober men with contracts in their pockets.

The barbarians are come.

Finally my City. Who destroyed us, who has always been too tough for the warm-hearted since she chilled her own to survive. God knows I'll miss her. And if you wonder at my deathlove, you haven't seen her leap from crone to

Christ's own Mary across an April morning.

I hope they stick me in the Canongate cemetery; this is the part I have loved like home. Her face is changing for the better; the single-ends and winding staircases are disappearing, and infant-mortality and bronchitis with them. Less and less is our City the angular noblewoman titivating her shining skin while her bowels rot with cancer. But there was good singing dialect in the tumour and I saw fine angles of stone and slate; Nichol used to say a sight of every grey close should produce a work of art. Not for me.

Every step of progress, they say, produces its own particular neurosis.

And nothing more I love or care for. Break the strings, burn the print, lie once on your back, Kate, and wonder what it was we really found. Sing for me a lift and plunge of bitter-sweet, Murdo, and try and forgive. Nichol...

Through the corridors of the fatherless and the trails of the tinkers I came to the sour, lovely streets of the City. And I met a sage who made my mind alive and a sorceress who turned from a square meal to an Iseult, and a brother who put his hand on my shoulder. Together we raised a new rebel standard, then like all the others we went the way of history, turned on each other and ...

Salvation or perdition is yellow and now, for the flames I feared are less than those I have ignited in my present wreckage. So different from a short time ago when a death wish was bloody great fun.

Kate, darling.

You know why I have done this. After all we've been through I know you so much better now—and yet the last wonderful creation that our fusion produced has given you fresh impact, almost as powerful as the first look you gave me on that weird night of last year's Festival, when I thought you looked a sane and steady good thing.

Please remember that my greatest regret is my failure to salvage pieces of our winter and enshrine them in your testament, starting with—...

That crazy Night. When I jumped from the toe of Mad John, father of our unique sacred poetry.

> Sweet God of John thy gracious hands into
> I poor vile sinner in thy mouth but spew
> With cries for mercy my soul give now do.

CHAPTER TWO

The last night of the Festival, the final amens droned, the strange accents departing and the City coffers groaning with genteel joy. Suburbia thought Haydn a wee bit tuneless, but Janacek was thrilling even if you couldn't quaite understand all the Italian. Connor's, temporarily revived by an itinerant column of Irish folksingers of the old school, was suffering a most affronting insult.

A modern Highland drama by an ancient Lowland playwright had been playing in Chambers Street, an odious device calculated by Whitehall Intelligence to obliterate pro-Scottish sympathies in America for ever. For this travesty a lifesize plaster statue of Mad John had been borrowed from the King's Theatre, and after the last performance its return entrusted to two schoolboys. Lads of undoubted integrity: having pulled the scowling prophet round two corners on a trolley they realised that two shillings each was small compensation for public loss of self-respect, and consequently abandoned John in the gutter five yards from the door of the Scala café. The bonneted figure snarled forward from its pedestal, pointing with wrathful forefinger across Woods Street into Connor's, the moderate wonder of all passing by. The Festival, after all.

Starkey Shearer came back white-faced from the door. 'Sten, the drink's gone for my head at lest. What is it?'

Joe the Rat and Ollie the Bull ventured across the road, returned to report that it had tangible form but refused to take a match.

MacAuley and I, the culture-vultures, fidgeting on the red tile floor, each wondering who should ask a loan from Connie the barmaid first. Then the last bell, and through it Ollie the Bull's counterfeit City: 'Denis, come and look at this!'

I recognised it instantly: 'Come on, Murdo, I'll give you an act of symbolism to end this pretentious pageantry.'

Woods Street stung my feet through cracked soles, mottled tenements swaying at me in raw air. My hand slammed on the pasteboard book under John's oxter, and I hoisted my bum on his feet, mine dangling over. Damn those wheels, keep her steady. Pit-patter of feet, and shapes following.

Murdo's pitching voice said, 'Very funny and remarkably agile, but where's the symbolism?'

'Gentlemen, we are the neurotics this man has made us. The flames of perdition are ever in our thoughts save when they are expelled by the sinful shapes of bottles and buxom unrobed women.'

'This performance is getting tedious,' said Murdo, but more loudly. 'Don't be a fool, that car would have chewed you if you'd jumped! '

'What more fitting end can an artist ask?' I asked him with dignity. 'Booted to destruction by the arch-destroyer of the Scottish arts, on the last night of yet another celebration of their impotence. Aside, oafs, I leap symbolically!' In fact I have no intention of anything dangerous but we're short of amusing stories at the moment. Move fast or they'll pull you down. Loyal friends, the bastards.

'Come on, Denis,' said Ollie the Bull white teeth shining out of his huge head, 'this is undignified. There are foreigners watching you.'

Whine and lights up the street. A Volkswagen coming, nice and slow.

'I thawt,' said a wizened foreigner in a plastic mac, 'that this man was a Scawttish hero.'

'Madam, you are misinformed. This man silenced the music of our realm with the stridence of battle, preached up with Glasgow Rangers and similar treasons, but worse, madam, do you know what he did?'

'No, I guess I don't.'

'You should be ashamed, madam. This bearded chimpanzee is the founder of our local Temperance Society.'

'Denis,' said Murdo, 'I've had enough.' His hand creaked on my jacket. The Volkswagen—JUMP!

A quick scuttle on side-thigh, shriek of swerving rubber, crunch and rip—Oh, my ankle!'...'you bloody fool, Denis.' ... 'that guy is crazy ...'

It stopped twenty yards on; the bald heavy owner panted back, loomed over me, muttering in German.

'Go on home, sir,' said Murdo kindly, 'you're just not used to our streets. My friend will hold nothing against you.'

The German ignored him, peered down at the ruin. 'You have deliberately sprung,' he wheezed in outrage. 'My wife is already vomit in the car.'

'By God, Murdo, this Festival is going too far. A native can't roll in the gutter without Huns driving over his helpless body.'

'For Jesus' sake, Denis,' said Joe.

'I want to see the police!' shrieked the German, his face violet under the patchy lighting.

Wet pain flooding my ankle, cautiously I came to my feet with indignation: 'Do you realise who this saintly figure is? Have you no respect for our Christian history, you pumper- nickel Papist?'

'The police!' shrieked the German to a crowd thickening like instant porridge, from whose edge came the Rat's warning: 'Murdo—there's two Black Crows comin' roond the corner!' Sudden fear in my bowels. Reality, Denis.

Murdo's voice, clean as a whip-stroke: 'Whose turn is it?'

'It's mine,' said the Rat squeezing through stocky and scared. 'You've given me a beauty this time, Sellars.'

'Greater love hath no man, Joe.' Don't faint, Denis, hold on.

Then the Rat was on the street-crown, jacket thrown off, traffic screeching to a halt. 'Come on, ma darlin's, here's a fightin' man of Connor's that'll make ye wish ye had a feyther!'

'No!' screamed the German, but they were diverted, running, the checked caps bobbing along the shadowy pavement, furious behind the quick yellow shirt that flickered like a match-flame in and out of the people-streams, down Woods Street and the Row towards the graveyard wall. The German lumbered hopelessly after them: 'Police! Attention! Police!'

The crowd were laughing now, sympathetic, God bless the war in which I would have been a coward. Murdo shouldered me through them, real tears of pain coming. Bloodstain on my shoe, slimying over the instep.

'Where are we going, Murdo?'

'To that fine hospital on the corner called the Royal City. I'm taking you to see Pat.'

Hirple, scuffle, sob, and the wind leaned round the corner making our eyes bucket. Sounds of Rat-pursuit dying away, tenements still.

'Murdo, I have reservations about letting that man touch me. He's been off the booze for years. How do I know he's still a good doctor?'

We stopped, swaying, before the wooded lane of the Middle Meadow Walk, chilly and twenty yards from the Casualty Gate. Murdo's eyes glinted through my silly pain-grin, that narrow scowl will not countenance witty dishonesty.

'The act's over, Denis. Stop it.'

Over, Murdo. Why do you put up with me?'

We were moving again: scuffle, ah, drip, drip, ah: 'Because I know what a pathetic idiot you are deep down. Calvinist hell-fire isn't preached only in orphanages.'

'This word Calvinist is used too loosely in Scotland, Murdo.'

'Meaning what?'

'It's lunatic Lutheranism that's really taken over

now. The mad Baptists, the Plymouth Brethren, these are the real hell-fire boys who cut Scotsmen apart—as that great man James Hogg predicted they would.'

'Hogg? You mean in the *Justified Sinner*?'

'Indeed I do. Remember that he called the devil-villain "Gil-Martin". Remember what "gille" means in Gaelic, and remember that the Antinomian heresy came out of Johannes Agricola, Luther's disciple. That's the twisted kind of election that fundamentalists believe in now.' Grunt, this eloquence has got me out of breath.

Now we were within the gate, heading downhill towards the parked ambulances, oh this bloody cruel tarmac.

'You're a good Highlandman, Murdo. You scared too?'

'Just a bit, like you. Forget the death-wish, Denis, it's poor art.'

A yawn of white light. A helpful porter in brown coat supported my other side. We clattered over green tile, past white checked tile into a sickening antiseptic stench. I saw blue skirts and white aprons, nice twitch of hem against a shining black calf. Then glass doors and a long bench. Bliss, ah. A drunk with a jelly-nose in the corner, and a frightened wee chap about three who'd swallowed a shilling said his mother. Threadbare coat, poor soul, couldn't afford it.

Murdo returned with Pat Leitch, surgical registrar, big Glasgow face, rusty hair. 'Into the treatment room, Denis. It's a long time since Connor's supplied me with business.'

'We're not what we were, Pat. It's the Welfare State.'

The red crown bent low under the fierce arc-light, red fingers woman-gentle. 'Nothing broken, but he's sliced you. I'll have to stitch it.'

'Do your worst, my trust is in God.' High above my recumbence the floating white ceiling was cracked into a squat Spain-shape. I'm feeling frightened. Bravado-sing! 'All people that on earth do smell—'

'Shut up and keep still, or I'll throw you out. Mr. Jamieson—hold his arms still, he's certifiable.'

The porter's face blotted out Portugal, smiled with elderly sympathy, 'Easy son, it won't be long.' Thank God, what a mixture of hot light and inhumanity.

Pat: 'Staff-nurse, some xylocaine.' My ankle drenched in coldness. Yaah! A needle. 'Denis, it'll go dead soon.'

'Mr. Jamieson,' I said nervously. 'You look an intellectual. Do you realise that life is a tragedy, and that even Joyce was inadequate on tragedy?'

'Ah'm sure she was, sir, just you lie still.'

'Mr. Jamieson, the great Irishman described the physiology of the Dreadful Thing in terms of terror and sympathy applied to the observation of a death. But what is the true physician's definition of this abstraction in terms of its aetiology—where is its genesis, Mr. Jamieson, this that infects us all?'

'Pat,' said Murdo, 'if you've any catgut left, use it on the bugger's mouth.'

'Ignore this cruel man, Mr. Jamieson, and retain the following sentence until you are hoary. Tragedy, as it affects us, is the eternally procrastinated fulfilment of an inevitably postulated hope. Blossom and red lips, the blind faith of youth, and the decline that comes thereafter.'

'Right,' said Pat—quick snip—'that's you in one piece. Go and talk to him, Staff Fraser, while I strap the sprain.'

She came up the table, a young woman in dark blue and white, a face good-looking but for its roundness and health. Cheeks blushing like washed baby-buttocks, touch of jowl crimp-downed. Short nose straight but rather wide, well-spaced blue eyes (a soft pain deep there, Sellars?). Brow full and vertical overhung with blonde curl. Soft throat, good teeth, she's a juicy one, by Jesus. Good strain of breast under starch, average waist, legs, I suspect lustfully, thick but definitely characters. And your accent is West, sweet nurse; altogether your presence is creating an awful tension in my manhood.

'Hold my hand, dear, what's your name?' Kate Fraser, lovely name. I'm Denis Sellars, the famous folksinger and writer. I hated my father, so he got rid of me and went off to the war.'

'Dry up,' said Murdo. Jealous.

Not a muscle of her face flickered but something internal was illuminating her expression; it was developing an uncanny intentness and simultaneously assuming visible refinement. Madam, there is a sliver of my personality in which you are interested, even although the twisted right side of my face is full in your view. I feel half-hypnotised by the strangest tenderness I have ever seen, and the temperature of those moist eyes is rising. Well, well.

'This was a silly thing to do, Mr. Sellars,' she said.

Disappointing. That was a silly thing to say, nurse.

'Nurse Fraser, I am an artist, consequently a destroyer. I hunt the heart of human darkness. When I glimpse my own Calvinist face in it, what am I to do?'

'You haven't found it yet,' she said with a headshake, and too quietly for the others to hear.

My God. 'How do you know?'

'Because you're enjoying yourself. What you're trying to talk about isn't really so very funny.' That ruthless twin-eyed sadness filling me with wonderful unease.

Murdo, you've been spreading stories behind my back. How does she know? Idea. I'm attracted to you, nurse, and I have a feeling that you're past the lip-blossom stage. I dream of a secure haven of complete uncomplication.

'Do you believe in the power of human communication, nurse?'

'I don't quite know what you mean, but I think so.'

'Staff Fraser,' rattled Pat, 'go and check the plaster in Treatment B. Off you come, Denis.'

Disturbed I watched her sail away graceful, carrying the few extra pounds without clumsy consciousness. At the door she turned and stared; that look wanted to touch me.

Murdo's arm round me again. Stamp on tile, pain but slight. 'Thanks, Pat, I feel much better. And who's your Staff-Nurse?'

'Why?'

'I'm impressed. I have a strange feeling I have looked in the eyes of a woman who sees deeper than my poor scorched husk.'

Pat came up to me slowly, strangely serious. Both hands on my shoulders. 'You've caused enough trouble for one night. Leave her alone. She's the most dangerous wonderful woman I know.'

'Don't understand.'

'Denis, according to popular legend, you travelled the roads with tinkers when you were a kid.'

'Sure. They kept Rob and me for years after we jumped the wall at Dunfreckie.'

On your travels did you ever see a ewe with a look of death in her, scanning the heath for a small body to cherish?'

'You're a lousy poet, Pat.'

'Have a good look at Kate Fraser again, but from a safe distance. By the way, I saw Rob on T.V. last night. He's really in the big-time.'

I reared forward venomously, steering Murdo to the cold relief of the corridor. 'I'm grateful to you, Pat. Don't spoil it.'

'Tut, tut. Brotherly love soiled by artistic envy.'

'Goodnight, Pat,' said Murdo hastily. I swung more easily now, needing only his shoulder behind to butt me off my bad foot. Outside west wind and elms were dancing a witch-trot before the stark University, and a faint spark of scarlet preened in the broken murk above the vague serrations of the Castle, the crown of the Cathedral.

I hear quick feet and a girl's giggle. A fingertip of night is stroking my ugliness. The Dunfreckie servant-girls giggled and pattered; the porridge tasted of their stale fingers on Sunday morning. Then the bells. I'm frightened, Murdo. My mother was lovely, and it didn't save her. I wonder if they told her to stop acting.

I was beside Murdo in the taxi, sailing down the narrow hill to Tollcross. A climb of garrets, a steeple, then the undulating Links streaked with supple shadows, a smell of space and the suburbs ahead. Splay of quiet green avenues back from the main road; the old village, working-class at heart despite the music-hall gibes.

Tell me, suave Morningside thoroughfares fronting the hills with dignity, have you also become disciples of election?—'*And all Mine are thine, and Thine are Mine; and I am glorified in them*'—do your cool bourgeois hearts soar like the Pentland lark on the warm wind of a paraphrase, does righteousness guard your doors?

But we've adapted the dualism, Denis, and the scripture's a bit barbarous for here. Were decent folk at heart, eles! Elect now only in terms of cless. The mark of God's own is pi-e-nos and kippers, our fur coats are braw so we cen't afford knickers.

'Where we going now, Murdo?'

'I thought we might have a midnight chat with Rasputin. Have you any better ideas?'

'No.'

We spilled from the black square, sorry I can't give you a tip, Jock, I've just been bled dry by my private herbalist. Funny bugger, Ah'll remember you.

The opening moaned and thrashed like corn its hedgelong length, dull silver scuds glancing off the waning moon, not a star to sing to us, but the shriek of a child's hot ear from a window. We skirted a market-garden; next villa to the left we saw him at the bay, sighting the southern hills beyond the bouncing crescent.

The red glare of the fire behind threw that finest of heads into awesome focus. Dance of a flame on the hooked nose but it remained handsome and steady, legacy of Rome or Normandy, straight slabs of nostril seen flaring through glass at forty yards, fearless rhomboid chin above the beard that shivered in the window-draught. Perfect semicircle eyesocket, a knuckle of high cheekbone back into grizzle. The brow bossed heavily above the eyes, higher a sweep of mane to the balding crown, then the long curls that dropped to his collar. In profile the gentleness of the full mouth was enough to prick the sculptor's eyes.

Murdo rang twice, and the steps were heavy, ever louder, the confident tramp of strong bone. He was six-foot-three in the doorway, stooping, blinking. 'Denis, Murdo—*Feasgar math, a chairdean*—I've been waiting for you; I had an aura of your coming an hour ago.' He turned, time for the throwing of a secret smirk between us.

And upstairs, the same old room. Leap of firelight into three walls of books, fiction, non- and his favourite which held the mystics from Buddha to Boehme, three shelves reserved for everything the Celts imagined when they were plastered. Three tacked leather armchairs by the fire, come away in and make yourselves at home. Coffee bubbling through in the wee kitchenette.

'You're limping, Denis?'

Murdo told him.

'It's as well you came down here to-night. I've got something important to say.' Voice quietening, he was angry over the cups there. 'You're becoming a disappointment to me, Denis, overplaying all this neurotic stuff. What's worse you're writing damn-all at the moment. How's the novel?'

'Nearly finished in my head, Nichol, but too fragile for print. I'm frightened it gets blown off the paper.'

He came with my cup, cuffed me on the left lug but muffled with fondness, big shoulders quivering with suppressed wrath: 'You're gutless. A dozen stories in periodicals, a few songs on BBC, and you're willing to wallow in your madness and consider your life fulfilled. Don't you realise that talent is a responsibility?'

Sudden hot blood. 'You know damn well I do! I also realise that I have nerves that tear like paper, and that at the moment, I need a new set of guts. And I wish people would leave me in peace to work out my own bloody salvation! '

'Easy now,' said Murdo. 'Easy, Denis.'

'Talking out of ignorance, the pair of you,' I snarled in ecstasy.

Nichol came across the room, grizzly proportions stag- lithe, crashed into the middle chair which rebounded a foot. 'Murdo, we will ignore these infantile sentiments of a supposedly twenty-six-year-old grown man, for we have better things to discuss.'

His head bolted characteristically between his huge hands. Murdo and I another quick glance. What is it this time? The exposition he keeps promising, the knowledge of the Enlightened, who conversed with stars before they were swamped by God-fearers? The only illogical power that can eradicate the blight of illogical anxiety? The revelation of Love, haw, haw? No, the hands are coming down, it's not the bland orbs of the seer we are facing, but the stiff eyebrows of the angry Scot. God help us, it's history or literature to-night, and I have a pathetic Freudian aversion to Scottish history when sober. Crackle, crackle, bless the chuckling bravado of the black-and-red demon-dancing fireplace.

'The Festival has finished to-night.' Nichol, you are an observant man. 'It's been a wonderful three weeks which I'm certain you two have spent entirely in Connor's and the Folk Clubs as usual.' Six-sevenths true, Nichol, how could you forget the Sabbath? 'I've seen African ballet, Brecht, I've listened to readings of Dostoyevsky, I've been to a superb production of *Othello*. And instead of being elated I am depressed. Why?'

'I don't know, Nichol,' said Murdo politely. Personally I think African ballet is no cure for frustration.

'Murdo,' he said, and now his voice was rich and sonorous, 'do you know what Voltaire once said?—"It is from Scotland we receive rules of taste in all the arts from the epic poem to gardening!" A slight exaggeration, yet there is what Europe once thought of us.'

And now I know why you're depressed, Nichol, for I saw the piddling morsels of Dunbar and Henryson advertised in mousetrap closes and your own Jacobite play performed in a tiny Church Hall, and a few good songs and readings hidden in the Lawnmarket. But the glorious stage-Scots who made the bright lights: tailored tartans and little bald city men warbling Gaelic pop-songs in the Usher Hall, the Yankee Ladies' Pipe Band playing out of tune in the Gardens and the French photographers squinting up their short kilts after heather, that moving exercise in clumsiness about Montrose in the Assembly Hall that made every Scot a saint and every Saxon an Enoch Powell.

'—The good stuff all relegated to the shadows, Murdo, and all this damned rubbish misrepresenting us! '

Time for the trenchant tongue of Sellars: 'For God's sake, who cares? This lopsided heap of peat has over-written its silly little problems to such an extent that whenever a real man-of-the-world appears, the publishers run a mile, expecting another jackets-off-in-the-midden. Look at dear MacAuley there, the sentimental parochial whose wonderful wide world stretches from the Butt of Lewis to Barra.'

'May I remind you that I recently licked you on Modern American Literature,' said Murdo quietly.

Nichol's chair screeched as he came forward. 'And may I remind you that Voltaire was one of the greatest Frenchmen ever?'

'So what. Scotland had a living culture then. Now it's dying, or merging into English. Probably a good thing too. I'm sick of northern mists and bonnie lassies, Nichol. Let's go to Monte Carlo for the winter, Murdo. I need material for a book.'

He should have struck me, but no. Nichol swelled majestically to his feet, long raking strides to the fiction wall. Back with a book. 'I think you need to read this.'

Oh, *A Scots Quair*. How dare I have opened my lying mouth.

'I've read it, Nichol.'

'And yet you still—'

'You've made your point. Thoroughly bad taste, I didn't mean it and I'm sorry.' There was a night at eighteen when I smelled the wind above Blawearie and my heart shredded and poured through my eyes to the grate, the music and seething wit of a master's craft lifted my head against heaven and the Lord looked through and said dinna worry, laddie, for I know how you feel and I've just read him too, although he'd never believe it.

Again Nichol over to the fiction wall, back with another book. 'The publisher is not always averse to contemporary Scottish fiction, Denis. Where—ah, here, listen to this: "*Harris Tweed Macpherson looked down at the corpse. 'Oh, Lord,' he cried, 'you have chust given me the bitter sorrow to thole! My only daughter found dead of the exhaustion in a peat bog, joined in the devil's gymnastic with her Papist lover!' Grief-stricken he removed a herring from the dead girl's corset and began to chew it.*

' "*At the door of the tin shack, Peigi Mary was rocking to and fro on her tartan bloomers. 'Ochone,' she cried, 'ochone, Fat Morag, it is I who am sad that you were the daughter with the burning bush and why were you not found wrapped round a Christian in your death?—'* " '

'Stop it! ' shouted Murdo.

'Yes,' said Nichol, 'all the picaresque Hebridean ingredients. Nobody ran from this book of caricatures and lies, Denis.'

'The bastard who wrote it should have his neck stretched.' My illogical hot blood.

'Aha,' said Nichol, 'the cynic's mask is slipping. The tribal consciousness is still there, Denis?'

'Yes, it is, and I'm sick of it. That mickey-taking sensationalist is a skunk, but I'm not a Highlander, and this conversation is getting nowhere. What were we on about,

Nichol? Oh yes, the glorious Festival, God bless the talent it brings to town, and I don't mean oboists—'

'Shut up!' He stood up, shook my shoulders, I never knew I had so many teeth. 'Now, listen, both of you.' Nichol collapsed easily in his chair, crossed the long supple lines of his legs. He spoke quietly, the dominie act just audible above a giggle of flame.'I don't intend to voice too many platitudes. We know why Scottish literature isn't all that it should be, for tragic reasons of racial division, religion and history. But we do have talent left, and situations of tragedy and comedy and drama are round us every day.'

'Tragedy,' I said, and smiled wisely. I know it, I know it.

'The facts are,' said Nichol, beaming now in florid enjoyment of his own voice, 'that our inhuman religion is retreating, we are fast becoming hybrid in blood, and that recent literary history has demonstrated the value of roots—look how regional the modern English novel is. And we have *big* talents—in MacDiarmid we have produced the greatest poet since Yeats. Moreover we are producing new writing whose subject matter is original and profound. My present novel is a brilliant metaphysical statement with which any man of genius will immediately sympathise, and young Denis, there, is trying to probe the scented skin of modern love. And I'm certain there are three dozen writers out there who are ready to make the pen of another Voltaire erupt with admiration!' He leapt to the window in three great bounds and slammed his hand against its chattering. 'Do you see what I'm after? A means of catapulting our written arts back into the mainstream of European culture.'

We stared blankly; back into the firelight he cat-footed, hands opened like a warlock raising the dead. 'Listen. The Festival is the one time when we have the cream of European criticism within our courts. What if next year we had a salvo of established *and* contemporary works ready for it; drama, prose, poetry, all under one roof, brilliantly produced every night in the three weeks, not scattered throughout the culture-backwaters of the City, but in the Ewan Hall?'

I laughed. Sorry, bad manners, he's angry again. 'You'd never fill it, Nichol. There's too much first-class competition.'

Still pacing restlessly, but his voice quiet now and conspiratorial. 'I've thought of that. We'll have to use our cunning.'

Oh God, my old hero, I'm frightened again, but for you. Is this a tang of madness I smell from the wild glow of your eye? 'What d'you mean, Nichol?'

'Many forms of artistic endeavour are poor commercial propositions just now. But one element of our northern tradition is riding the wave like a porpoise—Scottish folk-singers, genuine and fake, are real money-spinners.'

Nichol, I have new tarnished respect for you. There is an exciting red dawn rising in the east of my intelligence. 'You want to use folksong as bait?' Splendid, splendid bait. The voice of the proletariat, fifteen shillings a ticket.

Of course. We could use it as aperitif and savoury. An hour before and an hour after. And in between a judicious two-hour medley—drama, readings, the quintessence of our contemporary talent.'

Nichol, this sounds pipe-dream fanciful, but not impossible. And *my* flagging spirit requires goading towards an end or this beautiful novel will never be finished. Across the fragments of firelight I have a feeling that Murdo's rigid attention bespeaks similar thinking.

'It sounds a bit crazy,' said the Lewis voice. 'But, my God what a challenge! '

Nichol leaned back satisfied, knees covered by spread fingers, Abraham has re-convinced the children there's a kick left in the patriarch. 'You're both interested, aren't you?'

Sellars: 'We'll need time to think about it, Nichol. It's so full of courage that I distrust it utterly.'

Up he came to his magnificent stretch again. 'Stop this nonsense, Denis! Are you for me, or against me?'

'If you put it like that, I'm for. You're one of the few valuable things left round here.'

'Murdo?'

'I'm interested, Nichol, but I have my doubts.'

'Listen.' He was lobbing coal into the embers. 'I've

called a meeting for next Saturday, at the house of James McNeill the playwright. I've asked a few of the local writers to attend, also Rollo Wilson Craig and his Spontaneous Fluid Poets.'

'Oh, no!' Murdo had donned his critic's upper lip, disdainful curl. 'Not that decerebrate bunch of idiots?'

'Idiots be damned. There is a glimmer of gold behind their apparent misanthropy.'

'What about the folksingers?' I'm really enthusiastic. I intend to be second-in-command at least.

'It's up to you to bring them in. I'll consolidate the literary front first. And I want genuine singers—from the North-East and the Borders, and as few of the urban arse-waggers as possible.'

'Careful, Nichol. The hand that plucks the chord is the favoured of the Lord—it's the groups who draw the crowds,' but already he was assuring Murdo that Gaelic song and story would definitely have its place in this unique revival, and Murdo said he was really beginning to like the idea. Violent colour washing your freckles, Murdo, tension in your white knuckles.

And we would have to work like hell on all potential patrons, and God only knows if they'd even consider giving us the Ewan Hall, but I know a man, says Nichol, on the Festival Arts Committee who realises only too well that I am a writer of rare genius, and I think we have a splendid chance.

The challenge was out. Midnight thickened into the pitch of the small hours that diluted into a buff pre-dawn fashioning slowly-sharp lines of slate under a scum of drizzle, and still there was a tingle of excitement by the replenished fire, round the walls of the smoky brown room, in the Vietnam problem, in the lyricism of Ossian, in the paranoia of St. Joan (Nichol smiled secretively here and said nothing). There, burning brightly at the back of our accustomed polemics was the torch of Nichol Ross: *This night I have shown to you a purpose for a season, and for its length you may know yourselves as men who mean.*

We tried to broach his favourite subject through Spinoza, but by now he was falling asleep. On your feet, Murdo, it's a long walk, and what a topic we have to shred in the rising light. A new short-circuit to Europe, starting here on our own doorstep.

The big hand held my shoulder over the wooden gate. 'You mustn't let yourself get too hard, Denis.'

'You know I'm not really hard. I'm with you all the way.'

Pain on either side your nose, Nichol, and this always puzzles me. 'You're one of the few people I would be hung for, Denis. Keep writing. I'll teach you all I know.'

'Thanks, Nichol.'

Turning back, crunching gravel to powder, he said, 'Have you heard from Rob recently?'

'Certainly not. My dear twin is too busy prostituting his talents in London.'

'Denis,' hand on my shoulder, but colder as though a ghost had passed through him, 'you're too hard on Rob. Are you sure you're not jealous?'

'In all honesty, no.' Eye-to-eye and angry, and I mean it. That Beatle-furred folksinger turned entertainer, the rubbish of him.

'There are many vehicles of progress, Denis, and the

right kind of love is among them. Kinship is surely one of its starting points.' He shivered in the fine water-clouds, tartan rug fluttering round his shoulders.

'I'd better go, Nichol.' Raw City air breathing on my country neck.

'There's so much I still have to teach you.' This damned hand will not let go, the man is a Titan. 'He wrote me last week, asking for you.'

'Tear it up, Nichol. He knows better than to write to me.'

'He'd met some Colonel in London who knew your father in North Africa. This chap gave him some photographs. He wants you to have some of them.'

'Look.' Twisting away at last, voice rising angry down the gutter,'I want to know even less of my goddamn father than I do of Rob! '

Nichol, your face is pathetic now, when your side-curls aren't blowing across it. You worry too much over me.

'Don't you want to know more about your father?'

'No!' Back for handshake. 'Good-night and thanks. I think your idea is terrific.' Good-night, Denis, but lifeless. I've hurt someone else.

Run for Murdo, ankle makes me hobble, thirty yards down he's waiting by the jut of the garden wall. Damn that smooth TV idol Rob Sellars and that swine his father who threw little two-year olds into the most hideous up-bringing a child ever wept in. Love, haw haw, don that controlled sarcastic smile.

We turned into the bluish channel of dawn between the houses, a chimney clutching a spark from the crimson ball that I know is clambering the Crags. Dank autumn harsh in the lungs. We stopped, looked back as always. 'Yes, there he is! '

'It gives me the shivers, Murdo. I love that man for his honest-to-God humanity, but every time I see this I wonder if there isn't something to his supernatural blarney.'

'It's all part of the act. He knows we're watching.'

Arms spread to the east, a Druid in suburbia. Stop that fire-dance behind him, I'm seeing a bullhorn headdress and a snarl of savagery on those sympathetic contours. But brighter now, there's a shaft of dawn playing with the fire, it's mixing, purifying, there's a gown whiter than Greek, we're beyond the clock's cold hands... I have seen a curtain drawn.

'You've no idea what the sensitive imagination can conjure up, Murdo.' Hair on the back of my neck settling again.

'Conceit, Denis.' Clip, clip, clip, our feet. Morningside Road ahead, waking sleep-shapes muttering half-pace on wheels. 'What was he on about at the gate?'

Clip, clip, 'Same old tack. My father and Rob.'

'H'm. Strange, isn't it, the terrific interest he takes in you.'

'Slander, Murdo.'

'You know what I mean. His desperate involvement in your welfare, almost as if you and Rob were part of his great plan of universal salvation.'

'He knows an artist when he sees one.' Clip, slither, the main road. 'Taxi! '

I've no money, Murdo. Never mind, come over to

my digs, we'll give him a post-dated cheque. I've got a half-bottle untouched. Bless you, *a bhalaich*. Sweet comfort of leather on my lumbar spine. Dunfreckie stank of leather. Stop it!

'Denis, d'you think this scheme of his has a chance?'

'Who knows? At least it's a change from bloody politics.'

'Yes, yes, Denis. As a mystic he may be a fake, but if there is a solution for this fucking place I'm sure he knows it.'

'I couldn't agree more. Strange.' Whine, screech, Murdo's sharp skeleton stabs me on the Churchhill corner.

'Strange. Wake me up at Newington.' Murdo snoring, three bad teeth.

Life is soundful again. A milkman clanking into a rich man's rosebordered garden at 5.30 a.m. Pert niff of lawn and scarlet crab-apples through my window. I'm alone with myself, too tired to be scared. Drowse in the quiet shades: pearl, dove, slate, salmon-pink fatbelly cloud glistening through an inkgreen yew.

Strange. You are strange, Nichol Ross, for you claim to know it all and won't tell us yet. You are strange, Murdo, for your couplets can make the trees weep, yet you paralyse your fingers with the amber. You are strange, beloved Denis, for you are very tired of life but too terrified of the brink. Life is very strange.

What is your verdict, slateshine waking City, on the torch that has been fired? Have we your blessing, above the engine of your minion? Sing us the death of the night.

City, you know we pray for light.

I rule these sad hearts, Sellars, still. Vanity, vanity, beware! Beware!

John! Wake up, Murdo, we're nearly there.

But blessed be he who may yet safely keep
Our trembling souls from John who made us sheep
In whose black face we laugh and fear to sleep.

CHAPTER THREE

In the smoky back room of the Crown the Saturday afternoon performance was nearly finished. Ricky Slater and his trio were singing the *East Virginia Blues* in three parts, wonderful how that mountain-pick of Slater's can dance like jewelled light on the hairiest number. Around me jeans and sweaters and ecstatic young faces, a few bare feet, and one apathetic monkey on a girl's knee. Alcohol faintly sour in breaths. The front three rows occupied by the Legion of the Great Unwashed, yippeeing in their middle Jesus Christ and the twelve apostles, the monkey leaning forward to chew the ringlets of Doubting Thomas.

Thunderous applause. I slid along the fourth row towards the descending smiles and sweat. 'Ricky! '

'Hello, Denis. You're on last, after young Ann.'

And I'll need to put all my genius into my golden larynx. Thin-sweet slide from modal to modal, thrushsong in frost. Trip of lovelorn lady's feet, she fell in love wi' her feyther's clerk, this kid can sing. St. Peter, stop ogling her ankles. Whisper. 'Did you get my note, Ricky?'

'Yes *man*. We're being asked to appear with *real Scottish writers*. My heart's overflowing, you patronising bastard. Does Rasputin realise how well we're doing without his help?' Ricky's horsey face was unusually livid.

'Don't be like that.' So I sit and explain it carefully, Ricky, this could mean big money, think of what you're doing for culture, and we'll have Maisie Hay down from Banff to keep it ethnic.

'Look, man, she's no longer a big pull. You and I know what a magnificent ballad-singer she is, but nowadays we're singing for T.V. morons. To them she's just another fishwife.'

'The March of Time, Ricky. But please come in with us. You're the pick of your tender generation, and I make not jest.' Ann's brought the house down. I'm scared. 'Lend me your guitar, Segovia.'

'And now,' said a platform voice, 'a very popular singer, one of the few in Britain who is capable of wedding oral tradition to modern accompaniment. Denis Sellars, brother of Rob Sellars, who learned the real Mackay from the tinkers of the North-East!' Crap, mate, if I had a real voice I wouldn't need this guitar.

My stomach a wee bit squeamish and down below that first three rows is enough to make an atheist of the Pope. But a good harsh minor chord and we're swinging: Come all ye lonely lovers, and listen now to me. That's how auld Jock Stewart scared the rooks in regiments, and charmed the evening glades with a deadpan bawdry above dirty laughing, while the potted water burped and bubbled in the twang, *the boiling water—there's a girl there to my right staring at my face,* cut the last verse short: Go where he will, yet I love him still, he's my darlin' ploo'man boy.

But they liked it. Solid young hands paining each other, how I love you for the ringing sounds your silver made at the door. My sustenance. They let me have their worship for ninety seconds, all except that wee monkey clutching his navel, not long for this world now, poor victim of gluttony. Jesus and the apostles, however, clapping as loud as any, sweet hair of them bouncing like horse-mane, gentlemen I can forgive you anything. That's it, boys, have a bath and bring your sister to-night.

She was turning to go at the end of the last row. The profile was split-second, a clean sheen of blonde falling to her shoulder and that navy costume trimming the fullness to unforgivable provocation. Down through the milling shufflers I slipped an arm to her waist in the sunlit doorway.

'Staff-nurse Fraser, isn't it? Kate?' She's blushing.

'Mr. Sellars! I didn't think you'd recognise me.'

I took her elbow, pointed her east under the high sun. No resistance. Your arm is satisfying, Kate, and that sweet strong face looks as soft and yielding as it smells faintly of lemon. In my present state of infatuation I would bounce to Ballachulish for you on my balls, but I'm sick of looking into eyes that I esteem and smelling Lear or worse. Your big blue too.

'Kate, I have nothing to do this afternoon. Would you walk with me, madam?'

'I'd love to. Your name is Denis, isn't it?'

There's a blue shine more dangerous than Lear now, careful, remember Pat Leitch's warning. 'Denis it is. Take my arm, sweetheart. It's a wonderful day for the Park.'

'A good idea,' she said solemnly, sliding under my

arm as naturally as thirty years of practice. Solid and affectionate, but not leaning. A lady. That sun on her sparkling hair, stab of icy heartlessness deep in the beast in me. This is too easy.

Her stalk was stately downhill to the bus route, her ankles shapely in high heels, and Saturday people staring. In a reflecting window I saw a medium man with waving hair prematurely grey, good-looking were it not for half his face, a fine nose and vulnerable mouth gone to waste. They think she's mad, and so do I.

'You like folksong, Kate?'

'I love it. It cleans me out, somehow. Listening to you and Ricky Slater I get the most peculiar thrill, almost as if the song were creating a sort of life inside me. D'you know what I mean?'

Allowing for words being lying abstractions I do, and I'm surprised. We're heading through the shabby cobbled Pleasance, and the grey-breeked kids of this City are screaming peevers. I love the earth right now, that smells of stew and northernness, but you are dangerous. I've learned never to forget the necessity of fear.

'Where are you from, Kate?'

'Kilmarnock. My folk were Highland.'

'A sweet mixture. This land is your land, my lovely girl.'

Off the Pleasance, down a dreich lane, and soon I must come to terms with both of us. Infinite space and colour are approaching our gaze, and stone shapes carved before Adam's babyhood. Darnley's ghost is down there, and the meadow that was churned by Douglas horses witnessing the dreadful parting of the lovers. Waly waly.

We're striding against a screaming rise of volcanic rock, Kate, we're walking into sun and sky and history and all these do awful things to the unwary. How to raise it? You look past the lip-blossom stage, but I must be sure.

'You can stop worrying, Denis. I've few illusions left.'

'I beg your pardon?' We stopped, right on the vista's rim. This is impossible, I didn't say a word.

'When Dr. Leitch was taking your stitches out yesterday, I was behind the screens with a patient. You know it all, and I know you know.'

'Oh, my God, I'm terribly sorry. Look, Pat didn't mean...'

'He's out for my good. He helped me through the worst of it.'

Wind swirling at her skirt, but lust gone. 'It was Johnny Castle, the surgeon?'

'Yes,' she said in a cool voice remote from self-pity. 'The love of my life.' That statement too level to be bitter. 'He took cold feet. But his pal did a neat job on me.'

'Didn't it shatter you?'

'For a while. But I'm O.K. now, except for the complex. Don't worry, Denis, I'm a selective mother. I came for a walk in the Park, because I'm lonely and so are you.'

'Christ!'

'And I—I think you're sensitive, and you've suffered a bit too, though not as much as you pretend.' She blushed fiercely.

This golden larynx of mine is tight with pity and excitement. 'Sit down, Kate.'

We gazed across the wide scooped tunnel at the green flank of the Crags, its razor-spine and ochre terraces. Prehistoric monster. To its right the greater heap of the hill, scars of black rock, fading scabby whin. Half-left beyond the patterns of smoke the knife of sea. All this steeped in the blood and sweat of people dead. Much observed and scrawled over the page, old Sir Walter and all those stony ruins and silver lochs. But I cannot summon a word to accompany the lifting sweep of my eyes, Kate, not even if that mass magnifies under infiltrating sun. Before the wall of the City I have heard a great anti-Romantic sentiment, and I'm exhausted of expression. I'll find my way to your secrets not as a selfish lover, but with the incestuous kindness of a brother. The comfort of your shoulder, sister, you're shivering highly-sexed as me.

Yes, she agreed, what a lovely simple game to play. We both know the folly of transgressing the snow-line, let's be pals down in the undemanding Alpine pastures.

'Kate, I'm sure that we're made for a good old time together.'

'That's what I was thinking too.'

'Dammit, we really are! Are you sure you don't find me repulsive?'

'You're rather good-looking, despite the scar. I liked your face the first time I saw it.'

We parodied this leap into honesty, her shoes off, down the stubbly scree like ponies, dancing at the foot with the sheer smooth joy of road. Her sadness gone in a soprano giggle. Up the loin we bolted for the path under the cliff, normally a hell of an effort, but never on this crisp September day with such simple hope of happiness perfusing me, and this luscious girl fleeter than myself. Breathless we sat to smoke on the path's edge.

'What happened to your face, Denis?'

'Och ... it was a long time ago.' Anger and ugly memories must not intrude, I must vindicate my philosophy of life which is presently so apposite.

'Kate,' I said, 'think how privileged we are. We sit at the mercy of Nature, yet its lies are not for us. Most lovers would be damned for good by all this—imagine how they would rip each other to pieces in an attempt to recapture it.' Inevitable hope, eternal procrastination.

'You may well be right, Denis,' taking my hand. Beautiful she looked, her thick hair sweeping into my face, thank heaven for our protective scars. And this light hung between the fragrant smells and proud forms, how dangerous it could have been but for a sadist's belt and a curette, calm over Old Town reedy water and sheer slope, like a great pure pool of paralysed quicksilver.

'Denis, can you make much sense out of life?'

Cue for my wisdom. 'Not much, Kate, but we all hang on for no good reason. There's a thoroughly unscientific answer somewhere.'

'Unscientific?' she said. Of course, you're a disciple of Nichol Ross: "*The answer does not lie in the hieroglyphics of the test-tube, but in the dark language that flows from heart to heart across Time.*" '

'You've been reading his books. He's got something, but heart to heart isn't enough. It's in the pelvis and the larynx and the fingers we talk to each other, Kate, not in the holy incantations of Lawrence to a God who doesn't exist, but I suspect in a tongue that embraces humour and kindness and need, and the will to survive.'

'And how are you going to decipher this language?' The freshening skin did not smile.

'I can't ever manage it all, which would be a tragedy had I not given up hope already. No man could do it without consulting every Good Samaritan for ten lifetimes and screwing every Molly Bloom for five. But I'll find a wee piece of the answer, Kate, maybe with your help and the odd vision that a snatch of music gives me.'

She turned, warm breath into my face and two healing hands on my cheeks; her lips were moist and long on me. Lovely, Kate, and I yearn to lift your skirt in sheer gratitude. Against me I feel the promise of soft beds and so much Truth.

'You're blethering a bit, Denis,' she said. 'But I'm on your side. I haven't ever talked like this to anybody.'

Another warm embrace, breathless, the heavy hanging fullness of her long-nippled breasts. Trembling beyond control she was in my groin. Red crags keeling suddenly to starboard. Careful Kate, we can't here unless you can do it rolling down sixty feet in horizontal revolutions. And the City's watching.

We sat up, smoothing ourselves. But not a vestige of shame in her, and my heart leapt to the light, trout to fly. This is it. Simplicity. Here I can learn a kind of lieless love and write and learn more.

'This is what I believe in, Kate. Honest human communication at every level. Poor Nichol, with all his dreams of unseen spiritual forces. In all modesty, I assert that he's off-centre.'

'You never know,' she said.

She's not entirely impressed, it's lucky I'm not in the process of pretending to fall in love. But what value for a Saturday walk, this unfortunate turned sensible as myself by sorrow. Surely here is a fragment of progress, untainted by the passion for fidelity and possession. I'll love you and leave you, Kate, and neither shall cry.

She shook her heavy head and laughed with a soft undeclared mirth; for a moment I was gripped by the folly I despised, for this natural animation of feature rendered her younger and quite innocent, and me more helplessly aware of a tenderness that transformed easily to guilt. My soiled manhood and its history backwards to Adam.

Thus irritably I answered her queries about my manner of living. A flat in the Canongate, Kate, decrepit and cheap, and the brilliant folklorist Murdo Macauley is my friend, and so is Nichol Ross the self-confessed genius and my life is the odd brilliant story published and three folksong evenings a week and Nichol and Murdo and I are always discussing intellectual ways of staying alive and next year we're going to make Scottish Literature the most important export to the moon. All else I call dear are a few crazy amateur Folk in Connor's who wash their throats and stomachs every day and believe in God only when he's on the bell.

'Do you believe in God, Kate?'

'I don't know,' she said and began to cry. False move, Denis, ask why later, so two cool kisses, a comforting pat on the crown, and she said 'Sorry.'

'It's O.K.,' I whispered against a blow of easter

round the cragstail, and I told her one of Murdo's Highland tales that dissolved her tears in a chuckle.

'What a queer place Scotland is,' she said, 'so much natural gaiety beneath the black surface.'

'Aye. Most of us were never made for Knox, no wonder he drove us mad.'

Snuggling into my shoulder, she grew quiet; the straight steady usefulness of all this, how I need warm female. 'Sing to me, Kate. Let's have a song of the folk.'

A note came low from under my shoulder, gaining strength and shape, amazement and pleasure suppling me though her voice was only moderate. But despair she sang, the soul-cleansing despair that we both know, Denis, of the champing Douglas hooves and a fragile love fouled by a third tongue and this very earth we press saw it all down there so long ago. Her heart tearing with every ripped blade of grass that her horse left between them:

And that my little babe was born,
and set upon his feyther's knee.
And I, poor girl, were deid and gone,
the green grass growing over me.

That song can shatter the rocks, Kate, though I've heard it sung better. Stark tragedy, and yet you and I are beyond it, my brave friend.

'To-night, lovely maid. I'll buy you the finest steak in the Scala, then we're going to see Rasputin Ross presiding over an unprecedented literary event.'

'I'd love that, Denis. But first. .. would you take me to your digs?'

'You shameless hussy!'

'Denis, I haven't had it for three months. In the light of our mutual discovery I feel we should celebrate appropriately. But—be careful.'

And it was after two minutes of cuddling and laughing that she squinted her first artful look at me: 'Denis, I know old Rasputin probably doesn't have your great experience of life, but you know, I get those queer unexplained feelings sometimes.'

'You do, St. Joan?'

'I do, sir.' She reached to my shoulder for steadying. 'You know,' she said, 'right now I have the feeling...

That was when I stepped back into space, open-mouthed and incredulous.

So had I, Kate. So had I.

How are you happy here, New City, brave white schemes of stone?
Warmer and further from John, Denis, but five miles far from home.
Nae mair slime at the stairheid, exiles, nae mair rats in the ha'?
But nae mair smiles across narrow streets, nae faimily left at a'.

James MacNeill the playwright lived in an avenue of terraced villas, above the working-class scheme cleared from the Fishmarket and Grassmarkct, below an old square village church half-shrouded in darkness, girded with crescents of bungalows.

Modest little man James, he shook us warmly by the

hand, admiring Kate with a shy middle-aged smile. Through the narrow hall into the bright contemporary living-room, the two of us hand-in-hand in white light. Black angled sofas, flimsy modern chairs, mauve and yellow cushions. All covered with sallow people.

In the far corner the patrician face of Ronald Johnstone, swerving lines of handsome integrity and a mane of silver hair. We have the interest of the City's best poet; well done, Nichol. Bald bumpy head of Carson Hall beside him, we have also the interest of Scotland's most popular novelist. A few pretty and other women scattered around, some actors, and a few literary provincials come loyally from far places. Grouped truculently in a half-circle on the floor the Poets. The sharp-hacked face of Rollo Wilson Craig brow-fringed with sandy scurf, surrounded by the penners of the New Movement. The finest exponents of complete incomprehensibility since Mad John. I smell trouble.

Nichol was pacing the middle of the floor, head forward, baggy tweed suit and Ross tartan tie, red-grey ringlets brushed and shining. His glance swept the expectant faces incessantly and with ceaseless change of emotion as a northern sun smiles then snarls behind black cantering cloud. The arrogance on Rollo Craig's face ebbing and flowing as the burning eyes left and found him.

'Nichol, this is Kate Fraser, who is dying for a kiss of culture.'

'You might have come before the pubs closed, Denis.' Then they looked at each other, sexlessly hard and penetrating, but with such appreciative intimacy that I felt right out of it. 'You're a fine girl, Kate, please look after him,' were the surprising words.

'Thank you, Mr. Ross.' Flattered and blooming with pleasure.

Murdo half-asleep behind a large dram in the window-alcove. We squeezed down beside him. This is Kate, Murdo. You're a lucky man, Denis, but I'll take her off you to-night and sing her the balladry of kings below the white pinhead watches. She laughed with delight, but hugged my hand reassuringly.

Nichol's voice, head back: 'I should like to thank you all for coming here in answer to my letter.' He repeated the long speech that we had heard in firelight the previous week. '—Do I take it that you are all with me, allowing for the fact that the mechanical obstacles can be overcome?'

With you, Nichol, they chorused, although they all foresaw several problems: money?—'Lord Kincaid has promised to back me': adequate material?—'Don't be so pompous, Carson, there is not one writer in this room who hasn't something new to offer': I trust that you mean new in its Spontaneous Fluid sense, from one of the Poets—'I trust. Sir, that you understand what you are bleating!': will the folksong ruse work?—Of course it will, Ronald, I thought it up! '

'Right,' said Nichol at length. 'We have a lot of hard work ahead of us. Carson and Ronald and myself are agreed that the backbone of our programmes will be drama—a new play by our host, a dramatisation of Carson's splendid novel *The Seal Man*, and an inspiring mystical allegory which I shall write during this winter.

Ronald's poetry-reading is sure to make great impression, but all this leaves the New Guard with a lot of space to fill.'

'Mystical allegory! ' said the soft sarcastic voice of Rollo Craig.

'Craig, I'll wrap your arrogance round your wooden skull! ' thundered Nichol, advancing with intent. Beside me Kate stirred with surprise, Murdo laughed softly.

McNeill and Ronald Johnstone slipped hastily into Nichol's path. 'Now, now, simmer down.' Nichol nodded: 'I apologise—especially to the ladies,' he bowed with irresistible flashing smile, 'I get rather carried away at times. However, the younger elements of the New Guard are here to-night to give preview of their potential, and by God they shall! Denis,' he roared, 'what will you contribute to our noble cause?'

And now I can really show off before Kate. On my hind legs, and ladies and gentlemen I have the delicatest gem of a short novel which can be read in serial form. Tale of young love, sweet City schoolgirl floating happy as water lily on a serene lake of quiet-life, pitched into a glorious epoch of love by the advents of her seventeenth summer and a young Frenchman, but oh, the horror she discovers in his diary when he has burned the passion from her flesh and sublimated it all into his paper intention. Last chapter she stands same place as that first breath of eternity's promise, same scents, same stars, but now despoiled and different, down to the shore at Dunbar for the last swim—but, aha! Here I must cheat you of five pages, for the final twist must be saved for your tears beneath the hushed cupola of the Ewan Hall—

Mutter of approval, Craig smirking into his beer. I must make the Iago of the piece like him.

'Promising, Denis,' said Nichol. 'I want to vet it chapter by chapter.' Kate squeezing my hand again, between Murdo and her I am so proud.

Two specimen readings from Ronald Johnstone, incredible how that man can set nature to music, and then a very reasonable imitation of Dylan Thomas from a young surrealist, quivering-voiced with Nichol poised to scream contempt and breathing ferocious in his ear, but the giant clapped his shoulder and said, 'Not bad, but these internal rhymes are crude, you must work on it.'

'Yes,' said Nichol, 'we have plenty new material. You know... it has long been my contention that in all the traditions that have made us in Scotland the writers that we are, in all of our attitudes to Man and his true place in the Universe, there are hints of a greater knowledge, born not of modern science nor any organised form of learning, but of what Durrell loosely calls attention. I am at present finishing a novel which describes the sublime experiences I have had over many years among the surviving elements of this true and timeless tradition. I shall publish this work in the spring: I declare that its acclaim will prove an invaluable inspiration to our project.'

Murdo and I grinned, yet the old uneasiness inevitably present, and I could see the conflict on more faces than ours. The conviction concentrated in the words, their deep, melodious utterance, the hypnotic flash of the roaring black eyeballs, seemed somehow to belong to the mechanics of revelation, challenging mockery of the melodrama. There was silence even among the Poets; I saw Carson Hall shudder slightly.

'... be that as it may, I now call on Mr. Craig and his friends to demonstrate their right to a place in our ranks. We have not been the best of friends in the past due to Mr. Craig's unfortunate lack of humility, but our present issue demands solidarity, and I as ever am willing to welcome anything new.'

Craig's squeaky voice polite after all this, but his meaning difficult to clutch. Seemingly there is a hidden language that waits vibrant between words, the spontaneous fluid heart of poetry. Murdo and I quizzical, what is this bugger on about, Nichol bobbing now on his haunches like an angry kangaroo, champing his pipe-stem. 'Come on, Mr. Craig. Let's have some of your revolutionary stuff to replenish our sad hearts.'

'Right,' said Craig. Oliver.' He beckoned to a plump youth in tan duck trousers and dirty white shoes, 'Give them a taste, man.'

Oliver stood up, pointing a forefinger at the yellow ceiling. 'Here,' he said in an American accent, 'is the sort of consonantal image that has been so sadly lacking in poetry hithertoward.' Clearly he delivered:

> Strp—b—b—sht—sht
> Kn rr rr—r—pss—zz—blmp
> Pp—yr—ft—hi—grrrr.

He's growling now, throat swelling I presume with diarrhoea. Utter concern on all faces, Nichol unwinding to his feet. Murdo and Kate biting their cheeks with politeness. Oliver, friend, you should keep that stuff locked up, it's more lethal than your namesake's Model Army.

Nichol bore down on him: 'Are you attempting to be facetious, sir, or do you suffer from inverted intestines?' Poor Oliver, growl gone, retreating to his corner.

Craig came bravely to his feet: 'You damned philistine, Ross! This man has achieved a real breakthrough! '

'You, my friend, will achieve eternity in ten seconds unless you can personally redeem this disgusting exhibition of the velocity of spittle!' Nichol turned, beard quivering at bay.

A slight sneer invaded Craig's upper lip. 'Very well,' he said. 'You have reviled this man of genius, but out of pure love and forgiveness we will now show you a foretaste of *the* art-form of the future. Right, men, let's give these imbeciles The Happening.'

'This,' said Ronald Johnstone's clear tenor voice, 'should be interesting. Sit down, Nichol, give the maestro a chance.' Scurry of jerseys and slacks into the hall, solemn intonation of a directing voice; a tall ugly trousered girl appeared first, the light-switch operator and narrator. Tense anticipation when the fights went out. 'The Happening of Scotland,' trilled the narrator.

One minute, two minutes, heavy breathing, then Nichol erupted from the lower gloom; 'There is a decided *lack* of happening, Craig. I reluctantly assume you are still alive out there?'

'Ross, you're an idiot,' came the reply from beyond

the door. 'This first phase represents the Dark Ages when nothing of any consequence happened here at all!' Nichol's breath whistled indrawn to retort, but now a flicker of light. Oliver the poet pranced in bearing a candle and crooning an unintelligible falsetto plainsong. He hopped from foot to foot, thrusting his candle hither and thither, a scream from Mrs. James McNeill when her hair briefly caught fire, Oliver pranced away.

'That was an impression of Druidism?' asked Carson Hall seriously.

'No!' Craig's voice was utterly contemptuous. 'If you had listened to the announcement of the title, the Druids and ancient Celts were hinted between the words. That was St. Columba, the first bearer of civilised light to these shores.'

'Was that another poem he was reciting?' drawled Ronald Johnstone innocently.

'That, my ignorant friend, was the Lord's Prayer in Esperanto, a modem parody of his ecclesiastical influence breaking down the barriers of language.'

A pale young woman appeared now, draped in a white sheet and bearing two candles, Rollo Wilson Craig treading weasel-furtively behind her, his face smeared with the soot of the kitchen fire. Outside the voice of the Poets rose in a bloodcurdling chant while one athletic member kicked time on the lounge door. The grotesque pair panted toward diagonally opposite corners of the room: the faithful virgin splashed a cross of candle-grease over Ronald Johnstone, reciting shrilly: 'Light, light, Saxon light!' in rapid repetition. Craig was screeching, stamping a weird Pan-dance that smelled of brimstone against the unnerving distortion of the frail candlelight, his party-piece 'Night, night, Celtic night!' synchronised with his partner's, declared over the horrified face of a bespectacled little actress. A final splintering crash on the door, and the two leapt to centre-floor, embraced and departed, each bearing one candle.

In the darkness again the stunned silence was general, even Nichol, but for Murdo's soft guffaw. James McNeill's stocky shape moving apprehensively to examine the door, poking his head round to enquire if that was St. Margaret taming Malcolm Canmore. Of course it was.

Now the lights, and the little actress being led out in hysterics. Rollo Craig entering with a paper crown on his head, screaming like a wounded horse then taking a nose-dive over Carson Hall to lie prone on the floor. Enter two to carry him away, accompanied by an unseen piper.

Nichol was on his feet again: 'This is farcical lunacy! I suppose we are now moving surrealistically backwards in time, and that was the Great Lord Christ come down to save us all! '

'You have just seen the death of Alexander III over the cliffs at Kinghorn,' came the patient, humouring voice of Craig. 'And now, Ross, for our finest phase, just made for the Ewan Hall.'

The narrator woke up, glowered ferociously across the room. 'Bannockburn!' was her cry. 'Bannockburn, burn the bloody bannock!' Hallelujah said Murdo piously and Kate patted his shoulder for comfort. Strained agony in every crevice of face from wall to wall.

The three biggest Poets came loping into the room

in overcoats and James McNeill's three hats, brandishing the three largest knives from his kitchen drawer: 'The English invaders!' screamed the narrator, foaming at the mouth. 'Kill, ravage, Saxon lust—for our sovereign Lord we must!' The audience decidedly queasy now, with instruments of manslaughter being waved all over and around it. One invader retreating in pain from Nichol's boot, and if you tried to shave me like that, friend. I'd take that bread-knife to your goolies.

'... repelled by the Scots Crusaders! ' screamed the narrator.

The three smallest Poets appearing in column of route armed only with nail-files, the gangsters retreating in mock fear towards the door. Involuntary scream from every woman, every man including I rising flabbergasted. Nichol to his feet like a line-out-leaping forward. Mrs. McNeill holding her head between her knees.

'By God, you've gone too far now!' bellowed Nichol. 'How do you propose to excuse this sordid spectacle?' Gallantly Craig came forward before the three shivering patriots. 'Look, Ross, there is no better way of demonstrating how lightly-mailed and armed the Scottish army was at Bannockburn.'

'Lightly-armed be damned,' roared Nichol, squinting fiercely over his head. 'The buggers are stark naked! '

Rollo Wilson Craig leaned forward until his wet forehead was almost touching Nichol's tie. 'I didn't expect this to work before you cant-ridden anachronisms,' he leered. 'But our day will come, man, and here is our last word! Narrator! '

Nudists departed, Nichol's shoulders slumped in momentary neutrality, Rollo doing the nettlestung-bum act again, leaping high, shrieking with highly-selective insanity. And outside the pipes and Cherokees at it together. Murdo, I think we should be Christianly prepared to phone for an ambulance. It's O.K., Kate, hold my hand, Nichol won't let them get us.

The room now in full light. 'Much fight, such light,' screamed the narrator: 'Independence, joyous peace, a king who loves the tongue of Greece!' Aye, aye, James IV, not bad, boys, Nichol half-impressed.

Then all light extinguished save a torch focused on Rollo Craig. Hideous lamentations and shrieks from outside. The broken pipes were hurled at the narrator's feet. Rollo picked up a glass of beer and poured it over himself. 'Flodden! desolation! destruction!' he screamed, and spat on the floor. 'Destruction!' screamed the unseen chorus, but now Nichol was stretching like a panther, reaching for Craig's throat, the narrator fleeing.

'Desolation!' howled Craig and threw the empty glass at Nichol who ducked; the missile parted Murdo's hair and shattered the window behind us, then we were all after them, Johnstone's stick and Nichol's fists flailing, ill-garbed bodies blundering fearfully through the hall, the door, the gate, down the road screaming bloody revenge. Nichol, our ranks are somewhat depleted.

Coffee was required and consumed by all, the various debris removed, an ungodly draught whining through the smashed pane. But Nichol, cool, calm, commanding. We can do without these failed psychopaths, gentlemen, the rich voice of the general who seemed to stretch from floor to ceiling. Steady reiteration of all our functions in the coming campaign, then a few excerpts from Somhairle Maclean's poems translated by Murdo. The fragrant imagery of the Old Tongue, deft, exciting, mysterious as a queen's hand making love.

'Thank you, Murdo. Perhaps nobody here save myself understands Gaelic, but you have admirably demonstrated that no thinking Scot dare ignore the enriching heritage of his northern brother.' Murdo smiling, attempting arrogance towards the barbarians, but the man in him flushing with insecurity and gratitude. Approval was consolidated.

We muttered and talked and got to like each other's admiration, happy narcissists, then a rather less coherent and more ebullient speech from Nichol attempting to equate the agony of the writer with the Divine travail of Eden's Creator. Bottle ever gurgling to his glass, and by God, we are all saints and shoulder to shoulder.

It was at quarter to one that Ronald Johnstone rose. 'I must admit,' he said, 'that I have been moved by this new vision of Nichol Ross. Before we go, here's a wee bit of MacDiarmid to which we can all look, proof that at its best Scottish writing is firmly-rooted yet utterly universal in its message.'

Quietly, quietly, caressing on the Scots:

I met ayont the cairney
A lass wi' tousie hair
Singin' till a bairnie
That was nae langer there.

Wunds wi' warlds to swing
Dinna sing sae sweet.
The licht that bends owr a'thing
Is less ta'en up wi't.

Silence knifed the smoke, Nichol's head low, and suddenly the coldness on my neck sweet and mother. Murdo lean and disturbed in spite of himself, and when Kate turned to lean her head on my shoulder she was smiling and her eyes brimming with tears.

Ten minutes later we walked wet-faced into a blast of night. Murdo in the gutter, Sellars, Kate, Nichol pulling handfuls of privet, occasionally leaning down to question her on books and songs, a quiet excitement on his face. She's doing well, he likes her.

Then to me, as we struck up the South Side slope through large Ionian-pillared villas towards the jagged skyline, 'Denis,' he said, 'you've found a rare lass here.'

He's right. If only he'd seen her white and moaning in the Canongate this afternoon, and all that gorgeous sweating and the sudden spurt wilder than pain was so honest and unassuming. With a bit of practice she and I are going to dissect the anatomy of need.

'How am I rare, Mr. Ross?' she asked.

'Call me Nichol, Kate. I've seen Denis with a few, but I'm sure you're the one, my dear. I get those feelings, you know.'

Easy on, Nichol, this could be dangerous. But Kate quite matter-of-fact, laughing with control she says she hopes you're right, she understands the limits of words, the wise princess.

'So the pair of you are about to join the privileged?' said Nichol with approval as we tramped a crossing into tenements.

'None of this ethereal love-slush, Nichol,' I answered scornfully, 'I've told you before it's the greatest hoax in life.'

Clip-clip, but he's ferocious now in the headlights of that rattling night-bus. Denis, you must jettison your ham-tragic philosophy, this young woman is made for love and no other use. Grabbing my collar, and slapping my red ear behind her.

It stung more than intended in the cold; on the sharp brutality of the pain I flared: 'Ham-philosophy is more your province. What the hell would *you* know about sexual love, anyway?'

Kate and Murdo together, that's unfair, Denis, but worse the effect on Nichol, clattering to a stop, his face suddenly old and grey, brooding at a shop doorway. I'm sorry, Nichol, I swear it.

'It's all right, Denis.' He waved us slowly on: tension among us as we marched under the rickety skyline of Buccleuch, across George Square and up the Walk towards Connor's. I feel like tearing out my tongue.

'You shouldn't have said that,' whispered Murdo while we pattered under the graveyard wall down to the Grassmarket, 'There's supposed to be something hellish in his past, you savage.' Sorry, Murdo, I'm the bitterest swine on earth when roused.

Nichol stopped us by the hillfoot corner, Jesus that

awful ice in air shrieking up the black Cowgate. His great bulk sank across Kate, face screwed very close to me, black eyes fighting alive again.

'Denis.'

'Yes, Nichol.'

'Never regret hurting me ten minutes ago. I deserved it more than you know, laddie. But,' and now a return of the wild arrogant gleam, 'I still say you're talking nonsense about love.'

'Good lad, Nichol,' said Murdo, black quiff standing in the wind, relieved that warmth is among us again.

'... In the face of all your cynicism, Denis, I am convinced that passions of the flesh are heralds of a Greater Power whose face I have seen.'

We were waiting, but awful disappointment this time, for his face suddenly crumpled, and weakly he said: 'What am I on about? What right do I have?' Shrinking to a whisper.

Kate's arm round him: 'We're just not as long in the head as you, Nichol. Give us time.'

'Great girl,' said Murdo, now we're standing crazy, all maudlin-tipsy and wrapped round each other. This is very strange.

Nichol's face sprang alight with a sudden weird joy. He kissed Kate gently on the cheek. 'By God, there is something operating here that is not mortal, lads. This girl will show you one day, young Sellars. She'll show you!'

'I hope so,' she said. 'But at the moment I feel just as down-to-earth as Denis.'

'Never mind,' roared Nichol, out on to the cobbles

and jubilant; a terrified meth-drinker spilled from a doorway and ran for his life. 'Are you going to live together?' he demanded loudly. Easy, Nichol, John's around, the moon's blanched and scampered into cloud, the Castle's scowling up there at your blasphemy.

'Why don't we?' So small her voice, but so determined and pleading; how often since Heartbreak have you tried for peace and failed, sister?

'Careful,' whispered Murdo, 'we're all half-pissed, Denis. I don't want this kid hurt.'

Right, Murdo, but is it a bad idea? Secure haven, extra money, how I can write. And learn. And fuck. And learn and fuck and learn and write—Kate, I'll repay your mothering with such gallant friendship. Flesh on heat in the bitter dawn, we'll laugh at the Canongate sleet. And yes—you are unpretentiously simple and different.

We spoke it soundlessly, man-to-woman.

I said, 'We're going to live together, Nichol. And *you* have a new Art-disciple in Katherine Fraser.'

Nichol came to us, Murdo looking just apprehensive but I know his ten possible objections, and they're kind but invalid. 'Denis and Kate,' said Nichol, looking at us now with a timeless pagan dignity: 'Promise me one thing.' 'Yes, Nichol.' And she echoed me, grave and calm.

'If by any chance you find in each other a proof of my preaching, you will not run away from it, no matter what its responsibility.'

I don't understand, but I'm frozen. 'Of course, Nichol.'

'I don't understand, but I'll try,' she said. My God. Coincidence?

'Come with me,' he shouted, more drunks scattering. 'Come on, come on!' Across the wide Market, past the old square drinking-well, a walk of uneven stones, dirty old pubs and lodging houses, shabby human derelicts clumped for warmth. Up the curving Bow and across the lights to the Cathedral. We stopped by a plaque in the cobbles. Montrose.

Nichol scanned the street for Crows, but not a speck of black to be seen. His arms upthrust to the tall sharp roofs. 'In place of the conventional hypocritic oath that binds most lovers, let us be more reverent. Here he died, one of the noblest of our poets, and all the Black Ministers drooling with blood-lust and the whole City black with shame. Stand on his blood, children, stand on his death!'

The night wind stilled; strangely powerless we obeyed. 'Murdo,' he commanded, 'bless them in Gaelic!'

Murdo intoning, his voice an elegy, but so slightly mechanical, brother you are also hypnotised. The round diphthonged vowels faded through the night; Nichol's flat icy palms on our heads:

'And I order all that I hold sacred to bless and guard this union that is right beyond all calculated knowledge,' he muttered in a voice charged with affection. 'As I know that your feet now point towards the light, so I beseech you to love each other out of lust and away from darkness.' Lawnmarket, cobbled square. Cathedral moaning Amen.

Nichol, you are drunk and off your rocker tonight, and still I cannot move, nor Kate. Oh God, this wild northern day of shine and carnage and tragi-comedy has bound us with such a terrible simplicity, Kate, that I am beginning to fear even simplicity. Hold me, love, guard my back, Murdo, I'm frightened. *They shovelled her from the camber in pieces, her face still lovely.*

But the gale that rose in the High Street's throat to scream 'No!' died as Nichol wheeled to smile at it. Hope lies somewhere inside that uncanny skull. And here we stand on martyrdom, knowing nothing, but I feel your hand in mine, lassie, and above the last note of a rebel benediction the tolerant stars wink and watch like wedding women.

Dear Man of Men so strange thy words and strong
Below the spires that John had screamed among
Yet under madness in my heart a song.

CHAPTER FOUR

The wedding was on Montrose, and the reception was on Connor's one week later; a golden City evening when the shop-fronts glistered the furlong of Woods Street through a moist muslin of intruding haar.

In aid of our kitty Starkey Shearer had pawned his camel-hair coat—an article of sentimental value, for Ollie the Bull had done one of his few successful burglaries on an unsympathetic pawnbroker's to retrieve it. I had sold a story to the *Scottish Universal* for £2; a truth-watered-credible fragment based on a recent *affaire* involving Joe the Rat and his fifteen-stone landlady which had actually ended in his exhausted flight and vow of future celibacy. In addition Murdo supplied £3, most of which he drank, Nichol £5 and Ricky Slater a generous four.

The men of Connor's honoured our bond with unaffected gaiety and sincere unsolicited advice; Kate was solemnly informed by Ollie the Bull that he had never seen a pair so classically devised for the seventy-second position, and the Rat warned me out of his bitter experience that my mistress was a glory, but should watch her weight.

Timorous at first, then gaining confidence as her

scars sensed the sympathy of theirs, she joined them in song and laughter which was only once interrupted when the Rat, moved to sharper insight by the fumes of carousal, remembered a comic passage of my story and challenged me to come outside and fight. And the music leapt through every mood, Ricky's guitar-strings resonant with bothy braggartry or bass-melancholy fearful and a death-knell, burntrinkling clear and seductive when he warbled the Great Hoax.

A night to remember and we marched singing down incandescent Woods Street, on the High Street brae Nichol bending in his stride beneath the clock-tower to boast that the Festival Arts Committee had half-accepted our proposal, and we were to have a two-night trial on 4th and 5th April, and if we didn't draw the crowds the Ewan Hall would be given to the French Ballet. Wonderful, Nichol, how did you manage it? Influence, and a mysterious smile.

Two hours of music in my cloistered home that was already beginning to look like a house for clean and Christian people—kitchen-smells and white tablecloth and the two wee rooms shining with a nurse's hand, a mat on the iron balcony outside and the sharp-turning stairs washed to shining. There's a woman's wages blessing this house, boys, it's sweet to sleep in this dark alley of history.

Nichol and Murdo left last, Murdo unusually nostalgic. 'Thank you, Kate,' and he kissed her cheek.

'Come again.' Slowly said, and I could see she meant it. 'Yes,' said Nichol, sweeping his heavy locks to his nape, 'this is the best thing you've ever done, Denis.'

'The best thing,' said Murdo, his expression haunted by inner thinking. 'For God's sake, both of you, if anything should go wrong, stay friends.'

'But,' I said with a smug smile, 'that's exactly what we are, isn't it, Kate?'

We were in the close-mouth, blinking in near-darkness, but against a farside lover's match I saw her face nod as it sought to hide a secret thought. 'I suppose so,' she said. 'That's just what we are.'

We embarked on our honeymoon at the end of September; Kate secured two weeks' holiday, wc hired a Volkswagen and drew our respective savings. Sunwards we turned towards the south coast and the green and spume of the Channel, for I still had friends on the North Rhine after my National Service. You'll love it, Kate, where the nutbrown skins are smiling in autumn and they sing unafraid at café tables on Sunday. So different from here and yet how my heart lurched when the City receded out of sight.

The honeymoon another brainchild of Nichol's, a suggestion partially convenient to his own needs, Murdo and he having been commissioned by the School of Scottish Folklore to attend as delegates the European Celtic Congress in Geneva. We purred through the rounded hills and long river valleys of the Borders, over the switchback hillocks of Northumbria. Yorkshire soft in a mist, farmsteads of still-northern-looking stone, moorlands, squalid clumps of city exhaling smoke. Asleep through the grit and green of the Midlands, then I woke in a level foreign land of slow rivers, round mills, bright-painted villages. And later the Downs flowing apple round crops of white.

After a rough crossing we drove easily to Brussels, Nichol maintaining that Belgian manure had a more virile smell than the English variety. Flat road, ruddyskinned women working, lanes of fine trees. We crossed the frontier at Aachen, wound up through the drab expanse of the *Niederrheinland*. Narrow villages of red-brick, green doors, taverns glass-signed in German script. Tired, we saw Nichol and Murdo off from the Düsseldorf *Bahnhof* and found ourselves a small hotel off the Duisburg road.

This is real post-war Europe, Kate, our destiny. A city of straight lines, glittering shops, elegant flats with flowery balconies. New bridges and flyovers weaving patterns of traffic; white suburban villas, purple roofs, regal chestnuts, gracious willows, the drone of the long mustard *Strassenbahn*. Jackets off in October, yet I'm slightly edgy, no womb-smell in all this mildness.

Big Arnold Schulz was crazy-glad to see me again, showed us around his artist colleagues, Arnold himself showing unhealthy signs of being influenced by the European fake-school presently obtaining vast commercial reward and unenlightened favourable criticism by blowing up bicycles and corsets and unfortunately no artists under cover of daylight. Sad, Kate, pop-art *ist überall*.

But Cologne Cathedral in one lovely Gothic piece, and the quaint eating-houses hung over river were snug as ever. We toured the steepwood Eiffel, visited Bonn. North into the Ruhr we gazed at the belching monuments of the risen New America. Strong men and bold women working with relish—what power, what energy, Christ grant its end be quiet. *Bockwurst*, *Pils*, *Mayonnaise*, easy, Kate. But we're holding hands that are calm and honest, I think I've found a piece of Peace.

Here I can learn and write (yes, I have started 1,000 words) and learn and write and ...

There was a night that dun-and-olive Düsseldorf sank towards darkness—flat skyline, feathery poplars, maroon sunball, rows of lights across the Rhine, a constant drum of engines heading townwards into pleasure.

We were already half-naked in the central heating: rasp of a zip, slide of nylon, and she was completely; heavy-prowed and falling warm against my manly torso, moist and inviting me between the resilient plumps of her inner thigh. Need is jabbing us, Kate, as surely as the smells of sausage and polished wood slide under the door, what can you do to make that bed sing more than oblivion?

'Come on, Denis, come on, I need it.'

Slow circle of fingertip accelerating to raise the stalks, web-flimsy reciprocation on my rockhard heat, rev up to the thrust gasp and ask what are you thinking. I can't think of anything, hell Kate you must sense the root of this immediate desire, come on, Denis, come on, dammit she's screaming, the dirty filthy beast. Anchor to silt, slam, recoil, I know damn well that I wanted it too but why? Slam, recoil, very pleasant, a shaft of thrill but surely more, oh Jesus there she's opened my back, I warned her to cut her nails. Two films of sweat mimicking the inner union, a thirsty elephant between our breasts, disgusting. Screw the eyes above the short breath, Ovid, Donne, Dryden, Lawrence, I can't hear a word of one of you. I must know what you knew, Aeneas, halfway up the royal mile, no good, no good—shriek! And the he-thing bolted away powerless in its wake. Sticky failure, guilt, I'm palpitating; I've lost touch with the visionary gold in all this unpretentious agony. I've lain in a passion-lair of beasts. *No! No!*

'Is something wrong, Denis?'

Dressing by the window, 'Why should there be?' Too sharp, betraying.

'It's just that I've never seen you so irritated afterwards—I almost feel I've failed you in some way.'

Cigarette floating deep into me from the red point, renewing. 'Don't be ridiculous. In our terms there's no room for words like "failed".'

'But—'

'But nothing. We both needed a good fuck and we had one. That's all.' Stop that pacing, Sellars, inside you're wondering why that statement seemed not to come from you.

Soft-hearted lass, the tears coming you brute, over and caressing her on the damp pillow, her hair a spill of white in the early moonlight. 'There now, it was just a question of need. You're all right, Kate.'

She crooked her arms, pulled me down. 'My need's satisfied, Denis, it always is with you. Please tell me what's wrong.'

Oh, hell, stop it!' Storming in two thumps to the

latticed window. 'If you must know. I'm disappointed.'

'With what we did?'

'In a way.'

Oh, no. Are you—getting cheesed off?'

I smell fear and luckily my answer is honest beyond stricken conscience. 'I'm happier with you than I've been with anybody.'

'Thank God, Denis.'

Marching to her I soothed her splendid meaningless body, held her sitting to me. 'Listen to me, my angel. We've got a great relationship here, but this makes me even more ambitious. I can't help feeling we should be teaching each other something new down there.'

Hair wildswept, breasts against, she pecked me, cheering and coquettish. 'You give me contentment every time, isn't that enough?'

'Maybe, Kate, you're certainly the best ride I ever had. It's just that... I had the hope that some queer revelation was coming a few minutes ago.'

She got up, began to dress. Fruity autumn mocking through the window. 'Just what did you want, Denis? I thought you had pretty cynical views on hope.'

'Simply some explanation as to why vital affinities are vital affinities—you, me and the planets. This is nothing to do with the moonstruck hope we've both left behind.'

I was pillowed on her, head pitched deep in her rustling slip. 'Denis,' she said, 'Rome wasn't built in a day.'

'You know, Kate, I believe you're telling the historical truth.'

'If we're ever going to understand why we need each other, we'll have to work at it. And I'm not sure it's all that important, anyway.'

'You're not? Heresy!'

'To me feeling as contented as you make me is all I ever want.'

Danger, danger, the inevitable postulation rising, I must knock this one on the nut. Up to her expression of controlled conviction I twisted my savage face: 'Now, Kate, you're talking like a lover. We agreed that this won't last for ever.'

Her lightning flicker of pain was less unnerving than its successor, a remarkably successful understatement of Nichol's omniscience hinted in her recovering dimple.

It vanished, she tilted her head bravely: 'I know.' The window's swaying beech-shadows flitting across the tranquillity of her round dreaming face. Depths in those blue eyes I have yet to dive. Talk gone long enough, desire is resurrected through its overmuch discussion. When I turned her back to the bed she shivered, then sank limp, her flesh relaxing, mine apprehensive. 'Not just yet, Denis—just lie—and sort of feel the quiet. Relax, dear.'

Resentment flared, died, I lay beneath her white arm watching the leafy shapes take their time over the generous pink of her cheek, unable to detect anything but the satisfaction I had given her. My need subsiding with the realisation of an artless achievement, but to-morrow I must write.

Strange, Kate, you have clouded the vision, but this contentment is so infectious—small star fading between my flagging lids I know I must have things to learn from this woman who to-night is not my answer. For through the swish of beech-leaves, and against the pound of your big breast, Kate, I hear for a too-short moment as my eyes lock a wordless couplet that Homer never dreamed.

Murdo and Nichol returned to Düsseldorf well-fed, tanned and enthusiastic about the Congress. Some excellent Germans and Swiss there, said Rasputin, their knowledge of our folklore should put us to shame, and by God, the spirit of Calvin kept quiet for the ten days I was there.

I introduced them to Arnold Schulz: delighted instant harmony flowing both ways, so once again we did the Galleries, The Opera and the narrow lanes of the *Altstadt* where urchins stand on mercenary hands and whoop for *pfennigs*.

A glorious *Rheinland* evening to send us off, and we sat under the planes of a riverside tavern watching ten flat miles of west beyond Neuss ripple along the spectrum from scarlet to darkness. Kate and I holding hands under the table, Nichol puffing blue clouds from his pipe, explaining side-mouth his coming triumph to Arnold's patient blonde head. Murdo brooding unfathomable thoughts across the embankment wall, through the vague barge-caravans that coasted on the gleaming nightsheen of the Rhine. Behind us a tableful of dark-haired men and women were singing, an accordion whining softly through the rich Slavic harmonies.

Nichol drummed his approving fingers when a powerful solo-voice burst through its kin like a wild bird rising in fragrant air: wild and high it swooped, for the slender exile threw her head back and demanded the night's attention. Kate's hand tightened mine to whiteness; the *Stadtmitte* was suddenly quiet. Soldier's song though woman-sung, said Nichol softly, his girl stood at the Turkish window, and by God he waved and knew the awful knowledge that soldiers sometimes know. Serbian I think, or Bosnian. '*What's wrong?*'

The song had uglied to a gurgle of words, a wild lock—vomiting headshake; her body bent with racking sobs, the swarthy men trying to comfort her, another dark woman screaming. Nichol rose gallant, Arnold Schulz following. Kate nodded, patted my hand, you go help as well, darling, but I had seen Murdo's sudden snarl.

'God damn this stinking world! ' His *Stein* crashed down, and he was striding blindly down the riverside avenue through autumn lovers lit by shafting car-lamps.

'Murdo!' I missed death narrowly twice, a Mercedes and a swearing Opel, caught a glimpse of the spare form leaning against an equally gaunt chestnut of the shore parkland, staring across the void. I panted for a minute against the trunk; no recognition of my presence, but through his slim head I guessed the despair of his eyes.

'What's wrong, boy? Another mood?'

Turning he shook me, his hair flapping: 'What's the answer, Sellars?' he hissed.

'I don't even know what the question is, Murdo.'

'You bloody heap of smugness. Do you know what that woman was suffering?'

'Homesickness, I suppose. Now take it easy. This is Denis, Murdo. Your friend—'

'Friend!' Pulling free of me he wiped his hands on his jacket, eyes loathing me. 'I have no friends outside my own kind—Gaels. People brought up speaking my own God- forsaken language! '

A tiny knife twisted into a cell of me and killed it; Murdo sobered in a flood of compassion that washed away the contempt, reformed the snarling demon face.

'I'm sorry, Denis.'

'It's O.K.'

He was dreaming over the river, murmuring low, mostly for himself. 'Decaying minorities have such lovely homesick music ... like a sugar gloss on a cake of shit. That girl and I are dying all over Europe, but we die with a sentimental song and our murderers love us for it.'

'Come on, back to Nichol. Maybe I don't understand what you feel, but I'm on your side.'

He straightened with a sudden movement, smiled, ridiculing the situation he had created. 'You're not a bad chap, Denis. Why do you put up with me?'

'My grandfather was a White Wog like yourself.'

We returned through soft-footed shadows to the thorough-fare, Murdo saying, 'Tragedy, Denis. Tragedy has been written with the death of every language since words began.'

Tragedy, Murdo. Sung beside this screaming motorway of the most tortured majority-culture of Europe. Thank God I don't know how you feel.

But we hesitated astonished by the first pavement table. Laughter bubbling by the far planes, accordion skipping on the peals, clinks of friendship, Rasputin has turned the winds of darkness again. Arnold and he linking arms with smiling southerners forgetting their *Heimweh*. Kate under the arm of one. I'll screw his bloody neck.

'You know,' Murdo's voice stated through the harsh metallic air. 'That man is just not normal.'

I'm for going to Kate, but Murdo's hand unusually urgent. Walk back with me, Denis. I forgot to tell you something.

Clip, clip, out of their sight. 'What?' Hum, drum, Mercedes, Volkswagen, Citroen.

'Coming back from Geneva Nichol insisted on stopping at a wee inn in a village south of Fribourg.'

'So?' Clip, shoulderbump, it's colding, dying leaves burnished under savage orange lamplight.

'The proprietor and his wife fairly fell on his neck, evidently he had done some writing there before the war. They all finished up in tears.'

'You're an old gossip, Murdo.'

'Just a minute.' Murdo lowered his tail on the embankment wall. 'While I was helping the old woman to open the bottles she told me how delighted she was to see Monsieur Ross looking so well. That summer before the war, she said, they thought he wouldn't last a month. D'you know why?'

'This is getting interesting.'

'He arrived looking like the wrath of God, wouldn't say a thing, just kept sousing himself rotten.'

'"*C'était terrible, monsieur,*" she said, "*il restait couché tout le temps dans sa chambre, á crier 'Jine, Jine, Jine!*"'

'You think this was the result of the catastrophe he's blethered around so often?'

'Sounds like it, Denis. That's what they heard him screaming—"Jean, Jean, Jean!" '

A sudden gust of wind froze me from the open Dutch north. 'Come on, Murdo,' I said. 'Let's join the party... Strange...'

'Well,' said Nichol five miles north of Darlington and thirty hours later, 'our personnel are now complete. A good winter of writing and rehearsing, and we'll be ready for the fray in the spring. Are you happy about the folk-singers, Denis?'

I changed gear, slid round a misty lorry. 'Perfectly, Nichol. I'll give you the best there are.'

'Excellent. And we are returning filled with the spiritual inspiration of Europe! '

Three enthusiastic voices: 'Yes, Nichol.' Purr, purr to north, the pulse lifting with the dawn and the first sensation of slope under whirling rubber.

Later still. Border hills russeting against a smoky October haze, Murdo and Nichol were dozing behind us. Listen to what Murdo told me, Kate.

She heard it nodding, finished pitying and wise-eyed. 'Poor Nichol. His tragic love would have to be a Jean or a Morag, wouldn't she?'

'Aye, the Violettas and Ramonas of this wicked world weren't made for our Messiah.' Laugh as we bump over a home-feeling bridge. 'Jean McGregor's Scotch Broth, Jeanie's Black E'e, Jean Armour, Jeanie Deans—Jean was the first lassie that opened her legs in Scotland.'

Over a crest we swoop, glorious psalm in my gut for the City and Firth and Fife beyond spread blue and stone on a giant postcard before us, clean and shining as their Creator's imagination. Smell of pine by a long row of cottages, I have brought my friends home to their destiny, the land of Jeans, including the lovely gentle one I hardly knew. Back to Mad John, and death to the enemies of the written word!

Dear Love I know not yet the song
That sings from flesh where truths immortal throng
But help me find it then shall we belong.

CHAPTER FIVE

October flowed along the City walks, a horizontal eddy of yellow flecked with scarlet hearts, and the sun dancing on all the lovely dying. The moon plump and near in the placid mellow void, stars floating swollen against a thick tide of purple, but the east or north-west rising late one night in three to whine an overture of winter. Spread them, Kate, thrust into shelter, there's an age of night to be tholed.

Nichol raged through the streets and taverns, a literary lion ravenous for a gorge of success. Having formed his actors into obedient ranks he proceeded to direct rehearsals in a church hall near Tollcross. His first vehicle of publicity was a blistering correspondence with himself conducted under several pen-names in the *Scotsman*: Flora J. Stevens demanded to know why Scottish literature was so poorly represented at the Festival, Caithness Stranraer replied caustically that there was no Scottish literature to represent; *Alba gu Brath* launched a vicious counter-attack on Caithness whose counter-counter-attack was decimated by one Nichol Ross, who ended his thundering essay by challenging the 'snivelling milksop' to a duel with sabres at the West Gate of the Queen's Park. The Scotsman refused to publish

Caithness's acceptance, but it was circulated with due mystery through the pub-grapevine, and his non-appearance at the appointed hour was observed with considerable disdain by a large crowd composed mainly of journalists, students and policemen. Rasputin seized the opportunity to deliver his standard speech followed by an announcement of our two-night trial by Ewan Hall jury in April—the undergraduates were reported to have cheered and promised their support.

And in the background everybody was writing; Denis Sellars was also writing and developing a sexual friendship with Kate Fraser. There was a smell of witchcraft in the pungent dusk of the Canongate; inspired by Nichol's enthusiasm we were prepared to be surprised by absolutely nothing.

14th October.

Dear Brother,

From a far country I salute thee, oh bitter one! The love of my fellow-man has arrived hand-in-hand with success, Denis, and I feel obliged to declare that our reconciliation is overdue.

How about it? No doubt my brilliance on T.V. has filled you with envy, yet even from my lofty pinnacle I'm prepared to admit that you always were nearly as dazzling as me. I hope to come up to the land of pride and poverty on Friday the 11th of next month—how about sharing a glass and weeping a few tears of forgiveness on a TV idol's neck?

Seriously, I've missed you. I'd very much like you to

join me here in London where a talented singer can't go wrong, for audiences are much easier, and the birds come running in droves.

Incidentally, I hear you're 'married'. I hope she's prettier than the last one. I hear also that our mutual patron Rasputin has got some crazy scheme for next year's Festival involving folksong—I'd very much like to help him, if he's forgiven me for forsaking the sundrenched heather of our dear and ruined homeland—you've no idea how much I've learned about turning music into filthy lucre. I'll have a friend with me next month who is the last word in commercial sharpness. Nichol really should have him in on this. Who knows? We might all make a packet!

Think it over when my name crops up in your prayers, remembering that I am as ever.

Your loving twin

Rob.

16th October.

Dearest Rob,

Fuck off.

Yours sincerely,

Denis.

'That's just childish,' she said over my shoulder.

'Is it hell! The swine thinks there's a quick buck in Nichol's idea, and he wants to cash in on it.'

Her floury hands busy round the shining ironwork

by the grate-fire, girdle scones rising. 'He's your brother, Denis.'

I turned from my writing-desk at the kitchen window, the chewed stone of the breweries and the saddle of Crags behind me through grey curtains of evening. 'I used to be very fond of him.'

'And then he went all commercial, and laughed at your patriotic scruples?'

'That didn't help, but the trouble had started when we were still with the tinkers.'

She waited, her face gleaming slightly wet by the fierce heat, saw I wasn't continuing; back to her baking. Why still seek more when so much of her is already so soothing? But last night wasn't much further, John is somewhere between our endeavours.

A cordial breath of ham and eggs giving courage to my pen, the yellow lamplight swamping our brown leather chairs, and she said, 'Life has really kicked you around, hasn't it, Denis?'

'No more than others, sweetheart. I'm just another thinking denizen of a small country, fighting against the arbitrary process of civilisation. A mixture of sensible intelligence and senseless emotion.'

'Senseless?'

'Every thinking iota of me yells that all wee cultures will be swallowed by the really big fish sooner or later, and there's no point in trying to delay the evil day. But the old tribal scars are there, and logic can't obliterate them. It's neither a morally good thing nor a bad, it's just there.' I moved over gratefully to the heaped round plate, the clean-cut bread and cake, the gleaming fresh butter.

She asked me, her hair piled high and her mouth half-full, 'And your hatred of organised religion, is that just there, too?'

Clink, hot tea on my dry throat, then a forkful of juicy pig and yellow champed leisurely to soft mush. 'That goes back a long way too. I can only tell you that when the church bells ring I want to run for cover.'

She smiled across the snowy cloth: 'I'm finished with churches too.'

'Why?'

'Remember how I howled when you first asked me if I believed in God? I lost my old Church of Scotland God when I let that terrible thing happen to me. From now on God exists only in people who can shift my despairs ... like you.'

'You've come a long way, Kate.'

'So have you, Denis. I haven't heard a tantrum or a death-wish for a week.'

True, there's a noticeable lack of tension in the old musculature these days. Except for the ten seconds after It, when the empty silence still tortures me tense. Treasure the peace of this safe chamber, Kate, for I must discard what does not drive me forward, ruthless are the most noble purposes of man. Haha, my splendid thoughts, always creative.

Hot water thumping porcelain, she to the sink with elegant arms, Denis back to his fourth chapter where the moonlight is silvering such a tender seduction. Clambam on the door. Bugger.

'It's Lily,' she said. I grinned resignedly without rancour.

Brown beret cocked on wiry grey hair, eye-darts of mischief, two reddish plaques of health and hard work shining in the middle of cheeks that tightened puckering near the eyes. Neat slim figure for sixty-eight. Lily Drummond crossed her legs and helped herself to tea.

'Whit're ye scroungin', ye auld gowk?'

She grinned above the steam, showing her cracked plate: 'Canongate folk dinnae scrounge, Denis, ye ken that. Nae cheek or Ah'll skelp yer lug.'

Kate passed her a huge piece and jam. 'Quite right, Lily. Don't listen to him, he loves you all.'

'Aye,' said Sellars, 'I must be crazy. What a shower!'

'The greatest shower goin',' said Lily complacently, 'but they're no' whit they were. When Ah wis a lassie, Kate, it was Scotch or Irish every night. We used tae fill tin cans wi' yon stuff and throw them—Ah've seen the gutters runnin' in blood right doon t'the Abbey.' She spat aggressively into the fire which leapt in alarm.

I love you, Lily. And your flabby old Jock as well. The kindest, gutsiest neighbours in the City. Round the medieval sanctuary the folk are still untouched. Papes and Pro'estants are both preferable to policemen, and Saturday night is usually too damn wild to let the heralds of oppression resound through Sunday's stupor. Here we've been accepted into one of the last tribes who possess their original totems of humanity; in a mildewed close we lie guarded by centuries of independence.

Lily scanning the room, her live eyes fragrant with approval: 'Whit a grand job this lassie's done! My, when Ah think o' the midden this place wis last year. Remember yon awfy pairty, Denis?'

'Shut up, Lily! ' My face grinning helplessly.

'Shut up yersel'! Him an' that daft Hielan'man Murdo had a do for a' their queer friends wi' wine and cheese, o' a' things. Me and Jock wis the only decent people there—they wis slobberin' ower their dames an' singin' daft songs an' yon glaikit Nichol wi' the whiskers wis shoutin' tae hell wi' the bloody Kirk till Ah wis feart lightnin' wad come through the windae.'

Shut up Lily I was saying, but Kate bending back with chortles: 'Go on, Lily.'

'Aye,' the Doric crackling with devilry. 'Yon big French cheese that wis left, it wis as black as a whoor's repitation—this dirty bugger threw it oot in the back close. They say it killt fower pigeons an' Meg Crossan's cat an' Sandy Black the tramp had tae g'up t'the 'ospital tae get his intestants washed oot. An' the smell! It wis the shame o' the Canongate!'

I winked at Kate: 'Have you just come in for a blether, Lily, or have you got more news of the balcony?'

Oh! ' The small body leapt to the alert. 'Ah wis roond at ma daughter's the day. They've had the reporters doon, and the Council have got the wind up. A' the balconies on the new flats are tae be sealed up.'

'I should think so,' said Kate. 'That's the second one fallen in three weeks. If kids had been playing underneath it—' A shudder across the broad rounded shoulders, cosy in white wool.

'But,' said Lily venomously, 'they're no' daein' anythin' aboot the neighbourin' blocks—Craigview and St. Giles. An' they're a' built the same wey! '

'Stay away from them, Lily.' I glowered through the

window at the tall dusky erections right of the brewery, Canaan of the new-cleared Canongate young. 'Our heroes up in the Chambers have slipped up this time.'

'Denis,' said Lily, 'Ah want ye tae write a letter for me tae the *News*. Ah'm worried aboot this.'

'Come on over, hen.' The moonlight can wait.

The following evening a colder drizzle and the night of an important meeting with the folksingers at Ronald Johnstone's; Murdo and Nichol invited to tea, delighted with Kate's baking and confident hospitality. She kissed me ostentatiously when we left, don't be late, darling, I'm on duty early to-morrow.

Up the slippery rise, cobbles mottled red and onyx, our feet squeaking on wet asphalt, Murdo and I climbing breathlessly on either side of Nichol's raging strength, dusty droplets raw on our mucous membranes.

But just what is it, Murdo was saying, it's high time you told us, Nichol. It's all in a certain manuscript, lads, one day I shall publish it and set the world alight! I have quested after truth in strange places, boys, I have learned how to mock the voices of loneliness and darkness and evil. *But what is it*, Nichol? Patience, Murdo MacAuley, neither you nor the wide world are quite ready to understand my revelations. Clip, clip, lost-soul bus-screech, splatter in the gutter, but think, Murdo, you have known people with the second-sight. A series of genetic accidents, like eleven fingers—never! Vestiges of the Knowledge, Murdo, of the race who knew more than the primitive skill of the broch, who could see a vessel far from sight on water and who sat audience before the dramas of ages yet to dawn!

Let them yatter, for Sellars is communicating with live pictures of the present. Musty coal-smoke writhing against layers of darkness and slimy stone. Whiffs enfilading from side-closes: sour malt, savoury supper, fresh-hacked flesh out of a brilliant square butcher's, *Eau-de-Cologne* and varnish from a draughty curio shop. Clitter, rumble, didya hear that Jeanie there's nae mair bargains, brumble, clack, clip, so Ah got twelve quid in the Bingo an' no' afore time. And thank you very much, sir, screech, clip, so Ah ses t'the cunt just you watch it mate, yer fur a errly News! errly News! Cliffs of high dwellings right and left, plainstone, redpaint, blue, cream curdling under lamplight, lace curtains. Across the road sheer rickety morgues with square blind eye-sockets mourning in rows, the inevitable pointed crest awaiting execution. Below illumined by the endless tangents of running polar light the small grocers and antiquaries, the fashionable tartans for the Festival, warm fawn coffee-houses, SURGERY in peeling paint, Tolbooth Inn, World's End Close, *Blankets, Bedding, Sheets required*, JOHN KNOX'S HOUSE quaint in black and white, souvenirs in the charming little window. Head-squares, sootstained skin, dungarees, old dames with hats not much younger, erect in their shabby coats. Courage. Humour. Home.

Pale daughters of the Canongate your forms are slight and fair

Give me your lipsticked fortitude the pagan in your hair
We cannae Denis laddie though we smoke and drink and swear
For if ye try the lobby ye'll find John ahint the stair.

'—So you see, Murdo, there is good reason to suppose that those two things can be linked. The mysteries of the ancient psyche and the creative potential of freely-expressed modern love. Around their fusion, that is where one of my answers lies.'

I heard it faintly, turned with interest, Murdo nonplussed pretending to understand. But my question was baulked by our present position; crossing George IV Bridge into Woods Street, opportunity for a quick visit to the shrine of goodwill. Swing the opaque glass squares and wood. Into warmth and somewhere a guitar. A forest of legs on the slimy red tile.

Starkey and Ollie the Bull staggered immediately to us under the Connor's arch. The long dark shelves and counter rattling with voices. 'Nichol,' said Starkey, 'we've heard about your Crusade. We think we can help.'

'Indeed we can,' said Ollie the Bull. 'Starkey's face is an act of tragic drama in itself, and I'm sure my genius can bequeath your cause another masterpiece.' Silent comprehension among four, another schizo attack imminent. Ollie the Bull's fingers gesturing wild.

Sympathetic, Nichol said, 'I'll be glad of any help you can give me, Ollie the Bull.'

Rubbing the bend of his huge nose, Starkey chortled: 'We're going to raise some money for you,

Nichol. Folksong means a lot to us old Connor's men, and so does culture, by God.' He planted his hand on Rasputin's shoulder.

'Thank you very much, Starkey.' And God help the honest citizen.

The Legion of the Great Unwashed shambled out of the battered door marked 'Gents', singing *The Lily of the West* at a hairy, malodorous pace. Jesus stopped, fag-ash in his beard, nodded amicably to Nichol: 'Evenin' Mr. Ross, we'll see you later at Mr. Johnstone's.'

'You'll what?'

'We're comin' to hear you discuss things with Ricky Slater. We got an interest in contemporary culture, you know.' His head lolled an imperative doorwards; the apostles scuffled after him into the dark.

'The integrity of your support is acquiring a question-mark, Nichol.'

'Shut up, Denis! '

'Man,' said Ollie the Bull, 'that hairy creature tries my patience. I'm beginning to revise my opinion of Pontius Pilate.'

Roaring fire warm at ten feet. The *litterati* gathered once more around Nichol. Easy tea-drinking and soft well-tamed furniture. Ronald Johnstone a tolerant man, and the Legion admitted, though relegated to the wall underneath the large window so that much of them could float out into the reluctant terrace. And by the neat tiled hearth a woman hard to ignore.

'Who is she?' whispered evil MacAuley.

‘That’s Lisa Kendall, Murdo.’

‘My God. D’you know her?’

‘Spoken to her once or twice.’

A long white neck, Lisa, and delicate features spellbinding in profile, narrow nose less cruel when full-face. Lanky body and legs, bright chestnut hair tied in a Hunnish top-knot to fall long and left of her lean jaw. Feline eyes examining us all, wavering to pierce the next victim of a whim. Danger, she’s looking hard, and I can hardly resent my helpless return. I’m frightened, Murdo.

Ronald signalled to Nichol and Ricky; Rasputin pointed young Slater to his haunch at the fireside. Beside Murdo I broke the spell, my eyes screaming for quiet after drowning in the all-demanding green.

‘And who will your principal artistes be, Ricky?’

‘We’ll have Maisie Hay and Peter Douglas for the ethnic stuff, and some of the tinker fiddlers from Perthshire.’

‘Excellent. Will we need any more?’

‘If it’s a packed hall you want, we’ll have to use my group. The Moonshiners, and one or two of the commercial type.’

A hubbub commenced, various tone-deaf purists screaming disgust on ignorant principle, the only sensible comment from Sellars drowned by anti-olde-ballad tirade from shrill St. Andrew approaching premature martyrdom.

‘Shut up!’ called Ronald Johnstone, his cheek a perfect longbow of flame by the fireside. ‘I must confess, I see both arguments. The older tunes are tougher, the lyrics of the big ballads are far better,’ voice rising and impressing us, 'and Maisie and Peter have probably the best styles in Northern Europe. But—'

'But they don't have young attractive voices and their music is full of intervals that the modern ear doesn't understand,' said Ricky flatly.

Angry lightning sparked in Nichol's eye then a miraculous rainbow as he smiled acquiescence. 'I see your point. All right, Ricky, but I don't want anything too jazzy. All this damned pop-folksong—I've a good mind to get a guitar myself!' Hysterics piping round the pastel walls at Nichol's imitation which would shame a masturbating orangutan.

The guests chattered one great hubbub of conflicting sentiments. Damned trite banjo-stuff balls who wants to hear that old drunk Peter Douglas. Look man there's a new dimension in the group-folk this is the pop of the future. Nichol finally crashing through the barricades of chaos, I am thoroughly satisfied with the judgement of my friend Ricky Slater, and Murdo MacAuley will introduce such traditional Gaelic singers as he sees fit.

Lisa uncoiled languorously to her five-feet-nine, rubbing her narrow hips. The movement drew attention as if she had stripped. 'Mr. Ross, I suppose you will allow me to sing with The Moonshiners at your Festival?' Infinite care on the penultimate word. Sellars not fooled, intercepted the sly malice.

'Why ever not, young lady?'

'Because frankly I come from London, and my accent can't handle Scottish lyrics. Ricky uses me mainly as a soloist for English songs—perhaps I don't really belong on your platform?'

Nichol on the spot, shoulders rotating in impotent anger; suddenly he spied the guitar behind her. 'Let me hear what you can sing, madam.'

Cold ripple of strings then her voice purer than the poetry of her plucking fingers. As I was out walking to Birmingham Fair. I saw lovely Nancy. A man's song, no matter, this woman is inside me already. A May morning on Tayside, blackthorn blossom ripe, she's made all that youth-nostalgia captive in a haunting melody that belongs elsewhere. And she rolled her dark eye. First love ten years ago, this is it in new dimension, the same shrieking juices behind my navel. And I said to myself I'll be there bye and bye. Come away croons the siren, my voice bells a wild anaesthesia not of this pleasant room. Oar through the green pools, deep to my reality. I'll kill the pain, Denis, I'll kill the pain. She feels It like me, the bitch has sprinkled tears on me, her voice is everywhere. God within four walls. She's looking at me, the sermon of her long notes inescapable. A solemn minor climax on the strings. Trr-ing—oh, Jesus! *Singing and pain and need and wanting-even-more are international.*

Magnificent, they said, after they had found themselves. Magnificent, and she forebore to smile, leaning on her guitar, eyes jousting with Nichol's.

He stood up, threw an arm to her triumph. 'Young lady, you belong in the same family as Dante, Nichol Ross and Shakespeare. A splendid evocation. Miss Kendall!'

'I think,' said Ronald Johnstone drily, 'that you presented yourself at a very choice time, Lisa. Perhaps she's saved us from becoming too smug, Nichol?'

'There is no fear of that. It is not my intention to illustrate the differences between ourselves, England, and the rest of Europe, but to show that we belong. And when the Ewan Hall receives the works of Ross and Johnstone and MacNeill, and the singing of this charming young lady from the same platform, my purpose will already be clear. Thank you. Miss Kendall, you have done something quite unique for me through the finesse of your talent.' He swept a florid bow, and returned to his crosslegged priesthood.

'She wouldn't make a bad night,' said Murdo wistfully. So they say. Murdo wants you, Lisa, so does James the son of Alphaeus whose neurotic eyes are lusting you, so I imagine do most men in the room. So, God damn me, do I. Dear sweet Kate, where are you? I want to claw my way to that woman's soul, to lay bare the cleft of hurt that made her cry such terrible majestic desire. Lisa, I swear by your unsentimental face and the solemn sincerity of your voice that my heart's molecules are the same shape as yours under the infinite microscope. Union, Lisa, Christ and his Church never felt about holy matrimony as you and I do about songs. It's all illogical and at the moment I am not the slightest bit afraid.

Aeons away the voices were very earnest: that last act needs cutting, Carson; yes, I'll have the script of my own play ready for next month; yes, Andrew, I know you're heavily committed, but I need you for this part. Writers, actors, singers, nodding, suggesting, declaring, agreeing. Then Lisa was talking from the wall again.

'Mr. Ross, in this age of nuclear terror don't you think that the only possible background for the big play or novel is the world situation? All the issues discussed to-night seemed to be of limited geographical significance.'

'Young lady, human situations create common themes from Iceland to Peru. We are all aware of the Bomb, but our fear manifests itself in different degrees and idioms simply because our heredity and environment have made us all that little bit different.'

'Perhaps,' from Ronald Johnstone.

'—There is no doubt that comedy and tragedy and the pursuit of happiness still exist in plenty everywhere to-day. Let every writer dissect these great abstracts to their pith; his awareness of their existence makes him a brother to all good men, but some part of his expression will be utterly his own, his village's, his language's, his country's, and will add to Art yet another precious piece of individual vision which the Bomb must never incinerate! '

'Bravo!' cried Sellars, to shut him up. 'Fine speech, Nichol!'

Then Ronald attacked him suddenly from the right, is Scotland anything more than an abstraction? By God, and Nichol was rampant again, Ronald you should have heard 120,000 people roaring after the final whistle at Hampden. Lisa dividing her attention between the talk and me, a silent spring poem appearing along the curved red lip I despised yesterday as profligate. James the son of Alphaeus seething with envy, combing City soot from his seborrhoea to the carpet, trying to distract her attention.

Nichol ordered Ricky to deliver some music; the whole company were soon jigging into the Gallowgate with *Johnny Lad*. In my present need of profound communication I am in no mood for the sharp garrulous wit of Glasgow.

'I'm going, Murdo.'

'Hang on a bit. We'll get a bottle and go back to my place.'

'Sorry, old son.'

'I see.' Those strained brown perceivers of my conflict.

'Denis!' called Nichol, but the hall was short to the door. By the bus stop under the large solid flats I found myself on uncertain legs. Dull orange glow of the Bomb-Age City licking the slates, wind and fine dust stinging my nose. Other people, precious individualities, reeling with me in the snell east. For this sort of brotherhood I do not yet give a damn.

Sharp words issued on the blast from two familiar figures struggling on my footprints 100 yards back. Disgusting animals said the old dame beside me but I was sprinting without thought towards them.

Clatter up to the far pavement. 'Jimmy,' I panted, 'you hairy accident, I utterly demand of you to let this woman go·'

James the son of Alphaeus removed his incisors from Lisa Kendall's neck. 'My name happens to be Fred. Get lost, Sellars.'

'Lisa, do you honestly love the smell of him?'

Scornfully, 'I don't like anything about him. He's been pestering me for weeks.'

'James, your name may be Fred, but I prefer to call you Jimmy. I command you to stop eating Miss Kendall, after which I'll find you a cage and a hunk of pauper in the Zoo where they're a bit low on cannibalistic primates.' Pushing Lisa back to the wall the apostle doubled his fists: 'We're always being set on by louts like you, Sellars. Just because we're sensitive don't mean we're soft. Put up your mitts!'

I might have expected this of the bastard. Wants a fair fight, these beatniks are capable of sinking into the infernalist moral quagmire. Lisa aware of the uncertainty in my actions, steel yourself to look like Lancelot.

My face as cherubic as possible, I slid a kind arm round his shoulders. 'Come now, Jimmy, we're both folk-people. Surely we can—' and then I had his ringlets twisted round my wrist before he tumbled to it and hooked me in the ribs, but my left leg was behind him. He went over sandals-flying with a chilling blasphemy, smashed his nape, sprawled full length, was about to rise and at me when Lisa interfered; a vertical plunge with the sharp end of her guitar-case. The son of Alphaeus lay knees-to-chin making an abominable noise on the pavement, hands clawing for the throb of his ruined manhood, then a large car howled out of the night to brake beside me: 'What's going on here?' Good accent, smart suit, a City worthy returning home from possibly the Masons.

'Thank goodness you've arrived, sir. We've just been savaged by this lunatic.'

'Lunatic?' The law-abiding righteousness rising uncertain. I pulled James to the kerb by his hair.

'My God,' said the horrorstruck driver, 'What is it?'

'An LSD-addict. Some crazy psychiatrist let him out of hospital yesterday.'

'I've never seen anything like him. These new-fangled psychiatrists are irresponsible criminals! '

A small knot of eye-witnesses dribbling from the bus-stop, and this portly gentleman seems on the verge of a public statement. We must move fast, Lisa, before we are immersed in the sort of truth to which I have a pathetic Freudian aversion.

'Do you know the police box at the lights, sir?'

'Yes, yes I do!'

'If you can get help we'll hold him here.'

'Good lad!'

Instant acceleration, three gear changes in 30 yards. A quick swing draped Fred the son of Alphaeus on my shoulders moaning gratefully I'll get you Sellars if it's the last bleeding thing I do.

'Come on, Lisa—these superstitious people may believe in telling policemen the truth.'

'Why don't you leave the rubbish here?'

'I'd die of guilt if the Crows abused him.'

Outrunning a few unkind insults we pounded three misty lanes to the bridge over the canal. James was left jack-knifed and slanderous over the hypnotising iridescence of its scum. I forgive your lack of love, Jimmy, but I declare that Lisa is not for you. Through heavy night sick with the stench of rubber we rambled hand-in-hand past the gaunt black works, up the hideous slum of Fountainbridge, into the space of Tollcross. A few confused police cars heading north-west and south-east. We hid five minutes in a stair, slipped up Lauriston to sit on a wall in a quiet avenue of softer tenements. I lit two cigarettes.

'Were you coming after me by any chance, Lisa?'

'You're a stuck-up bastard. As a matter of fact I was.'

'Why?'

'Why d'you think?'

'Because in your self-confessed search for lasting affection you've been laid by nearly every folksinger in Britain with the notable exception of Sellars.'

She came off the wall with a sob and lashed at my cheek. Then she began to cry.

'I'm sorry, Lisa.'

'You're at least honest. I shouldn't have done that.'

I took her elbow, pointed her south to the dark Meadows, a grassy face bright then pitch under the high bounding moon. 'I've buggered this up. There's so much I wanted to say to you.'

Clip, scuffle of her old wedges. 'Well, there's a change. Not a hard man after all?'

'Not at all, Lisa. Do you honestly fancy me?'

'Yes.' Her fine-boned face, footlongplus, unutterably desirable, a beauty born of pure situation. She smells of sweat and Capstan and scent. How sheerly inflammatory.

'Why?'

'God knows. I look at you, I sing to you, I look at you. I think I need you, and I keep thinking, maybe this time— Denis, what's wrong? You're as pale as bloody death!'

She settled me against the bole of a lustrous beech; before us the gentle lowland, rings and squares of shadowy moonbeams, stately minuet from the high tree-fronds but a dishevelled schottische when the wind fiddled a tune to the light's advances.

Broken, I told her: I had a conversation so like this over by the Crags. Need seemed so simple, Lisa. So it is, but it has conditions, Denis. It was song and need and progress, Lisa, and I think the world of her, but there's something missing. Of course there is, Denis, she can only go so far with you. It was to be simplicity and learning and vision, Lisa, but the vision never came. Times she understands me, times she hasn't a clue.

'You haven't read the best writers, Sellars. She can't share your most passionate experiences and longings.'

'She likes singing, Lisa.'

'Do you look at her the way you looked at me in Ronald Johnstone's?'

'I don't know. I don't think so.'

'Does she feel what we were feeling?'

'How the hell do I—?'

'Is a good song a succession of waves around both of you, pushing you nearer and nearer each other till you're locked in an underwater clinch too marvellous to be portrayed in any form of art under the sun?'

'My God, Lisa!' Rehearsed?

'*Do you have this with her?*' The thin features glowed fanatically; above us the scanty branches whispered soothingly, and Lisa gave a wild chuckle, burying herself in my shoulder with a wide swing of hair. 'I've had so much with so many, Denis. But never enough. I'm sure you're the one.' Yes, I felt it too, Lisa. For every second of your singing the hair was threatening to stand on my pimpling neckcrease. If I'd only died then I'd be jazzing away on Olympus right now for ever. We have a mystical communion whose intensity says This is It, and yet—you postulate too much hope.

'I don't know, Lisa.'

'You don't want me?'

'You'll never know how much, hen. But—there's something about Kate. Oh, God, you've mixed me up, you bloody witch.'

Kate, Kate, I've lost simplicity:— *I get the most peculiar emotional thrill, almost as if the song were creating a sort of life inside me*—a voice from another planet.

'Well?'

'I can't, Lisa, not yet. There's just something about her.'

She traced the car-lights across the Meadows, brilliant airworms noisily crawling. 'It's no good, Denis, I've seen her—she's just an overgrown sensation. You'll come round.'

Maybe, Lisa. If it means that my fractured striving becomes slightly less turbulent I'll dance a crazier triumph than those mad white feet of moon on beech and Barclay steeple. But there's something about her, although your chords hypnotised me to-night into the nirvana I thought I wanted.

The lithe London girl pulled me to my feet and kissed my cheek with level mouth, her small teeth grating. 'I write too, you know, Denis. And I'd love to see your stuff. There's so much we can do for each other.'

'Don't rub it in, Lisa! '

'I'll wait, Denis. You'll come!'

Warm lips clicked on my scars. 'That's one of the few chaste salutes I ever offered, Denis. All of me goes with it. I'll wait.'

The night took her, opened its black embrace from

the heart of the parkland and I watched her go almost in terror, that tired long-legged walk symbolising the pain of her rejection. With my back to the pliant tree I watched a woman walk away from a chance of time and people that should have made us lovers immortal. Through the traffic she misted, slipped ghostly up the Links into the callous streets of pride and prurience where she lived anomalous and would lie in wait for our second lesser meeting.

And cursed be she who gave me from her eye
A love that strove mine own to make a lie
I nothing know and pray once more to die.

CHAPTER SIX

Early November, Visibility nil. The thick banks sat yellow in our streets. Occasionally the roofs appeared above them, possessing a cold contrasting elegance. Frost at night crackling underfoot, adding sensuous silver capsules to trees and cars, the day-fog lifting briefly to display a sky of bland green ice or a five o'clock sunset of burning rose. And the City ever aware of a huge restless figure looming through the damp underworld, the ghost of some terrible importance.

Nichol's part-time actors began to whittle at the plays of James MacNeill. Ronald Johnstone selected a dozen poets to support his own readings; they came at weekends, drank, criticised the rehearsals, came back the following weekend for more. Readings and plays were rehearsed together; sometimes Ricky Slater's Moonshiners provided relaxation for the tired cast. And a difference on every face involved: there were glints of adventure among the shadows of fatigue and the tense-set expressions doggedly surviving the grand Sunday evening rehearsal when Nichol deliberately bellowed the whole company to the need of a drink. This is no longer a pipe-dream, boys, we really can do it.

Sellars now in his sixth chapter, but the going sticky

in places. Kate interrupts too much, doesn't realise the battles fought inside before the blank-faced enemy can be confronted. But the house is warm and she's loyal and kind; Jock and Lily and the rest of the Canongate worship her. *Get lost, Lisa!*

Repeatedly the lanky apparition flirting through my reluctant inner eye.

The curse lifted on a Saturday morning. We shopped up the bright dripping High Street and along George IV Bridge. A shaft of strained sunlight playing on Connor's sign and the dissension of Joe the Rat, Ollie the Bull and Starkey Shearer on the drying pavement below it. The big glass windows sparkling behind them.

'Ye're just a Yank! A stinkin' bloody Yank! '

'Joe, I'm being very patient with you,' said Ollie the Bull. 'I've told you before that I have adopted this country, and that I am a better Scotsman than you! '

'That does it! Come on and fight, ye talkin' panda!' Screams from the irate little drunk, moving gratefully behind Kate's interfering arm.

'Now, now, boys! What's going on here?'

'Good morning, Denis,' said Starkey. 'A most unfortunate altercation, this, deriving from argument as to who was Cain's wife.'

Kate moved to my side, whereupon Ollie the Bull threw the defenceless Rat into the gutter by his belt and double-chin. 'Now, Ollie, he's smaller than you.'

The madness passed from the huge countenance. 'I'm ashamed, Denis,' said Ollie. 'I've laid violent hands on my brother. What's worse, my hands are rotten with the odour of his unwashed skin.'

'That does it!' screamed the Rat. 'I've lost ma temper,' coming to his feet, hiding behind Starkey's narrow shoulders and small elfin head: 'Come on, ye big nutter!'—moving backwards dangerously into the hurtling weekend traffic.

Then Kate, learning fast, said Crows. Two of our heroes, seen the lot, coming across fast from the Scala.

The Rat's jacket was thrown down with great courage: seventeenth time this year and not even his turn as decoy: 'Come on, ma lovely boys! We're all fighting men here!' Refuge in Connor's was immediately achieved by all the other fighting men; betrayed to isolation by our judicious retreat Joe made his accustomed breenge for the Row and the graveyard, the police their experienced futile pursuit.

Connie served us with an excellent anecdote and a pint and sherry, indescribable the tart bliss of Connor's amber. 'Have a look up the top o' the bar, Denis.' Something odd in her voice.

'Excuse me, Kate.'

I clapped up the red tile, under the arch with the kiltie on it, through a bunch of coalmen to the two neatly-dressed visitors in the window alcove. Oh, hell.

'Good to see you, Denis,' said Rob Sellars. 'This is Len Hackett, my agent and producer.'

Saturnine face, close shrewd eyes and a hand like decomposing liver.

'How do you do, Mr. Hackett.'

A few essays at conviviality from Rob, God damn

that unmutilated twin-face so smooth with patronising amusement. Hackett not the slightest bit uncomfortable which any good man should be, ordered three doubles with the air of an animal that enjoys ownership of souls.

Quick gulp made in anger. I'm coughing. 'What do you want, Rob?'

'To see you.'

'You're a liar. What do you want?'

'Why can't you believe that I'm trying to do you some good?'

'Careful, Rob, you're developing a sense of loyalty. My medical friends say it can lead to the gas oven.'

'Mr. Sellars,' said Hackett's brisk whine, 'we'd like to discuss matters with Nichol Ross. We're honestly anxious to lend a hand in this project of yours. I've already written to Ross, but he wouldn't see reason.'

'We don't need you.'

'Come off it, Mr. Sellars, Rob's the biggest folksong name in Britain. He could make your show.'

'It isn't a show in your terms. And what's *your* angle, Hackett?'

The pale eyes said briefly ungrateful hairy-arsed savage I've just bought you five bobsworth, then they smirked unconvincingly. 'I can help too.'

'Len is a genius at producing folksong, Denis. If you let him run your wee affair, it'll be a sensation! ' Rob crimped his styled dark hair. Nervous. Aha.

Behind your silk shirts and white teeth, gentlemen, I think I can see the facts. You're branching out, new TV programmes starting up here, all BBC-directed; Ricky and Co. will be told what to sing, no tramps or hawkers or authentic balladeers allowed, far too rough and rabble. But Nichol and his project are threats: he won't wear your standards, and he could influence local singers away from your stinking fat offers. Oho, my beauties, it's the arm round his neck you're flinging. Come in, Mr. Ross, join the Club. Douse the heavy load of your integrity and realise how festal is the life of the thoroughbred parasite.

'Some sensation. You mean he'll kid the good people into thinking they're folk-fans when all the time they're listening to dressed-up pop.'

'Oh, for Pete's sake, Denis. This word is a myth. There are no "folk" left in the parochial sense. Pop-song is the folksong of this day and age.'

'I'd like to hear you say that to the tinkers. You wouldn't be so bloody affluent if they hadn't kept their traditions going.'

'And if I didn't dress their songs up with a bit of guitar and polish nobody would listen to me. Come off it, you do the same.'

'Do I hell, you lying bastard! '

Rob's eyebrow crooked with charm. 'Easy on our poor dead parents, Denis. Now, look, I know you're supposed to be breaking your heart about dying communities and all that jazz, but I doubt if you're any more of an idealist than I am.'

'You'd better watch your teeth. You've become so corrupt yourself, you've forgotten there are some people whose talent can't be bought.'

For a flicker the grey eyes keened as hurt and wounded as mine. He was such a nice kid so well I remember, why did it ever happen?

But sharp and suave he reverted: 'You can't turn back the clock, Denis. The songs of the bloody People are changing as much as their literature—this is the era of the entertainer and his musical druggery. The trogs who gape at me don't want sounds that think! '

'Some trogs round here still do!' One up your nostril, Hackett.

'Do they? I've heard people tell me this morning they can't stand the noise of Maisie Hay—nowadays they don't want medieval sagas any more than they want Plato or Tolstoy.'

A nasty echo of the despairing reflection of none less than Denis Sellars. Gazing deep in my glass for comfort I'm utterly grateful for Kate's reflected smile. I closed my eyes, speaking with less mettle. 'I don't know, Rob, it's not as simple as all that. But for me the loving and sharing of a real song are real experiences. I'll fight all the way to keep you money-grubbers out.'

Rob shook his head, superior yet hardly unkind; Hackett thrust his blue chin forward.

'Did nobody ever tell you that the greatest troubadours all sang for money?'

'I suppose you were their agent, Hackett. Lean back, your tongue smells.'

Anger squashed the dark oval blob of his face. 'We've tried to be nice, Sellars. I'd advise you to arrange a meeting with Nichol Ross.'

So, and temper, for I knew it. Rob looking apprehensive at this turn in events, especially when I leaned forward with a sour smile and took a handful of Hackett's bright green tie. But enter Kate the

peacemaker. Steady white hand from behind, conversational reproach, leave him go, Denis.

'I give up.' I drained my whisky and suddenly Rob and I were laughing. 'Rob Sellars, Kate Fraser. And this creep Hackett eats my brother's voice for breakfast, darling. I'd love to paint him green in Glasgow on the 12th of July.' Hackett snarling, 'You'd better be careful, Sellars.'

'He's highly-strung, Mr. Hackett,' said Kate with apologetic pride. 'It's nice to meet you, Rob. I'm glad you and Denis have finally got together.'

The confident face of Rob Sellars stared a short appraisal, but lost interest. She's beddable, but not his model class, one day I'll spoil his leering lean magnetism. Sparring with words to regain composure and hypocrisy, we let Kate insist on buying us drinks. Such an occasion. Hackett's eyes quicker from face to next than the evil thoughts of Satan. Small-talk. The weather, politics, then she told a local story and made us laugh. I think I love her for a second. The warmthless sun of November is glowing on her plaited crown, and she's adding a tonic of admiration to the spirit of their glances.

'Can I speak to you alone for two minutes, Denis?' Rob serious, hand on mine.

'She's not for sale.'

'Please.'

'O.K. Kate, look after Onassis here.'

We moved past the Legion (one of whom snarled at me) to the sweeter air by the arch. Connor's all shining glass and polished oak and amber compensation for everything that everyone here is not. Long jangle in my

pocket, Rob took the hint, two more, Connie. What do you want, brother dear?

'Denis, for heaven's sake don't cross Hackett. He's a very influential man.'

'Sweet advice, Rob, but too late.'

'He *could* do you a lot of harm. And I'd like to help. Think it over.'

'How can I ever thank you, brother? Come on back, Kate's prettier than you.'

I experienced pleasure when the sneer and brotherlook clashed. Something painful behind all his conceit and pride of life. My face driving him neurotic. I'd love to think.

'Denis ... I met a chap called Colonel Ferris in London. He knew our old man.'

'Back to Kate, Rob.'

'Listen!' Rob's voice was an ugly clangour of emotion above the clink and swish of Connie. 'He knew the old man well, and mother too. He was with our father when he was killed near Tunis.'

'This is all very moving, Rob.'

'Denis,' Rob was lost, angry, fists clenching. Very strange. 'You know we've always blamed the old man for everything—but Ferris reckoned that it was mother who drove him crazy.'

'Shut up.' I cherished the sinister control in my voice; my own features recoiled from me. 'From all accounts she was a poppet. Leave her alone.'

Jesus Christ, tears in those idol-eyes. 'You can hit me if you like. But some malicious buggers have even suggested that he wasn't—*please, listen, Denis!*'

'What?'

Oh nothing. Look. Ferris was certain she was an alcoholic. That was how it—why she crashed.'

'He drove her to it. To kill herself.' *I will believe this till I die.*

Rob calmed with the swill of his whisky, but his voice still urgent. 'Ferris said he was a fine man, Denis. Spoke about us a lot.'

'Spoke about us! *Spoke about us!* Do you remember Dunfreckie?'

Rob's chin slithered on his collar; turning to me again he was the veteran performer, glib grin for the plebs, and I resented this change on less explicable grounds than the obvious. 'Maybe you're right,' said smiling Rob Sellars of *The Folk Show*. 'I just thought you'd like to—oh, I forgot!' His wallet appeared, smooth yellow pigskin.

'Are you giving me a loan?'

'No, boy. Ferris gave me a photograph of Captain Melville Sellars. D'you realise you've never even seen what he's like?'

High above Woods Street an early winter cloud smothered the sun. Connor's was plunged into gloom, oaken shapes staining solemn.

And my stomach pitched in sudden reaction to Rob's droning voice. 'Put the bloody thing away! I don't want to see it! '

The apostles whispered in surprise, then sympathy was heard even from the son of Alphaeus for the livid misery that sagged on my face.

'Put it away, Rob! '

'But—'

'Put it away!'

Unsmiling my brother slipped his left hand behind his right lapel. He started to speak, stopped. Looking at me as at a horror film.

I want to scream. Kate. Murdo. Nichol. Nichol. Panic. Just couldn't help it. Stupid. Came right over me.

Tentatively we walked the long bar back to Kate, exchanging glances with the air of men who have betrayed each other to a sinister unknown fate. And will it deal with us together?

The spirit of John is abroad. Shrieking a sermon of arctic vehemence through our slanting streets. Wildest night I remember for years, yet every crystal lamp of heaven so calm and beyond it all. Turrets and blue ranks of roof, heavy lands rock and reel, creak with stress, stone gropes frantically to mortar. Dear Lord, prays the Castle, I've been so good lately. You will endure, Grey Woman, your slippers are set in solid rock.

And we who lie in habit, Kate, within these weary walls, can we create a constructive warmth to melt this ancient arrow from the sea that strikes ice into our City's marrow? To-night I need a sign, Kate, or weeks hence I'll lie in a crisp suburb with a heart that shares my deepest longings.

This day has made my night a thing to wonder in. This morning I was afraid to look at my father's face. There once was a rich young farmer who fell in love with a Peebles girl. And they lived their own version of love's

tragedy, they must have been given a wicked vision of the hopeless hope. The neighbours heard the strife that summer, screaming at her he was, the black beast. And Rob once told me he fancied he could just remember the sobbing. His earliest memory. They found the shattered Austin and Jean Sellars mixed like trifle under the moon. And two years later there was Sellars blood on the Tunisian vines and small Sellars tears all over Dunfreckie. Fine man be damned and yet I feared his face. So much it could tell I do not want to know.

My altruistic endocrines are ripe for revelation. I look you up and down, regret that our communication requires a physical focus. For so shimmering and desirable-white you are. From falling blonde hair to long wriggling toes. And not a jarring word in your mouth. Beside you I lie, feel life hardening, awakening. Explosion! Control away, she's shivering like a windswollen aspen. Ridiculous metaphor, concentrate on the deeper levels you seek, otherwise you'll realise that this is more like mounting an epileptic camel. Deep in her mouth I parody the vital demand. Iron in the forge, moist heat resenting withdrawal, thrust, pull, thrust, and I'm feeling a glorious absurdity. Hands lingering out of musty darkness down spine over thigh, this is not so bloody absurd. Fingers are talking truth, I'm burning into song up the belly *now find my heart Kate* I've got the feel of the language but my grammar-book's locked away. Crush eyelids, feel, feel, FEEL! Where is it Kate? Your body is a grip of chilling roasting joy from rubber-firm tit to satin calf. I'm short in the breath but weird cogent messages are binding us pore by pore. I feel you running into my knee-caps, my shoulder-blades. *But where is it, Kate?* I must find the source, the answer to Dunfreckie and the foreboding of the unfilled second. *Find my heart, Kate!* But come on darling I'm nearly finished she gasped all flesh weeping. I'm too aware of our skins now, Kate—GONE! And my thought at its going that the hair in your armpits is so coarse. I smell, see, touch as friend again your ripe carcass. This bed is high. Tears in my eyes. For this was so very near that I can't bear the old stale emptiness. If it had been Lisa.

'Oh, Denis, we needed that.' Slow light filtering through from the kitchen, slight shame flushing complacence from her smile and oversighed sighing.

'Physically speaking, my dear, that was the best fuck of my life.' But limp weariness was never my ambition.

'Don't use that word, Denis. It's not right.'

'I didn't realise you were so inhibited.'

Arms sliding behind her wild head, 'That's not what I mean. It may apply to ninety per cent of the human race, but that just isn't what we were doing.'

'Go on, Kate.' Still weary, but more interested than before.

'If words mean anything, that one is applied classically to a bull and a cow.'

'Your biological training, Staff-Nurse Fraser.'

'I'm prepared to believe that many people make love like two-legged cattle, Denis. I've done it myself. I've—I've been fucked. But with you—'

I welcomed the beam that replenished her full form. 'I'm almost inclined to agree with you, Kate. I nearly got somewhere just now. But careful—you're sounding like a romantic again.'

'No, I'm not. I'm being as honest as I was in the Park. We just weren't—I don't even want to say it.'

'Maybe we weren't.' I'm so confused. Simplicity is getting complicated. You have a wonderful body, Kate. Does things.

'Maybe?' Bloody hell, waterworks again. 'Denis, what more can I do? Don't you see how we're growing together?'

Almost, if only I didn't hate this noble falling-short so much. Something happened, but my swears were for its lack of purpose and direction.

'Kate, lass, don't you cry a bit. I know it all right,' and the half-truth quarter-satisfying. 'You definitely did something to me to-night.'

'Thanks, darling. I thought so.'

I was composed in the kitchen, whistling in neutral emotion as I cut and spread some Welsh rarebit. Her hair swept back into seductive order she came through; my eyes dickering to her magnificently-filled sweater while she ate with me at the window. By the holy rood I am slightly content and the kettle is singing on the hob. Wallpapers soft yellow. A nook of Montparnasse hanging above the gold clock and the ivory impala on the mantelpiece.

Cling, gurgle, hot sweet tea and mustard-pepper taste.

'Rob seems rather nice, Denis. But I don't like that creature Hackett.'

'Rob's tarred with the same dirty stick. You don't know him.'

'No, he's not. There's something honestly sad in his

face. Hackett's face has no room for sadness. Doesn't understand it.'

Just what I was thinking, but you have no right to jump my gun: 'Rob has good reason to have a sad face. He's done his share of destroying.'

She looked at me with sudden devastating sympathy. 'I knew it, Denis. Your face.'

I moved away, drew back the curtain, gazed into the howling abyss where my friends were huddled under stone awaiting a quieter morning. 'We were fourteen, Kate, in a tinker camp near Aboyne. Our foster-father was beginning to teach us his best ballads. One night I made a better job of *Lord Lovat*, and Rob couldn't take it. He was boiling water for a rabbit stew—I've never seen such mad jealousy on a human face. He was always prone to jealousy.'

'So that was it. I think he's suffering for it now. More than you know.'

'So he should, the bastard.'

'I know it's not easy, Denis, but try and forgive him.'

'You're a strange girl. In some ways I damn near love you.'

She was a torrent to me before I regretted the words, but she asked no more than my embrace, another increment of shelter against the cruelty of northern Nature. Her hair sweet up my nose, all of her pressing me and not quite as before. This reminds me of the plaque of Montrose, Kate, a reincarnation of my heart's September song. You and your peerless comfort, Lily and Jock across the balcony, all around us the muscular heart of a real people. Rob and Melville Sellars are a long way from this.

Near the end of the month Murdo bought a Citroen in loving memory of a dead rich uncle, and the last Sunday of November was a rare beauty. Nichol and he arrived in the Canongate for lunch, and were viewed from windows with the usual mixture of respect and suspicion. When a knot of youths gathered round the car, however, I observed with satisfaction that it enjoyed the protection of Meg Crossan, boss of the lower stretch: 'Git oot, ye interlopers, these are friends o' Mr. Sellars.'

Lovely day, Murdo's opinion after eating, where'll we go. How about Peebles I said before I knew why. Association of recent ideas. Wouldn't Haddington and Gifford be nicer, from Nichol, but Murdo and Kate liked the Peebles idea. We brummed a curving trail through the Park on to the South Side, down the new-chemical roads towards Roslin and Penicuik.

I sat in the front beside our lean driver, Kate enjoying a cool Sabbath dualogue with Rasputin in the back. In the mirror new lines of age and stress on Nichol, grey streaks in the hairy jut of his chin, remarkable creases high on the red-speckled pate. But gentle as ever with her.

He crouched forward, eyes relentless with worry. 'I hear Rob's up from London. Weren't he and his agent in Connor's the week I was in Aberdeen?'

Kate and I recounted the meeting, through the hard brown fields, the clumps of rheumatoid skeletons, the thin higher greens on the hills.

'So he's joined the enemy. After all I've cared for him.' Nichol reclined perplexed, smote his knee angrily: 'If they want to play it tough, they'll find this old dog is full of firm teeth. I wonder what Hackett's after.'

Murdo leaned back from the wheel. 'There's a new T.V. Folksong programme coming to town. I wouldn't be surprised if Hackett's the producer.'

'So that's it.' God help me if those black eyes are ever my adversaries. 'By God, he won't ruin our singers, boys— I'd murder him first!' He shouted it, through the window into dull deserted Penicuik, an unhealthy swollen throb in his temple. Kate took his arm, whispered, soothed, looking the queen to-day in a new red coat and her cold hair falling to it. My thoughts lyrical as I gloat her reflection.

Murdo's eyes were on guard, always irritated by pretty Lothian scenery: 'How's the novel, Denis?'

'Coming on. The Frenchman's easy, but I keep losing the girl a bit.'

Murdo's words hissing through his teeth, intensely critical. 'This sounds most unpromising. You're writing about people you don't know.'

You're right, Murdo. I should be translating Sellars and Kate Fraser into fiction. But without The Answer she keeps withholding I'm afraid our narrative would appear so retrogressive and unsanctified to the pundits. A document of promiscuity and the negative side of human nature. Depressing filth. It's so hard to present the mottled truth to people schooled in black-or-white, whose fleetest vehicle of escape is the dream of absolute virtue and whose last-ditch excuse is the devil. But the chaos of my own fight for survival. Where every tiny action seems to be the resolution of a dozen internal algebraic forces. Good and evil, polarised myths. And environmental stress distorts these inwishes even more, but we daren't write too much of that unfashionable squalor for we're living at the end of an incredible literary era where against all the odds the kitchen sink achieved deserved prominence through the honesty and integrity of a few and then vanished despised under a mountain of mediocre writing and avaricious publishing.

'I'd love to do a book on Kate and me, Murdo. But I've a feeling we're too ordinary and therefore too painful.'

'If you're writing a valid situation it'll survive its ordinariness. Remember Joyce.' After that a reverent silence, thoughts of Dedalus, stale crusts, and sour tea.

The first glens of the low hills, shallow and dark. A cold soundless river, serpent of frost beyond a few tough little sheep. Kate telling Nichol about her patients, she can make you see the indifferent exhaustion in their brave faces. Must be hellish to be old, but her description doing no apparent injury to Rasputin's insane faith in his own immortality. Absorbing every syllable of her low, loving voice. Murdo and I happily detached from the immediate by it, sailing into wooded falling country past Eddleston.

'Hey, watch your elbow, Sellars! '

'That corner, Murdo! That's where my mother was killed.'

'Oh, darling.' Kate's lips touched my hairline, her hand on my shoulder.

'It's all right, for God's sake, I hardly knew her. Did

you know, Nichol? That's the corner she crashed?' but he was turned, following the belch of our exhaust. 'Is it?' Half-dreaming. 'Is it, Denis? I see, that's where it is ...'

He brooded on, face hidden towards the orange west. Kate making friend-glances at me, she once said she was a selective mother. She can save me. She'll have to.

Strips of pine, clean low houses, trim gardens, Peebles. A wide country street, bordered by walls of tasteful quiet colour, filled with City philistines breaking the Sabbath.

Pretty tea- and other shops, nearly all closed. And a big kirk-shape watching from the street's end.

'Where now, people?'

'Let's follow the Tweed into Innerleithen,' I suggested.

'No! ' Nichol's spell of morose corner-slouching was broken by a bellow that nearly sent us up the backside of a fire-spitting sports car. 'We'll drive along to Neidpath Castle, Murdo.'

'Why, Nichol?'

His hot breath streamed between Murdo's shoulder and my cheek. His eyebrows shot erect with wilful passion, a vein thumping under the biggest fleck of his pate. 'You will damn well drive to Neidpath as I say! '

Now now Nichol said Kate it's a lovely day and we'll not spoil it.

'I'm sorry, my dear,' and the front seat grimaced in resignation.

Murdo's wheels spun us over lilting tarmac out of town, the high bank of the reivers' river. Nichol breathing heavily beside Kate, whose hand had slipped to my collar. A gesture used when in her estimation I need protection. I wonder why. From somewhere in this quiet leathery air there has come an unmistakeable odour of tension. The woods around us decaying audibly. A drumming sound in my ears like the four awful horsemen. Get a grip, Sellars.

We parked at the roadside. Nichol was out ahead of us all, through the gate and striding the springy damp turf and muttering to himself. The castle stood tall and watchful over his figure, declare your intention, sir, this is Border country. Below him the green shelf pitched to water, a fast-swirling crook of lateyear brown between the chilled grasses and naked sloping groves. History again, red fire and reddened Tweed through the long dying centuries. Thousands of crazy people smelling winter smoke and fear. A place immortalised by Scott in a moving poem that later inspired McGonagall. Only the cut of your coat, wild-haired man, tells me the time of your living.

'Coming up the castle, Denis? There's a magnificent view.'

'No, thanks, Murdo. I'm too damn tired.' I don't like this place, I think 'flu coming on, I'm shivering.

'Come on, Kate. I'll show you how a Highlander makes love on battlements.'

Her blue eyes enquired: I'm safe with the rascal, well you know, but if you want I'll wait with you.

'On you go, Kate. One good clinch with you would break his back.'

They went, dear friends, arms swinging, an awful loneliness stilling my world when their lissom shapes glided through the porch. Mankind has left me, and this universe of dark colours and no voices is hostile. Come back, my God I'm alone. Get a grip. There is something in this square of rural menace that demands my screams. Settle down you bloody fool, this isn't funny, no more Saturday nights for you in the Tolbooth with Jock and Lily. Look at Nichol. He's shrinking, quivering, his tie whipping his throat in a fury as he bends like a penitent. The blackness of that sky The look on Nichol's face. Madness. Black sky and madness, mad soundlessness! I can *hear* this silence, it's crawling into the car, oozing out of the dark forests, tin dungeons, it's coming for *me*! The dumb response of the damned before the Great Throne!

Slam, bound from the car and a vomit of panicky gas in mid-stride, all I want is that water. Lung-searing three yard bounds, foot screeched off a stone two somersaults and bounce off a cracking shoulder, twenty feet of slope in two seconds, but it's nearer, nearer, shingle strangely soundless under my feet, only water, cold brown security, knees struggling, DENIS! up to waist, DENIS! Jesus what am I doing. DENIS! feet away world all blind and breathless mouth full of sound and brackish spitting. I'm drowning! DENIS! A hand yanked my hair to the surface, masculine-sobbing cold-skinned something tearing me from the spate. Did I go crackers or something that's it Denis, that's it—slow to the dry stones and haven. Then trees and Neidpath and black clouds toppled drunkenly across Murdo and Kate sprinting down the incline. Did I go crackers or something as Nichol squelched me over his shoulder, and I fainted across the body that was trembling like a bullock in a slaughter-house.

*

Darkness. All-comforting.

Murdo's sleek turns forged us on through the flaring deserted town. Urgency of the motor, knows we all need home. Sellars shivering bare-legged in the back despite Murdo's pullover and jacket, Nichol's overcoat. The giant's hand massaging my numb shoulder.

'Nichol, do you think I'm mad? I don't know what it was.'

'What made you do it, Denis?'

Murdo and Kate motionless, like sculptured salt before me. 'Everything suddenly seemed hellish, Nichol, even you. And it all went silent. I must be nuts.'

'You had far too much whisky last night,' said Murdo, bless him.

'Shut up, Murdo!' Long streams of light flitted over the interest fixed on Nichol's pupils. Out of the town, the high road to hot beds.

'Denis,' quickly, 'look at me.'

Wet-cheeked I looked. Nichol, this was no death-wish, please understand or I'll be under the brown flood again and you'll never wrench me safe.

'Denis, look at me.' Lost in the black coals, fight them, lost again, can this be a sane experience? 'Denis,' far away and soft, 'I swear there is a perfectly simple answer to all this. It's happened to sensitive men before. I'll explain it to you before very long. You're all right, Denis, you're not crazy, I swear it. Do you believe me?'

Gleams of conviction slowly filling the entrancing

jet circles. Face I cannot see but suddenly I slackened and laughed at myself. 'It all seems so daft now, Nichol. Christ... what have you done? I feel as if you've exorcised something out of me.'

Too much to drink said Murdo, yes thought Kate post-alcoholic depression I'm going to watch you in future.

Nichol sank limply away from me, head brooding between his hands. 'So be it. We'll call it that, my dear.' But Kate never listened to silence bellying up on her, nor felt the comfort of a black iris kill a ghoulish memory.

He squeezed my shoulders on impulse, hugged me near embarrassment: 'Oh, Denis, Denis, laddie ... ye're all right, I'll watch you, laddie ...'

Murdo and Kate glanced, appeared to understand, slewed back to watch the road. Noble the solitary silhouettes of their lovely heads.

I was dozing, Murdo crooning a Rannoch love-song, Kate smoking with reassuring straight movements, when Nichol said, 'This is it, isn't it?'

'What?'

'Where your mother died?'

'Yes, I think so.' Cruel bend, not so well-banked then.

'Stop a minute, Murdo.' Screech. Nichol brushed past Kate into the darkness.

'What's he up to now?'

Under the brilliant lopsided oval that studded the endless night-space we saw his liquescent shadow tread the verge away from us, muttering loudly. I've never seen him so agitated. Mystified we let him settle in his place again, hardly questioning our lack of wonder. What a day, and I saw Murdo still alive enough to show quick curiosity when Nichol held me again: 'Denis, laddie... I just wanted to stand at the place... somehow it helps me to know what you've been through ... you're all right, Denis ... now I know you're all right...'

So we all sang the car home, four voices floating behind us, beautiful, filling us with pride, yet hardly the ones we possessed a few hours earlier. Something has happened to-day that our subconscious will chain for ever.

Nichol insisted on being dropped at the City's boundary, his arteries requiring a little exercise. I made a half-hearted tug at his coat-tail, dreading the return of my phobia, but he leaned in the bitter wind of the door, said 'You'll be all right, Denis,' with quiet reassurance. I relaxed in the sanctuary of his leftover presence, his Erinmore-smell a source of courage.

Still the voice of the car unreal, and Murdo and Kate aware of it, silently discussing the weird events till the Canongate flashed a sleepy green light to allow us entrance from the High Street.

To hell with further examinations, why are people so avid for reasons? It happens to sensitive men. Nichol said it. And I'm quiet. Dazed but quite apathetic and quiet.

Slow shudder to the close-mouth, wrench of hand-brake. The moon hopping down the rough pavement to welcome us home. Clash of cutlery through a window, Lily sounds in a temper.

'All for coffee?' said Kate.

'Kate,' said Murdo in his occasional authoritarian voice, 'you go on up. I want to speak to Denis.'

'Who are *you* ordering about, MacAuley?'

'Go on, Kate.' Sharp, Murdo about to spew something painful.

'I'll go,' she said, and kissed his cheek with a gentle movement that released perfume through the car. 'At times you're closer to him than I am, and I know it. This is something I'm learning not to hate.'

'You're a good woman, Kate,' he said in his tone of spontaneous admiration.

She swayed under the gloomy arch, disappeared with a flare of skirt. The walk of a native, belonging.

Murdo's face self-important yet desperately honest, enjoying and suffering the forging of another link. 'Denis, I don't suppose we'll ever explain to-day.'

'I went nuts, dear Gael. I'm stopping the booze, except for weekdays.'

'Be serious. Why don't you have another think about Nichol?'

'He's my great hero, Murdo, along with yourself, of course.'

'You bloody fool, you saw him stamping up and down that bend! Just what must I say? And he was holding you like—'

'Like a son, Murdo?'

Trenchant silence. Two fags lit. 'You're not so mad. You must have thought it, Denis, other people have. You're not all that like him, but there *are* odd expressions, you know.'

'I've thought about it often, ever since your story of Switzerland. It's incredible, yet it's possible—so much adds up.'

‘You’re not angry? I had to say this, Denis—it was getting in the way of our communication.’

‘Communication.’ Short dry laugh. ‘Until my last meeting with Rob I’d have filleted your guts for saying one loose word about my mother.’

‘What happened with Rob?’

‘He tried to show me a photograph of my reputed begetter, Melville Sellars. I couldn’t look at it. I was terrified of seeing an obvious resemblance. And I realised then—I want Nichol to be my father.’

‘Are you going to ask him?’

‘No, boy. There’s something mounting in him too, I can feel it. He’ll tell me in his own time if it’s true.’

‘Good lad, Denis.’

Confused and deeply grateful we shook hands across the driving seat, impressed by our absolute sympathy, surprised at our ability to observe and absorb the astounding without letting its emotional impact dwarf our mutual esteem. This is a sacred thing, my brother, another lamp to clutch in the darkness. Our hands retreat with added strength from such a clasp. Such a broth of sentiments and sensations, this complex narrow face. He’s a bloody mess like me.

‘Good night, Murdo. Thanks.’

‘You’ve got a good woman there, Denis. She’s stiffening your backbone—slowly.’

‘So they tell me. It’ll happen to you too.’

Wrong statement. I saw him clench the wheel too hard, the rebound in his masseters. ‘Maybe, Denis. I’ll find a good Highland girl one of these days, and then my tensions might go.’

The perfect night guided him round into the Wynd, and I stood alone in the freshness, happy to assign the consequences of our talk to some nebulous future reckoning. For the salt in the air, the jig of townpaper, the singing tremble of a bucket and this sleeping scree of City—a reality too precious to share even a minute with speculations on sanity or parental adultery. The Canongate.

She was waiting in the snug firelit kitchen, matron in her flannel nightdress. 'Well, Denis?'

'Kate, I think Nichol may be my father.'

'I know. It's a nice thought, isn't it? There's so much about him we still have to learn.' Relief and excitement stamped on her words.

Nichol's healing eyes were my last memory before I sank into dreamless sleep.

Dear Man of Men how patient and how brave
Your lonely quest an erring son to save
Be yours the cross to keep me from the grave.

CHAPTER SEVEN

Three weeks till the celebration of Bethlehem. I'll never curse frost nor mist again. I can love this City despite her shortcomings except in such a mood as this. Grey, yet the oft-abused adjective a pathetic understatement, for it denotes a quiet lack of colour; this greyness is a unique hellish way of life.

On the first of the month it engulfed the cold, pallid blue of the sky, then descended on the buildings. It drove pride from granite facings, warmth from sandstone, made the contemporary a lowering freak, the older streets forlorn cemeteries haunted by apologetic feet. Nor could the myriad visual surprises of the town renew her beauty: anachronistic tower might suddenly span a garret-gap, a fang of Crags or belly of upland spring out of a side-street, or a vale of suburban reds and purples recline under a mastered summit on a couch of green; colour and sweet shape dissolved after the illusory second, for the infection infiltrated windows and skulls and poisoned the receptors inside. One could pretend for only a breath, then the evil sorcery wrought change before and behind the eyes: not only did everything look, sound, smell dead and grey, but the City and her creatures were spellbound slaves of the relentless tyrant above them.

There was some relief in the early darkness, when Nichol and his followers argued out their lines in Tollcross. In the actors' voices and eloquent hands, a quality of watchspring—less than four months to go, most of us unknown and unfashionable idealists until this fanciful production, and yet we never knew such competence existed alongside our battered ambitions.

Sellars and MacAuley commenting from the back of the hall, Ross-styled critics of elocution: MacNeill's two plays a whirr of dynamism as Nichol cajoled pomposity into a speech, slanted a face, slapped a winded back to its proper station. The readings still rough in places: MacDiarmid and his younger contemporaries, the sages from Henryson to Burns. Carson Hall had insisted on Sir Walter, and Sellars would yawn under the drugging prose and turn for company to the tall shapes outside his window:

How do you stand it, City, this grey plague that deforms your winter daylight? How can you bear it with such ugly stoicism?

You're too young, Denis. For I've seen red murder, heard yellow supplication. My palace lawn was gay with scarlet sash and blinking silks, the sun stepped a gorgeous gold quadrille on the Crags. And I laughed and loved it all till the pendulum of Time swung into darkness and a BLACK voice screamed my BLACK sin and the laughter fled and the moon and the sun hid their faces till I feared none of my flesh should be saved. Too many awful colours, Denis: Rizzio's crimson life pouring under his howls, the flashing tartans of the doomed who danced my last glory.

This greyness has its own security. Quietness, Denis,

quiet bowler hats and pinstripes in Queen Street. . . like The End, Denis, so sure, quiet and grey. . .

Everywhere we went, the City was increasingly aware of us. Posters, questions, reassuring promises, sardonic mockery. Teasing from Stan and Connie. The Legion, many of them London and American exiles, had suddenly taken our cause to their bosoms: a new folk-chant was to be heard in Woods Street of a starless night:

> Oh, the burden may be heavy, but we do not count the cost,
> We are marching on to Europe 'neath the flag of Nichol Ross—
> Come and join us, come and join us, in the Ewan Hall next Spring!

'Denis,' said Ollie one night, 'I promised to help. How's Nichol off for money?'

'Not so good, Ollie, he's got a few patrons helping to cover expenses, but I think he's getting short. How about robbing a bank for us?'

'Wonderful,' said Ollie, 'at last I can assume a major role in this great battle,' and he slapped eight five-pound notes into my hands.

'Christ! Now look, sweet brother, have you been—?'

He seized my lapels. 'I knew it, Sellars! You're a police spy! The Crows got Rasputin to organise this thing just to frame me!' The paranoid eyes whipped suspiciously over my purple face, then along the bar.

'Ollie,' I croaked near fainting, 'I don't know what the hell you're on about.'

Ollie released me abruptly, shook his head with a gentle smile: Only joking, Denis. No, boy, an old gentleman in Marchmont has taken a fancy to me. I've been digging his garden—made a wonderful job of it. So he's given me a room in his house, and a small personal allowance which I am now partly donating to Nichol Ross, the father of our souls.'

'But, Ollie—'

'No arguments, Denis. This is a present from Ollie the Bull, King of the Celtic Beats!' He lunged up the bar with an eldritch whoop, hurling wild loving arms into the midst of the scattering apostles: 'We shall overcome, Denis— we shall overcome some day! And don't you tell him who gave you it! I am a true artist, and demand anonymity!'

'He's goin' worse again,' said Connie unnecessarily. 'Starkey,' said Murdo, 'is this the truth, traumatic as the awful noun must be to your hearing?'

Starkey's face too static to be conventionally dishonest: 'Ebsolutely. I was up seeing the place yesterday: the old chep's a retired commodore and he owns much money and a perrot and a smeshing big house. He's a bit crenky too, suits Ollie fine.'

'Well,' I said gallantly. Til deliver it anonymous to Nichol, like the man said. We must meet this old chap, Starkey.'

'Yes,' said the rake, 'he fencies himself as a culture-bug. Ollie was reading his own poetry to him. Only the rum made it bearable.'

'Loads of booze, eh?'

'Even the perrot gets it, Murdo. The old boy's off to

Cenada for Christmas. Maybe we should have an old-style Connor's party in the house?'

'There'll be nae parties, Starkey,' said Stan, 'till ye pay yer bill here. Ye know, Denis, it must be awfy tae be a bit touched, like Ollie.'

'Yes. It must be vile, poor devil. Come on, three drams quick, before we start thinking seriously. And put it on the slate—this filthy stuff in my slender hand is sacred.'

The lamps yellow and round above. Puffballs of steam from wet coats. Tired bodies leaning. Three dozen conversations from the door to the far 'Gents', I'll bet at least twenty of them are about us. Connor's the blessed is aware and rallying.

Tired eyes were surviving the dreary December streets, and in the Canongate the home-fires burned brightly below the dripping rows of wool and nylon, the teamakers sang above the creakings of the cheerful rooms. Wheedling love from my guitar, scratching over paper, I watched for strength and weakness, echoes of the shining Park or the rusty bedspring. Her head bent over needlework cooking and my manuscripts in its own expression of goodwill and tolerance, ever understanding, never inspiring.

I have been trapped, or I am a liar. This is the most satisfying friendship of the City, yet it gives me less than I deserve. She housekeeps like a mother-angel, and it irritates me. Her body takes with the abandon of a nymph after submitting with the longsuffering of a Jersey cow, and it hasn't given me a half-page of new philosophy, A cold snake of fear often glides through my creating cerebrum: she was past the lip-blossom stage all right, *but were you?*

Last week I watched her from the platform at the Crown, half-oblivious of my modulated arpeggios, the desolate splendour of my *Lord Lovat*, then Lisa, two rows back and ashen with communion and her hungry eyes sexing me in half. I turned back to look at Kate, dreaming at me with a he's-mine-and-you-should-see-him-throw-a-leg satisfaction—careful, flaxen woman, I don't like the smugness in your cat-smile.

Friday she looked through my chapters: not bad, the cheeky bitch, but that love-scene isn't convincing, this girl wouldn't give in with a silly statement like that.

'What's so bloody silly about it?'

'I can't put my finger on it, Denis, but it's not right. It's false.'

'Such criticism! Kate, you're a genius. "It's false!" Madam, you are a blade of razor heavensent to pare the woolly borders of my literary intelligence.'

'Say what you like, but you'll realise it if you look at it often enough.' Already back to the stewpot, dumplings for supper.

'Madam—oh, I give up! If only your intellect were as sharp as your appetite!'

'Easy now, Denis,' chuckling. 'I'll tell Nichol. By the way, are you going to ask him—about your mother.'

'I don't know, Kate, I'd rather he brought it up. What do you think?'

'I'd wait, darling. I'm sure that he's going to come out with something soon.'

'That's what I thought.'

'Well, now, we're agreed on that. I wonder if I used my intellect there, Denis?'

Laughter, lipsmacking, rich tender beef and suet. And after, while the iron grate hurled abuse up the chimney, the new dialogue that had become so popular, that had given us a cosy intimacy of speech that we both delivered with quiet, dedicated interest. Where could they have met? And all the years in between? Is it really possible?

If you cherish your happiness with me, Kate, pray for Nichol's long life and continuing proximity. Discussing him-we-love we occasionally plumb a depth of experience whose intensity reminds me of the power of Lisa Kendall's voice and the look yourself once gave me by a cliff of red rock.

Too much time spent away from the script just now, and three reasons. Vision of a wild shock of chestnut, diminishing fulfilment in writing the neo-Fitzgeraldian bitter roses, above all Murdo having a good spell and presently the finest company this side of Paradise.

His eyes off the torture-wheel and his voice less staccato, geometrically-precise metaphors and similes enriching every cubic foot of air he addressed. His manic phase, in which poems poured into his fingers like waterfalls falling on paper with an innocent purity of taste and tone. When he read his fragments in translation the striking quality was a blood-congealing simplicity almost beyond bearing whose full import struck at the second or third reading; this the great art deriving from the terrible honesty of an ancient world: *and when they were come to the place, which is called Calvary, there they crucified Him* ...

Wild bursts of elation in the grubby attic he infested in Newington. The bottle low, suddenly Murdo to his feet and a thumping howl of reel, forelock flapping like a gannet's wing, hands splatting together: 'Christ, boy, I could do with a good woman! '

A week of immortal arguments: existentialism, Wallace Stevens, the Hungarian uprising: infidelity is necessary for thinking people, faithfulness encourages the lust for possession which is the real assassin of freedom: rubbish, all of love's a circle (symbolism!) and all the lads and lassies merely segments—you won't find the centre by wandering haphazardly through the whole $\pi r2$. The fag-machines rattled, the nights spluttered into mornings. Kate, bless her, never reproachful, working hard for precious pennies to bolster her underpaid artist.

A precious week with Murdo and the great abstract words that pass for what men and women pretend to feel for each other... we all need women at so many levels, Denis, and so obvious his regretful insight on Friday when his eyes betrayed his silent loyal tongue: Kate and Denis running into trouble . . . Bloody pity . . . Lisa Kendall . . .

We had arranged to meet Nichol in the Red Eagle on Saturday evening; Rasputin had promised us a celebration in honour of some mysterious new personal triumph. He made no appearance, however, and after two hours in among the smoky tartan walls and the earnest voices imitating the Clancys and Joan Baez with varying effect, we had suffered enough. Down to the Canongate, Murdo, there'll be plenty tea to chase the three-quidsworth-of-malt on your hip.

We swung under the points of the floodlit Lawnmarket, a crazy otherworld bothy-song of High Street, past the disapproval of Mad John's wee hoose to find Kate in with Jock and Lily watching T.V. Come in, Denis, ye're ower late, Kate's been worried, an' Ah see ye've brought the dug along.

A kiss for my girl, Murdo's charm working swift magic on our host, the watery blue eyes and purple face shimmering with wit like canvas under a summer bracer. Then a colossal tale from scrubby-haired Jock, rubbing the cardigan on his pendulous belly, slippers up on the range: ye can say whit ye like aboot Germany and Cyprus, laddie, ye should ha' been wi' me on the Somme. Aye said Lily an' ye should ha' seen the postman goin' up the Canongate, stoappin' at every third door. I sympathise Lily but you must realise that my experiences are simply not comparable.

Balls, Murdo. In the corner I was hugging Kate, always damned attractive on Saturday night. Blouse and mohair skirt, small fleshy tyre sprouting out of her girdle.

Discussion continued. 'Thae big words o' yours are just eye-wash, Murdo,' said Lily with calculated sedition. Ordinary folk like us that really feel things, we dinnae need them.'

'Not fair, Lily, ye're pullin' rank.'

'Nane o' yer nonsense, Sellars. Ma sister's boss wis the same: when her man was killt at Gallipoli, he took her into his office: "Remember, Miss MacKay" he says, "remember, God is good and omnishyunt, but I'm afraid yet fyongcy's deid." D'ye ken whit Ah mean?'

Oh yes Lily.

We switched to entertainment: Murdo versus the Drummonds : A Highland yarn against a City anecdote, cut and thrust and Kate and I cupped our chins and grew blind to the spotless cheap wallpaper, the brown linoleum, the tough crockery on the bright black shelves. The rich, different voices. To-morrow I must remind Murdo that for half-an-hour he was utterly at home among Lowlanders. A strange deputy of love is Saturday night. Splutter on the window, our communication has broken the grey spell, this is the night that the rains came.

Thunder resounded on our door across the landing, making Lily curse drunks as she opened hers: 'Good grief—Professor Ross! Come in, they're here. For heaven's sake, man, ye're drooked.'

He staggered in, collapsed in my chair, covering his panting face; a frightened look of recognition swam across Kate's, and I rose in panic. But she was swift to him, took his pulse, rubbing his hands and feet, off with his coat and shoes, towelling his dull-and-fiery hair. Her competence stilled our anxiety, uneasily the four of us settled again, Lily pouring Nichol a stiff dram.

'It's all right, folks,' said Kate calmly. 'Nichol, you should know better than to walk about in a storm.'

He drained his glass, and my silent prayers accelerated his colour's return, piece by greyfled piece of his haggard cheeks. 'You're a wonder, lassie. Sorry to cause all the fuss, Mrs. Drummond, the rain caught me in the Park.'

'What's wrong, Nichol?' Kate's arm round him, instinctive cradle.

Very slowly, 'I had to see you, Denis. I'm desolate tonight. That novel of mine. I hoped to make us some money on it, do you remember?'

'Your metaphysical one, of course. Has your publisher given you a poor offer?'

'It's not that.' A shuddering spasm and a crackle of phlegm. 'He's refused me altogether.'

'Refused? But you were his bread-and-butter twenty years ago.'

'Twenty years ago.' His hopeless eyes were brooding into the hearth; a piece of paper was handed blindly—*but despite the obvious literary merit of the work I am afraid that the reading public of to-day simply would not have the stamina for even the early chapters. With the greatest reluctance, therefore, I fear I must—*

'God damn the money-grubbing parasites, Nichol.' Dostoyevsky, you weren't born a year too soon.

'There are other publishers, Nichol,' said Murdo. 'Don't give up hope yet.'

'True, Murdo, but I've got a feeling... the omens are not good, boys. First Hackett, now this.'

'Dinnae you worry. Professor Ross,' said Lily from the corner. '*The Evening News* wouldnae publish my letter aboot the new flats either.' She rattled on indignantly, and midway through Jock's exasperated counter-attack Nichol began to snore softly.

'Dinnae you go botherin' the poor auld craitur,' said Jock with disgust. 'She's crazy, Denis—organizin' petitions and writin' dirty letters aboot the builders tae her MP. She'll hae me in the jeyel.'

Lily rose to stand preacher among us. 'Ah'll huv the fat crooks, Denis. There's a loat o' things happened roond here Ah cannae forgive them fur. Just let yin mair balcony come doon.'

We helped Nichol over the iron balcony, the frozen wet landing, into warmth and our bed.

'Poor Nichol,' said Kate, 'what a Christmas present.'

In the shadows he was already sleeping, grand in profile as a king of Assyria.

'Kate, d'you think he's ill?'

'Yes, darling, I do. I'll try and get him an appointment in the Royal. He needs a complete overhaul.'

'You're a great comfort, Kate.'

'I suppose so. As long as he's around.'

'Holy crumpet!'

'What?'

'Oh, nothing.' For another second I'm close to loving you for your coincidental thinking. 'It's just that I'm with him all the more... but somehow I feel I can't ask him the big question for a bit yet.'

Though now high priests of letters him have hung
On that same gibbet where the saints have swung
No cry of cockerel shall indict my tongue.

CHAPTER EIGHT

A few snowflakes, then colder again, and some flawless skies to cheer our route to Christmas. The shops throughout the Old Town full of bargains and lies and smiling duped faces:

> Hark the herald angels sing
> Glory how the shillings ring.

Away from the podgy red Santas and the University clamouring round the East End for Post Office employment, Nichol refused to see a doctor, submitted his novel to a second publishing house, but decided not to write his play; the actors breathed relief and Sellars feared the implication.

Rasputin's Christmas party was a masque of splendour, however, a full rehearsal starting in his lounge at mid-day and ending in artificial light, followed by a sumptuous dinner (cooked by Kate and Mrs. MacNeill) and a roaring Valhalla set to music. Maisie Hay the ravendark queen of the travelling North-East was invited down to show her mettle, and the goblets were still for every cutting nasal sound. Also Peter Douglas, the elf of Galloway, a round face carved out of turnip and a baby

blue-plum for a nose, owner of seven hundred songs and three hundred stories. He sang the *Hielandman's Fancy Ball* during our plum pudding, cured Carson Hall's toothache and made our leading lady swallow a sixpence.

At nine o'clock a wild schottische bounding on the carpet to Maisie's mouth-music; Murdo slipped among us, christened with a sheen of Yuletide sleet, pulling me into a comer.

'Where have you been, Lothario, seducing the Christmas fairy?'

'I've been in Connor's, Denis. I've got news for you.' 'Don't tell me. The Three Wise Men are outside. Have they brought any drink?'

'Hackett's up again. The gloves are off.'

'You always had a weakness for metaphors, Murdo.'

'The TV programme. *Stringtime*, is starting here—on *April the fourth*, to be exact. Hackett's the producer, and he's on the hunt for singers.'

I hope I'm not to blame for this, Nichol. 'Where's he doing it?'

'Hold on to your indestructible courage. They're televising live excerpts from the Queen's Theatre—round the corner from the Ewan Hall! '

I crumpled into a chair. 'Showdown, Murdo. I wouldn't tell Nichol till after the party.'

Hogmanay was a marathon and the first two days of the New Year a slice of Angst and headache; Kate coped, and on the fifth of January I sold an article on Hume, seven guineas and we managed the rates.

The first Folksong meeting of this crucial

twelvemonth was in the Black Friar in the High Street. I was eager to see if Hackett and Rob would put in an appearance; already their prospecting in and around the City had created a sub-folklore of its own.

Kate tired to-night, go on yourself, love. Setting out early I was stopped on several stages of the hill by local tradesmen or worse, here Denis ye've no' had yer New Year frae me yet. Topple more fire to the scorching belly, only the strong survive in this land. So to the High Street's newest fake authentic quaint eighteenth-century tavern.

Upstairs smoke and chatter. City affluents set among the tablefuls of addicts. Pack-out. A Disneylike mural of the lovely queen and Mad John. Rob and D. Leonard Hackett smiling to starboard.

I was on second and badly, my voice still hungover. The kids gave me a short burst, generously prolonged by the Legion who were spread powerfully along the back wall.

Ricky Slater and the Moonshiners shamed my mediocre reception: loosening the roof with the *Overgate* (black glimpse of Dundee), *The Spanish Lady* (perfumed locklets, washing her feet by Dublin candle), *La Paloma* (the Emperor asked for it before they shot him)—around the world in eighty bars, good on you, boys, where's Lisa?

Rick heard my searching eyes, called her from a smoky corner. 'Lisa Kendall.' She shrivelled their conversation with a glance, the spotlight igniting carmine and gold in the hair tumbling across her left clavicle. Made a small movement of cheek to soften her hard mouth and remove the bitterness flickering at her fine nostril. Nobody can introduce a song like her, she's playing at Irish to-night. There was once a man of Ireland, and like most of us he was not one person but many. I know it, Lisa, you're giving us the lyrical cry of a drunkard through the throat of a bird. One day he found a bittern dead on the ice of the lake, couldn't break through, died of thirst. You're parching my throat, honey. Now she's saying he pondered and moralised upon the tragedy and here's the song.

> The yellow bittern that never broke out
> In a drinking bout might as well have drunk.

His white bones on the naked stone, Lisa, and your simple backcloth of block-chords knows the hell of it too well to obtrude. Mine are candidates for that hunk of rock. Miss Kendall, but when I dream in resonance with you I can forget the cold picking my flesh off.

> My true love said to me, if I drank any more
> My life would be o'er in a little while
> But I told her 'tis drink gives me health and strength
> And has shortened my sorrow by many a mile.

Damn you, Kate, how would *you* know? I worship you, Lisa.

The pearly grace-notes set in unerring pattern, what a tribute to agony and flaw, my kindred. Hunched to the table I gave all of me to this blend of heart- and soul-ache that might crack the frontal lobes were it not intermittently bewitched into a gem of all joys, its only formula listening need and a woman's telling.

Nerveless, I squeezed my eyes shut for her climax needing no crescendo:

> 'Tis strange that the bird of the long yellow throat
> Should die of the thirst when it came to the last
> Come Sun of my Soul, fill high the glass
> You'll get no more sup when your life is past.

I love you, Lisa. Too bad, Kate.

Cold fluid smarting on my skin, I resent the barbaric acclamation of men around me who only know and feel so much. Ricky's voice was faint from a mountain in Patagonia, introducing something special. My God, a big deal.

In the violet ray Len Hackett's sleek black hair and blue Italian suit were gleaming behind his Hampstead voice and the microphone:

'—the first night will be on April the fourth, and I want the best performers possible. Rob Sellars and I will be on the look-out for new talent in the next few months. Brush up your numbers, kids, and you may finish up on TV! '

All ears were taken aback, Sellars tempted to hurl his pint glass. A whine of contempt from Nichol's publicity-despising Legion, but Ricky and Lisa both reflecting their subconscious consideration of the temptation despite their sneering noses.

By God, I know these local folksingers, they're the salt of the earth and they won't touch Hackett's lousy commercial propositions unless he offers them enough cash. I must intervene, tender immortal souls at stake.

Hackett explaining it all so sincerely, you'd never believe his father's real name was Rachmann, but a commotion from behind forestalled my own interjection:

'You can sew up your tongue, Hackett.' Accents of rising storm. Nichol emerging in his cloak from the smoke, the lights playing weird tricks with his cavalier curls and harsh bloom of fury.

Hackett master of the contingency, 'How nice to see you, Mr. Ross. I welcome this opportunity for an impromptu debate!' Manager of the bar muttering to a bar- man.

The giant interruption bumped through the tables, stopped by the mike, eight towering inches over the money-man. An arm was flung above the plastered skull: 'Listen to me, all of you. This man is an emissary of the devil. He will defile your standards and squeeze the last ounce of individual talent out of you. I can do no more than advise most of you against him, but I can assure him that Ricky and his group will be at the shoulder of Nichol Ross on the fourth of April!'

Voicerumble: bravo-Nichol mixed with who's-the-cave-man-throw-him-out. Hackett leered into the microphone for a comeback. 'Don't listen to him, my friends, don't listen to *him*! What can you do for these youngsters, Ross, except teach them crummy old songs that are only fit for half-cracked antiques like yourself? We don't want to live in the past—I stand for good modern entertainment, and they know it! '

'Good modern entertainment!' Nichol placed his

hands on his hips, laughing a very unpleasant impersonation of Goliath. 'We've seen what you've done to Rob Sellars, reducing his performance to the inane level of your barbershop quartets and folksy beat-groups. I warn you, young people, avoid this viper! '

'Ask Rob Sellars how he's doing! You're happy enough, aren't you, Rob?' Hackett summoned a brief smile from my dear twin, modestly straining into the limelight. 'Look, young people, Rob Sellars is a very highly paid entertainer, and he sings good tuneful stuff. In spite of what this maniac says, he is the true folk-artist of our time!' Slight cheer, nasty indecision on Ricky.

Nichol smiled round the tables. 'Mr. Hackett,' inclining his head as to a C-stream pupil, 'let us be honest. You couldn't tell a pentatonic ballad from a diatonic fart.'

'Hahahaha.' Hackett setting out to act David but having to settle for a bumtickled spinster hyena. 'Who cares for these technical terms, that are as dusty as the so-called scholars who use them? My purpose is to entertain—to make people happy! '

Nice touch you bastard, watch the outflanking, Nichol. In enervating silence the great figure closed its eyes, rocking on soundless heels. Silence, silence. The initiative wrested without a word through sheer spectacular power, Hackett's eyes glued to his adversary as inevitably as the spotlight.

A low, pleasant tone to Nichol's voice, but every vibrant syllable heard from wall to window. 'I didn't wish to subject you to this, Mr. Hackett, but you force me to use my advantage. We must elevate this confrontation to the level of TRUTH!"

A glass crashed, soft scream of a girl.

'Hahahaha,' squeaked Hackett uncomfortably, 'you hear what he says—the level of truth?' Siiiiiiilence.

'Mr. Hackett,' and the spotlight gone mad, flooding from violet through green and yellow till the drawn faces of the antagonists belonged to some flamelit canto of the *Inferno*. 'Look at me straight, and tell me whether you honestly give a damn about these young folksingers! '

Hackett tried to sight Rob, but the two great hands had viced his twitching cheeks.

'Tell us, Mr. Hackett, the truth!' Nichol's features of chiselled bone oscillating three inches from Hackett's bewilderment, then frank fear. 'The truth, Mr. Hackett, you know what it is.'

The eye of Rasputin switched seventeen shades of ruthlessness; the audience hung on his words, a tableau of spellbound embarrassment.

He can't, Nichol, you've got him too terrified to lie, well done your regal phiz and imposing physique. The unimaginative might call it intimidation. Your stare developing an intensity of brilliance that I can scarcely take from here; Hackett must feel like a man without eyelids staked out under sunshine. Len Hackett grimaced, tried to speak, gargled. Nichol's eye forged forward, almost touching. Hackett's head snapped its reins; one demented blur of shaking till his features were indistinguishable, Brylcream running down his cheeks in rapid coloured rivers.

We were one minute from unprecedented drama in the history of entertainment, but the manager and four of his largest barmen had decided to join us.

'Get 'im oot o' here,' yelled the manager ferociously, a larger edition of Stalin in his prime. 'He's startin' a fight! ' Nichol pushed his broken opponent towards Rob's window table: 'Truth has prevailed!' he roared to the highly-impressed tables. 'Touch me at your peril, you dupes of mediocrity! '

Jesus and the apostles, inspired to rise to the occasion, danced a hastily-formed ring-o'-roses round the proprietor's column, waves of their subtle fragrance clearing the room ahead of their chant: 'Oh, the burden may be heavy, but we do not count the cost—'

Nichol still speechifying in the uproar and I slid to the corner where Hackett's face was buried in his hands. 'A further warning, gentlemen,' and I clucked their foreheads together with a whip of my strong slender wrists. Rob swore and swung, turn of my loin and I took it on the back, leaned fullweight on the flimsy table, upending it and their chairs as well. Hackett opened his mouth to speak from the floor but I poured a pint from a vacant table in among the gold fillings. Rob was swearing in very common fashion, trying to dislocate my foot that was pinning the table across his rosy sexual future. Galloping carnage appeared in my eye-corner, Doubting Thomas and a poor innocent barman inextricably tangled in hair and brotherly homicide on the floor, St. Peter baptising the manager with a double rum and coke.

Then Jesus came out of the wilderness and said get Rasputin out of here Denis one of them's 'phoned for the police.

'Thanks a lot, Jesus. We'll blow.' My victims groaning, beyond reprisal.

'My name's Paul, Denis.'

'Don't be modest, man. I won't forget you boys for to- night.'

'—and this is the final vindication of our community's integrity,' continued Nichol the Great waving his bonnet, 'for here is proof that the silver of lewd men cannot shake our faith in eternal values—·'

'Come on, Nichol! '

He backhanded the microphone to the floor. 'Wasn't I magnificent, Denis? Once again I have demonstrated the powers of light which lurk unseen to act as the handmaidens of noble intent!'

'Come on, the fire-escape.'

The apostles' rearguard action was over; they were now filtering through the roughhouse to mingle inconspicuously with the crowd in the front bar. Stalin and his largest aproned thug were left free to perceive my shoulder clanging the glass door wide to the open staircase. This is bloody madness Denis called Rob on his knees and the cold shadows of the High Street flickered against my modest delight.

Three tinny footfalls, what a bloody racket in there, a crowd gathered to welcome my triumph but where's Nichol. He roared for assistance from the door, huge mass stuck fast in the thin gap.

I swooped back to the exit, tried to tear his shoulders through by bumping his lapels. The big barman kicked him behind the knees; Nichol roared with pain and delivered a back-heeler of incredible velocity which struck the brute a thunk in his most unpublishable province, spinning him heels-in-the-air and headlong clatter over Hackett lying behind him.

I twisted Nichol like a great slab of chewing-gum, but Stalin the manager was delaying my act of mercy by pulling in the opposite direction, his head to Nichol's spine arms round his thighs, Ah'm savin' you fur the polis, ye big herry ruffyin.

One thing to do, Jozef, and as a younger man I apologise. Wait for your next heave then come with it. Running Nichol back through his prison I catch you a cracker on the Caucasian snout with his checked backside, pained and humiliated you're on your bum-hole among your own bestial kind. And Nichol reclaimed at speed by myself and the jolt of rebound, crunch on the doorpost and a shower of flaky paint into the applauding street. The two of us came bouncing down the iron steps, stood up valiant among our fellow- citizens.

'Are you all right, Nichol?'

Nostrils quivering with satisfaction. 'I've never felt better, my boy. This is just what I needed! ' He raised an arm to share the victory with the crowd, then saw the hideous sight moving through them.

I grabbed the first constable by the arm. 'Thank God you've come. Inspector. It's hell up there! '

'Whit happened?'

'The manager's gone berserk. Shouting the most dirty things about our Queen. The bugger needs a bullet in him, looks like a Communist.'

Stalin appeared to my dismay at the stairhead, but his slanderous invective was hardly begun when the plate-glass window of the front bar shattered before the onslaught of two locked and flailing figures. While the

Crows bent to restore order we cantered round the corner and caught a merciful bus.

'Sure you're all right, Nichol?'

'Couldn't be better.' He laughed into his beard, face lit by the garish stream of Christmas shop-signs. 'Denis, you are a man of great invention. You're the first chap in history to find a useful purpose for the corns on a novelist's arse! '

A chill evening peppered with volleys of hail. A warm glow in the Sellars-Fraser residence, Lily and Jock in for supper, two juicy kippers each. And as ever the conversation spraying around the walls with the relentless energy of machine-gun fire, punctuated by shell-bursts of laughter. Lily teasing Kate about this new pill that gives the act of love a clear conscience. Little knowing she's already on it. Jock and I discussing the sudden remarkable resurgence of the Scottish National Party, it looks like the political front is due for a real shake-up. What a pity I'm not a political animal. Finally Lily climbed back on her favourite platform, the next sign o' negligence in any o' thae flats an' I'm organisin' a march up tae the Chambers. The Canongate ready to renew a tradition of martyrdom, Lily, d'ye still spit on the Heart of Midlothian? I hugged them both as they left.

Back to work. By the comforting swirl of floral cretonne I worried and lost weight for two hours—no good, this suicide scene is something I know too little about. Struggle, struggle, Denis, think of your own terror, the red flames they preached at Dunfreckie, but I can't project my own neurosis on to paper, this girl doesn't know damnation exists. Only in some minds. More real than the mocker ever knew. If only not in mine.

'Kate, those knitting needles sound like a couple of armadillos on the job.'

She gave me that only-hers of frank bewilderment with the pixie of amusement pulling at the wide corners of her eyelids. A look I'd almost forgotten.

So much of your subtlety I no longer record, strapping woman with high-piled hair, and this the queen mystery that you always mitigate disadvantage with that disconcerting naive and humorous expression. And its counterpoint, the hurt look that often follows nothing I can explain, and revives a strange self-hatred I ought to understand. Stranger still I can watch Sophia Loren and lust her and you not, yet settle by this shining range and take time to wonder that I am moved and comforted by the incredible softness of your hair between the fire and the curtain. And be unmoved to touch you then but later moved and disappointed. Discuss Robert Lowell and shudder at your comments yet talk crass trivia and wonder why the hell it's just as natural to Sellars then you suddenly say something incredibly original. The warmth of your seeking tongue. Sudden sexiness of you one day in six conjured by a crossed leg, a slash of lipstick. Your perfume and figure and soft voice that fills this room already responsive to every twitch of your sharp ear-lobe. A serene new world created by you, Kate, your achievement, but not the one I want wherein artists of destiny should be inspired. Too bad, you've far too little to teach me. If only Lisa.

'Is it tough going to-night, Denis?'

'Yes.'

'I read through it to-day. I like most of it, but there's something wrong.'

'How would you know?'

Rustle of her legs, she crossed the quivering room to show me: *—and so the mirror of reality revealed the other Elaine to herself, as she had been invented by Jacques at the beginning. This was the only real import of Elaine Underwood in the eyes of the being who was her Universe. Through tears she saw the milk-skinned goddess and her hallowed giving disenchanted to the function of a wood-and-metal tool scratching holes in the soil that was his selfish literary ambition—*'

Bending over me, her hair warm and heady from the fire. 'You didn't need to say that, Denis. It's all in the bit of dialogue and action that went before. To me it sounds like some of Fitzgerald's worst overwriting.'

'I take it that with your inimitable clumsiness you're accusing me of making explicit what is already implicit?'

'Something like that, and don't be so sarcastic. You shouldn't analyse love-affairs too much.' Back she swayed to her roasting fireside.

'Indeed, Miss McCarthy, is this so? What the bloody hell do you think most writers try to do?'

'I don't know. But it strikes me that you can't put love into big words.'

'I said that weeks ago.'

'You wouldn't think it from your writing. You

should describe the kissing and what happens, but—oh I don't know, darling, I just feel this! '

My knuckled swipe filled the room with flocks of paper: I came to my feet and shouting: 'I've had about enough of your smugness. *You* feel *this*! You're incapable of feeling!' Thunderstruck her face, deservedly, the bitch. 'But, Denis, you said—'

'What do you know of the countless images that can come out of a kiss or a song? You and your superficial view of life! Do *you* feel a folksong like a great sea crushing you?"

'What? Not really, darling.' Eyes moist and bright.

Of course you don't, you're too wrapped up in your smug security. You made up all that guff you gave me on the Crags! You've got *nothing* to give—and you have the bloody nerve to meddle with my book when you're hardly interested in Art at all. You'd never know what I'm going through in a million years.'

She was slack on her cushion, speechless since the 'nothing to give', that shook her. I was stuttering, spluttering, reappraising my emotions, fury still the favourite: 'You're stifling me,' deadly quiet. 'You don't share my love of songs, or literature, or Scotland, or people.' I slapped into my coat, half-frightened by the vigour of her sobbing; 'Well, I've had enough. I'm off.'

'Where are you going?' I could pity that face for the length of ten millennia if she'd only left my novel alone: 'Songs and Scotland are just words, Denis. Why must we fight about words?'

'If that's not the stupidest statement of the year, it's

in there contending. Good-bye, Kate.' Stuffing half-a-manuscript under my coat.

'Please, darling, please!' Bang. A sad closed door. Scar suffering an uncontrollable tic, tears of outrage aggravated by a screech of hail ricocheting into the brick-walled ravine.

Lily leaning out of a window: 'Sellars, if you've hurt that lassie, Ah'll have yer dirty hide!' Fading through the white stingers.

Farewell simplicity.

The world a flesh-hating swarm of white pain. Keel into it, moaning timber the guide, down the Walk and battered in the open road, how people can bring little babies into a place such as this. Hate it, must leave, chills a writer's courage. Nice to write in yellow shine by a marble wall looking at azure seas and mahogany people. This filthy pest-hole. No warmth in our poetry, how fucking lucky you were, Dante. The Links slimy as a politician's tongue, two hundred more yards to Lisa. Romantic if I died of exposure short of her light-in-the-window. That bastard Kate. Like most Scottish people, too fucking retarded to have an inkling. No wonder. With the tinkers I watched Ross-shire crofters rescuing an emaciated harvest. I've heard soft city people in armchairs maintain the buggers are lazy. Haha. The Glenlyon girl two weeks overdue in January, they strapped her to a barn door and horsepulled her through the drifts, dead by Aberfeldy. No fucking wonder and damn you all the same, Kate. I once saw a buroo crowd in Clydebank.

Dante was a genius, but all things considered McGonagall was a miracle. Clip, clip, nearly there. Tall stone to save me from the blast.

Stately old hulks, conical turrets and weathervanes, the beezneez fifty years ago, but so austere and forbidding. Clip, clip that bastard Kate and this dung-heap of cold hearts and stabbing darkness. Nichol's round the twist. Bamslam Godblessyoudoor. Lord, what celestial bliss to lean in a middleclass City stair. Suddenly the place isn't so bad. Schopenhauer. One minute's panting up the helical flags to Lisa. And a sharing winter cannot touch. Eagerly I climb and knock.

'Denis! Come in, come in.'

Chestnut tresses, bed of a Muse. Aaaah. Lovely, sweater and slacks on a slim figure, long oval face finepencildrawn. And emerald eyes that sing.

'You were right, Lisa. I've had a basinful of that bitch.'

'Of course you have.'

Pine logs crackling Denis you old bugger. These are what I call civilised walls. Delacroix, Matisse, Picasso, Alex MacNeish. Folk-records and Bach piled unevenly on the carpet. Hospitable settee in front of sizzling pinesap, and the *New Statesman* opened at the fiction section under the fragile handcarving of a Dalmatian *tamburitsa*. Taste and elegance and intelligence in this house. I collapse and divest.

You must be hungry, Denis, her voice floating on a drift of French perfume. I love that greenlit bloodless mask dedicated to creation and reception. Wine-hued plate of curried prawns, Danish lager, real Brazilian coffee. She sits by my left knee, rubbing my cold ankles. Lisa, you are the mistress of all immortal sensations.

The hail melting to sleet then rain on the casement of our ivory tower. Lisa and I were kissing, our tongues playing like baby rabbits in a warren. This is the grail. Soon ram my way to the purifying chalice. Must perfect the build-up, sing me a song, Lisa.

Professional proudface over her strings. Mandy was a Bahamas girl (tragedy in Nassau), *Los Quatres Generales* (let me at the Fascist pigs), and a pleasant tear rolled down me for the jail of Clonmel. Stage one artistically perfect, let's talk.

'I've missed you, Denis.'

'Me too, Lisa. But we had to finish up together. I'll get my stuff to-morrow.'

'Did you get the old feeling just now?'

'Certainly did. There's nothing like it.'

'You're the man I want to sing to till I peg out.'

'You're my woman, Lisa. I've brought you some of my writing.'

'Oh, wonderful, Denis.' She turned the pages with her alabaster hands, her lean lips working with intense absorption. 'This looks good. You're an exciting bastard, Sellars.' Oh Lisa. I haul you up beside me, supple as a limb of young birch. Fierce whispers from the narrowed eyes, warm hair silking through my hands, the golden hedonism of these kisses, burned faces short-punching each other, the aphrodisiac aroma of our sweet blending spits. Right now I wish there hadn't been all the others, Denis, but it was just trial and error. I know, Lisa, yours was an honest asking, the dishonour was all your users'.

Baring me to the waist with deft fingers, it's only artists like ourselves who can perfect sex, Denis, we who are committed to enrich the grey lives of those to whom we owe nothing, how much more can we do for each other who need and demand the same level of communication. By the risen Christ how right you are, darling.

'What did you think of my *Lord Lovat* last week, Lisa?'

'Magnificent. What did you think of my *Yellow Bittern* last night?'

'Tragedy at its best, but a greater tragedy that it had only three verses.'

'Thanks, Denis.'

'Lisa, don't you think that a writer should grope like hell for every possible word to express what sex really is?' That bastard Kate.

'Of course I do. Don't you think the Yellow Bittern is a terrific song? I love singing it.'

'Me too, Lisa. You know, I've got a love-song in my head right now, but it just won't come.'

'Give me a week. Dick Jordan the Somerset singer used to write a song every time he heard me sing.'

'Oh, yes.'

Aha, nostalgic grunt, and Lisa, I preached movingly, do you realise that life is the eternally procrastinated fulfilment of an inevitably postulated hope. Of course it is, Denis, I've thought that so often. Oh, yes.

Hands of sleet clawing on your window, scarlet curtain fluttering like a startled cardinal. The firelight giving flame in your witch's eye, but cruelly discovering blackheads in your dark upper lip. I'm frightened. Stage two left unfinished stage three required for this moment is almost unfilled. Quick, Lisa, the flesh, invaluable colleague.

Terylene slacks and nylon were scragged to carpet, her goose-pimpled legs writhing round my back, hot pine-scent on my randing throblift, this must be It. Oh, Blessed Aphrodite, those timeless Mediterranean things we're doing to each other, Kate never knew the half. Fleshbitten finger-teased rumpsqueezed hear the darkness screaming on on strike the lance to the singing spring that eternalised the Yellow Bittern yes yes Denis vocal surrender cut off for I always had a marksman's eye, your tongue writing a poem on me—*a voice must come*. Perfect oblivion, now to beyond perfection with a raking slide to the deeper larynx of the purpler cords; Lisa, I'm going to love those clinging sinuous ridges flat. Using your every square millimetre on me you're in me outside above beyond me but leave me my mind Lisa you must let me use my intellect but it's impossible when your fingers are streaking so much electricity into even my cranium and it's all crazy Greenland's icy mountains land-sliding down my back and India's coral strand tearing fire-skin from my foreskin darkness rising and falling woops sorry I farted those bloody prawns get control, love, perfection, beyond, get control; DONE IT: now concentrate on these ridges and ranges first one just hurts that's Lord Lovat second one tickles that's the Ginger Man and Rabelais third one gives my cock taste-buds that's wonderful the absurd miracle of Jesus I can't find a literary analogy for it but I'm up up upping to where your womb hangs down somewhere in there the great pens must lurk and their answer it's coming Lisa you're screaming speak I say Hamlet Karenina Bovary Heathcliffe SPEAK you BASTARDS stop it Lisa hold hold on—NO!

Slime. Sweat of loveless lust and I've been spouting inside rubbish. And. The. Moment. Is. Gro-tesquely. Unfilled. Impossible Lisa—*we have been FUCKING!*

'Wonderful, darling.'

'You stupid Christless bitch!' Give me darkness I prayed exhausted and slept defeated on her far too bony chest.

Peace stirs uneasily before moonpaling. Shadows displaced from lighted nooks merge to form the angular silhouette of Lisa Kendall stooping in arrogant forgiveness.

'Forget it, Denis. You got a bit wound up.'

'Aye.' Sellars seeking solace in his guitar and Lord Lovat.

Wound up. Understatement. Her fingers nervously apologising to my hair, saying please Denis it seemed terrific to me you heard me yowl and what's wrong. Its O.K. Lisa, what's the loss of a dream between spoiled children. Please stop the hairpulling, lassie, it's sore. Two strings bust on the tamburitsa, I wondered how she managed to sing diminished chords through her arse. Go on now, it's all right, sure sure go on. I feel sick. Croon *Lord Lovat.* Passing his stable door, brushing his white horse.

She was making coffee one room away. 'You know,' she shouted, 'I love these old songs, but they're too long to sing right through. Don't you think Hackett's got a point?'

'I might have known, you bitch.'

'What?'

'Of course, Lisa. I've often thought that myself.'

She sat beside me. Her lovely hair, combed for me into a refreshing fringe and long curled flange behind. Bloody fool I was to condemn. After only once. Life and hope from her never-bettered coffee.

I spied the new opening, stage four. 'Lisa, I'm dying to know what you think of my book.'

'Slip it over in the drawer. I'll start on it sometime next week.'

'*Next week?*'

'I'm terribly busy, Denis. So many rehearsals with Ricky, and I've got a story of my own to finish. But I'll read it as soon as—Denis, I wish you wouldn't go on having those pale turns. It scares the crap out of me.'

'You've got a dirty mouth, Lisa.' Wearily I crept to my coat. The end of all stages.

'I beg your bloody pardon! Where are you going? Denis! '

I had to weave and scurry like a fox fleeing beagles, her nails clutching at me all the way to the door, her face frightened and frightening.

'You've had your fun, have you? Any port in a storm? You're just like the others!' The dark pouches under her dull green eyes, the gangling movements jerky as puppetry, you poor bluffing pretentious young woman.

'I'm sorry, Lisa. I made a mistake.'

She leaned out of her door; the dull red coffee cup glanced off my forehead, shattered to smithereens on the dirty brown stairwall. 'You made a mistake! You bluffer! You used me, you twit! God help you, Sellars,' hysterical sobbing, brief recovery, 'God help you! '

Forgive me, Kate. I shook against a soaking privet, little redemption showing to eastward. But the storm had washed across the sky like an indiscriminate tidal wave, destroying, maiming, yet donating to the debris a priceless atmosphere of near-tangible serenity; behind the zigzag forks of stratified cumulus the whitening half-moon was fixed solid as a shell in wrack-scarred beaten sand.

All the City save Lisa Kendall truculently intact, awaiting the rosy victor's wreath for every spearbright spire and turret.

The way to the Canongate was downhill; Kate was quiet on my shoulder ten minutes after daylight.

Hell should be his who scorned a Heaven so rare
Yet found this faith to temper all despair
That you are more than once I thought you were.

CHAPTER NINE

Snow, slush, rain, frost. Nights of groping blindness, and of clustered crystalline glory. The streets never covered for long, every now and a few hours later a great breath of clean smell scavenging in from the shore, lifting winter scum from sight. Ally of some men, angel of death for older others.

Tollcross. Battered benches and lack-lustre rooflamps. Andrew, you must watch Margot when her face flickers towards the doorway, and make sure your voice cracks just as the apparition leers in the window. I think we should cut that soliloquy, Nichol. All right, Ronald. Beautiful, Maisie when the sun and the moon meet in yon glen, that's when we'll really bowl them over. Press notified about conference next month, Nichol all set for TV interview next week Wake up, Denis, can you hear Margot, what are you dreaming about. Sorry, Nichol, I got lost in pondering the peculiar attraction of a yellow-haired wench who's cooking stovies for my supper.

Connor's. Hackett and Rob up and around every week-end being shadowed by Joe the Rat who has been expressly instructed that much is at stake and he must not betray his sleuthing presence by threatening fists on the

Crows or even human beings within Hackett's hearshot. Stan agreed to put up Hackett's poster, but absent-mindedly used it five minutes later to wrap up yesterday's steak pies for the starving Legion. Oh, the battle, boys, sharpen your broadswords, Culloden was never like this.

The New Town, Georgian and Victorian. Damp and misty round its spacious Gardens in early twilight. Pro-Nichol among the cultivated, unaware and apathetic in most of the professional and commercial residences. Might go to either, though, Fiona, David Hunting-Tower was saying in the *Aperitif* to-day that some of these folksongs are awfully good value.

The Outback, from the seaspicy lanes of Newhaven where fishergirls still learn to cry 'Fine buckies' above strippit skirts, to the villas and bungalows that threaten the rustic integrity of the Lothian slag-heaps—interest among the blazers and gym-slips, condescending curiosity among their immediate ancestors who keep reading in the Evening News and other children's dailies of the two rival ploys. And all those things that the eccentric Ross and the whippety Hackett are saying about each other, they've no breeding at all, can't have been schooled round here. The issue publicised even more by Jesus and the apostles carrying the Gospel to the heathen, one suburb a night for a week, proclaiming Nichol's virtues on every horrorstruck pavement. But on Friday an elderly schoolmistress turned a comer sharply in poor light and had to be resuscitated in the Western General Hospital. The Legion were taken to Police H.Q. in the High Street, shown certain bye-laws in black and white. Nae mair o'yer Jehovies Witness stuff if ye havenae goat authority.

Dear City burgesses, whose fathers carried the words of Mad John as a fiery sword against those who despised him, i.e, all men with an ungodly IQ over 70—revolution approaches, and your redemption with it; no longer are Church and Capital the rave of your highways, but culture, boys—comedy, couplets, and calypsos. Await the day with courage, Jock Corstorphine, when the Rugby Club gather round the spinnet of a Saturday eve and the wife denigrates thet common Mrs. Broon in iembic pentemeters.

The 15th of January; Ollie the Bull has delivered fifty pounds this month into the hands of the just. And this is worrying, Denis. Something fishy, and my principles won't tolerate any kind of dishonesty that can be proven. Must face Ollie with this, look Ollie, man-to-man I won't have anything to do with stealing from the rich, unless you're absolutely sure that nobody saw you. The rich are only such because they're all pally with lawyers and gangsters and so on and don't tell me that your old commodore got all his dough without slipping somebody lethal a backhander.

When Starkey pushed through the smoky maelstrom of Connor's, I was already half-prepared. Slithering into the hard bench beside me, biting his nails, cursing the kids who were hollering to guitar and fiddle outside the Gents'. His face the colour of the weather forecast, 'Let's get into the corner, Denis. Ollie's in trouble.' Starkey was given the needed dram.

'What's he done?'

Starkey slurping with unusual coarseness, 'It was all thet bloody perrot's fault.'

'Come again?'

Somewhere a glass crashed, an angry voice complained.

Ollie the Bull had a soft heart, and the commodore had a vast collection of valuable books and a parrot. Ollie also had the true writer's facility for remembering spoken dialogue and subconsciously adapting it to suit himself. The commodore gave him twenty pounds before leaving for Canada, but with an old-fashioned grin added that he could make some extra cash on the commodore's rubbishy books—one hundred and seventy paperbacks of doubtful religious merit usually read for light relief in the toilet. Ollie blew the twenty pounds, made four out of the naked blondes murdered in technicolour, blew that, then looked around the library without hope. Being fond of the commodore he was resigning himself to a spell of hardship when he remembered that Nichol Ross had once uttered some hostile reservations about the novelist Scott. Ollie's liberal and ingenious memory saved him from thirst; having found custom to the tune of forty-five pounds for Sir Walter in the Grassmarket, he remembered a French critic unimpressed by Balzac and made fifty on his volumes in the High Street. Byron fetched twenty-five in the West Bow and Tennyson was earmarked for big things in the West Port the day after his owner returned unexpectedly.

Ollie having a soft heart communicated with all lonely creatures whenever possible: 'Don't you worry, Polly, old Mr. Balzac is going to buy us a crate of rum.'

The commodore refused to believe the parrot at first, but on exploring his library was apoplectic to discover that the perfidious beast was indeed telling the truth in Ollie's impeccable accent. The trial would take place in the High Court next month, Ollie as always defending himself.

'We'll try and give him the dough back, Starkey.'

'Ach, his books are recovered. I thought your cause was a good one.'

'Maybe you're right. But if Ollie ever mentions giving us money—just think how Hackett could cash in on it.'

The crafty, disproportionate head vibrating angrily, 'You should know better than thet. Ollie's a dyed-in-the-wool Connor's men. Even when he's crazy as a coot like now he's loyal as hell. As long as Rasputin doesn't know where the money came from, nobody's going to gress! '

'Sorry, Starkey.'

Starkey Shearer leaning across the battered varnish to hold my elbow, wise in the crooked eye, 'You're developing a pious look, Denis. You're slipping away from us.'

'I'm getting old, Starkey. Ollie shouldn't have done it.'

'I knew it.' His profile more sensitive than his cynical creditors would ever credit. 'Connor's is nearly finished, Denis. It used to be the greatest brotherhood on earth, the cemarederie of the demned, and we know that's no romentic twaddle. But the demned have all died off or left. It couldn't lest. This town won't tolerate too many nonconformists, and people either stop being alcoholic cheracters or it kills them. Connor's won't kill you, Sellars.'

'And you, Starkey?'

'I've got no choice.' Giggling into his manicured hand. 'I'm what they call a psychopath. I don't appreciate the stendards of the stark event outside thet window. I'm getting almost homesick for hell, Denis, so many of the geng are there now. And my lest embition is to borrow a fiver from my mester the devil.'

You sentimental clown, Sellars, the beginnings of a golfball in your throat. 'Starkey,' I shook him by his thirty guinea lapels, 'Starkey, you old bastard.' But no word in the world to add to that. Pick up the shopping and leave him. 'Can we get him a lawyer, or something?'

Starkey shaking his pointed crown, clucking inside his small mouth. 'Denis, you write stories and I make an art of scrounging. Ollie defends himself in court once every two years. How would you feel if I cut off your right hand?'

Outside, snow coming says the tinker's nose. Thicksteam sky, Woods Street a long moving volume of frozen air, the refrigerated wrath of God. Connor's will never look quite the same. Good-bye to an era. Thanks, Kate. For I never could think of the fiery lake in terms of homesickness.

The saga of Elaine and Jacques is nearing completion. I'm not entirely satisfied, but within its limits it'll produce a couple of good readings for Nichol. It's a sparer narrative now, the froth blown off, much less analysis than before.

Silly Sellars, overestimated the bed, which doesn't contain the promises once sought. What did Pursewarden write to 'dear D.H.L.?'—he refused to build a Taj Mahal around a good—, or something. Quite right, and I still don't want to believe it.

But so much else A few weeks back I would say I'm off to sing at the Crown. I'm tired to-night, Denis, don't be too late, I worry about you. Aha, thought Sellars, this is further disintegration of my friend; her voice is betrayed by its veneer of longsuffering and jealousy. Kate, there are times I don't like your attitude; you haven't the all-consuming passion for lovely things that I have, you play at them, and you envy the people I can share with. I'm sick of telling you that I love the songs, Denis, but I'm a bit tired of those conceited faces and their gimmicky imitations of each other. Don't you get like that.

A few weeks later I know I shouldn't have slammed the door. Should have sat down and listened, because she says that the best way to share a song is privately, round the fireside. Hand me the guitar, dear, let's sing. It's amazing how much interest and more you have to give if I let you do a wee bit of the talking.

Back in December, my need for combat thwarted by the intransigent pacifism of those cornflower eyes and the attentive tilt of her kindcast cheekbones, I might push it further, touch of deliberate cruelty. Kate, dear, are you sure you don't resent those areas of experience that I can't explain? I feel if I could get them over to you, you wouldn't handle me so clumsily, asking me to go out and buy sausages when you don't realise I'm about to get on the blower to Musie. Denis, you don't sound like the boy

I met three months ago. Most people need other people, Denis, but it strikes me there are people who go on about needing people when they really want to use them.

In January I think I shouldn't have thrown that cup at the wall.

So we each sit with one cheek blistering, and together we commune with Lord Randall and Eileen Aroon and the Christ-child; the dove of Maximilian, the bonnie banks o' Ross-shire and the water of Tyne; *in einem kühlen Grunde, á la claire fontaine*, where the nightingales sing. No wild waves of communication here, Kate, but a nebulous something rising from deep inside that doesn't create uncomfortable eye-moisture till the song's sentiment deserves it. Our voices blend less than perfectly, but they rock the Christ-child's cradle by the fire. Happy introverts.

Your big red hands, and their speech that takes a while to become audible. The way they linger on a laid silver spoon, the infinite care that straightens white linen; little deft rituals, a craft learned of limitless compassion. The proud noonlight of your northwoman eyes moving over the brown leathers and gleaming metal and counterfeit flowers that you have gathered from your healing's meagre recompense to make my cave a home. Areas of your experience that I didn't understand, and I handled you so clumsily. You bend over my shoulder: at my desk I catch a glimpse of pride without hauteur, this lass who never shared my love of literature, who makes fatuous remarks about Robert Lowell.

That supreme first mouthful of yellowrimmed ruddy-fleshed brownskin steak when the coals are chattering and my papers laid out ready for five hours with Elaine and Jacques and I honestly don't give a damn if I never publish a page, till the plates are all cold and greasy and I'm mystified again that what Nichol calls the Eternal Consciousness is churning my stomach and throwing my impatient legs back towards that bloody worn chair.

I'm almost happy. Here I can write and I have learned a little. No more safaris into modish fakeland. But the country looked so sweet from afar. And here, Kate, are so many new areas of experience I can never understand; how can I ever be completely fulfilled? I watch you fondle linen and see what you need. But too complicated, not the answer. If only.

We rented a T.V. set after bitter heart-searching. To hell with intellectual snobbery. Rob appearing more often in Scottish programmes, lovely voice, smooth technique. Less criticism from Sellars his brother. Kate's insistence on finding the positive in people has become senselessly contagious, and Rob's got style, I assented with a shade of bloodconsciousness. A chiseller all the same under my breath. They say he goes through five girls a week. Twenty suits in his wardrobe; mother-of-pearl lavatory seat.

Friday night I left the desk early, Nichol and Murdo arriving to share our entertainment-slumming. I never realised how quick is Kate's witty satire. Murdo moves in and out like a rapier, wounding with hardly a malicious stain on his face to accuse, Nichol strikes with the force and accurate velocity of a guided missile, but Kate is a whiff of laughing-gas, has you joyfully dazed before you know it.

By the fire with my three friends this evening was the recreation-hour of our week; Kildare and Z-cars suffered comic indignities that the most dexterous critic could not match without the aid of intelligence. Nichol looking much better, how welcome the return of colloquial thunder, Murdo admitting modest satisfaction with his latest poems which must be masterpieces. Only one minute marred the rest.

'That woman Kendall was on the radio last night,' said Nichol at twelve o'clock, preening his beard in the blank screen. On second thoughts I distrust her voice; it has an unhealthy siren quality. I'm sorry I let her join us.' Phrases sonorous and vindictive.

Murdo looking at his laces and clearing his throat, but Nichol scowling at the white ceiling, ! have also heard that there's a very wayward, wanton streak in her.'

How would you know, you vacillating old loud-mouthed gossip, but I caught Kate's eye and hesitated. A look of incalculable pain crossed her face before she dropped her attention to her knitting.

The following morning, a surprise in the post.

7 Heriot Gardens.
Friday.

Dear Denis,

This must sound strange, but I should be very grateful if you could come up and have a drink with me to-morrow evening about eight.

I assure you that the invitation is made in your best

interests, and that I bear you no ill-will for the unfortunate incident in the Black Friar.

As we have something of a private nature to discuss, I think it would be best if you came alone.

Yours sincerely,
D. Leonard Hackett.

'Whatever could he want?'

'I've no idea, Kate, and I'm not going.'

'I think you should.'

'What?'

'Denis, you want to find out as much about that weasel as you can. I think you should go with your eyes and ears as wide open as possible.'

'You know, Kate, I think you're right.' And after reflection I told her to buy me a skate, a big slimy beauty.

The afternoon drenched the steaming football crowds, freshened around seven to give the students a pleasant walk up to the Union Palais and the East End ladies an early start with the Norwegian sailors; Sellars staggered down the Mound skirting the great valley of The Gardens and met the apostles singing their April hymn by the pillars of the Art Gallery.

'Evening, Paul. Have you seen the Rat?'

'Indeed we have, Denis,' said Jesus. 'We've been watching Hackett's house with him, like you said. Lisa Kendall and your brother have just left. Joe's following them.'

'Is he sober?' Lisa and Rob, by Jiminy.

'Not too bad, Denis. He's at the religious stage—prayin' for a fight.'

'Tell him to meet me at the Scala at ten.'

Padding on through young men embellished with bright scarves and women. Down Hanover Street into the New Town, what good and loyal soldiers I command. Heriot Gardens, elegant sculpture of a gracious era, Georgian remnant hidden behind a park of creaking winter woodland. Giant's bones snapping under torture in there. Hear the howls. Clip, thhrick, up the steps, very exotic. Distinguished- looking door. Hackett must have bribed a Councillor.

'Denis, how nice to see you.'

'How nice to see *you*, old vulture. What d'you want, Hackett?'

A mysterious beckoning to the interior, here goes. In the huge main room, cluttered with hideous bright furniture, I took a good look at mine host. Move away from that artificial snake wall-lamp, Lennie, it makes appraisal confusing.

His distinguished-looking face was softened to-night by a front of horn-rimmed spectacles that almost humanised the shrewdness. Black hair divided by a ruler, something almost shy tugging at his straight sallow cheeks, making his pensive lips twitch like thin earthworms. Pale blue suit giving away his lack of breeding, tastelessly garnished by his silk orange tie.

I sat on a mauve-and-indigo couch facing the Thin Red Line at Balaclava above the fireplace. Too dated for even Hackett to sell. Hackett humming to himself, he's bottling something.

'Come on, Hackett, this firewood's uncomfortable.'

'Whisky, Denis?'

'Juthst a thmall one, Leonard, I've heard thome awful thtories about you.'

'Look!' He poured and carried, sat opposite me with a natural weary sigh. 'If you're going to be rude, you can go right now. I've never known such people. You try to bring them some help and they spit in your face. I've heard this so often from businessmen down south—you can sell progressive ideas anywhere except Scotland! '

I drained the sharp Talisker softened with the correct amount of water. 'Typical big city platitudes, Hackie. You citizens can never appreciate that there are still parts of the United Condom which hang on to their own system of values. This is one of them, Lenny laddie. There are savages up here less touched by your civilisation than the dirtiest wog of the Duskydong tribe. You've been too long in the streets of easy money, you've forgotten all about human nature. It's made you hard.' Somewhere beyond the subtle presence of my skate I smell a memory of Lisa.

'You silly young nit,' said Hackett softly, a suspicion of outrage hovering behind his lenses. 'I was brought up in the East End of London during the bombing. If I was a sentimental Celt I'd start wallowing in it till I made you sick. To hell with you and your values—I've seen more of human nature than you'll ever smell!' Shouting and standing, for the first time there is one-millionth of him that I respect. 'I've learned *one thing*, Sellars: people need a bit of bleeding fun before it's too late to tell them just how late it is! And my business ensures that a few of them can grin a bit easier on both sides of the mike! '

One point to you, Hackett, though I suspect self-deception is involved. This is forgivable, but it's time for us to bare our horrible souls to each other—

The skate intervened. 'D'you smell something, Sellars?' Innocently, 'No.' My impassive poker face, capable of wrenching envy from Gielgud.

Hackett freshening my glass. 'Let me say my piece. I'm truly offering the olive branch to-night. Sorry I blew my top.'

A practised wheedle removing all trace of the sincerity that had surprised me; I doused my passing sympathy: 'That's all right, Lennie. How much are you offering me to leave Nichol?' Clash of crystal, got him.

'What makes you so sure I want you?' The old sugar warm on his measured defensive words.

'My crystal ball, Hackie. At some time after your brutal shaming in the Black Friar you asked my twin what would be the quickest route to Nichol's back, and the idol of the magic box said: "Get Denis away from him, and you'll kill the old crank without firing a shot!"

Silence, only the whirring of the huge electric clock below the Russian sabres. This skate is more veteran than I thought, old Charlie Reid in the Canongate knows an innocent soul when he sees Kate. As I fiddle it from sliding under my belt Hackett saying you're wrong Rob never said a word but surely you realise I can offer you the best deal in the country. Hackett whining he don't hate Nichol, just wants to bring him gently to his knees, make him move with the times, see reason.

Haha. Remember how vile the human heart is, try not to hear it all.

'—'s my offer, Denis. If you'll sing in my show you'll get thirty pounds for each night, and I'll make you an extra thirty a week with club work. After that I can guarantee you a fat year—T.V., radio, the clubs. I can get you records made, trips to America—you'll not want one penny as long as the folk-boom lasts, and it still looks good for ten years.'

One of the Highland infantry was kneeling wounded, lines of fatigued bewilderment.

'The bombing didn't do you much good, Hackett. One more drink and I'll go.' I fancy a complaining crick of glass beneath his blanching stubby fingers. But I'm tempted.

'Don't be a fool. You'll never make a go of it with that old fool.'

Relief in the dark canvas from the vulgar decor of beige and bile-yellow, the peagreen lamps, the round blue spots on one white wall.

'He's one of the greatest writers Europe ever saw, although you're too thick to see it. If this thing fails his big heart will shatter.' Harden that voice to sandpaper on granite, no slush. 'Even if I thought he *was* crazy, I couldn't let him down.'

Hackett lighting me a sweet Burmese cheroot, frantic fingers. 'Look, Denis,' pacing back to me. 'I'm facing the music too. D'you think that I wanted to force this issue? I *have* to establish my show, Denis. I have my own career to think of.'

The front rank broken in places, still belching smoky death into the Cossacks.

'You'll survive, sweet refugee. You'll finish up

selling pornography in Peking. Scope for a brave revisionist there, Hackie, market's wide open.'

His snarl was hard to remove, but the counterfeit smile was restored with sweating muscular effort. 'I'm going to win, Denis,' gluttoning his tall glass. 'And I won't be ashamed to stamp Nichol Ross into the dirt. Remember what I accused him of in the Black Friar.'

'Sorry, Hackie, I fell asleep during your bit.'

Squirming in his yellow triangular chair, 'You and he claim to be idealists, keeping up the classical standards. But you're no different from me, we're all backing different horses in the race to significance. You've backed the esoteric. I've backed the popular—neither of us is more moral than the other.'

That damn clock. Another rifleman on his knees, who had the time to bind his head up?

'That's good for you, really good. That impressed me, your use of English, Hackett. But it's not a matter of morals, Lennie, it's a case of fighting for subtlety and finesse that has endured a long time—that against Moodie and Sankey harmonies that the public'll be sick of next time.'

Cossack points thrusting at the red tunics.

'Subtlety and finesse,' Len Hackett acting a chortle. 'All those filthy bothy-ballads and that Geyelic dog-music that nobody can understand. I'm sponsoring what amounts to a national movement, Denis. Come on now, boy, think again; I can keep you right at the top if you do what I tell you.'

His syrup cloying, but smells of comfort. I do envy Rob and three nights a week of national recognition, five skirts to raise in six days. But the rear rank are flashing silver bayonets over their fallen comrades.

'One of these days you'll realise there's a difference between bawdry and filth.'

Big chuckle, Brylcream running again, 'You're weakening.'

Nearly was, you skunk, I'm too ashamed to tell you why. But something struck me.

'I'll tell you a story, just to change the subject. I'm a man who's had pre-marital sex.'

'Get away, Denis.' Off for another, really thinks he's there, mincing happy feet.

My big white teeth and golden larynx in the spotlight, I could take my pick of the front three rows. Lovely. For a while. No, Sellars. No.

'But even stranger, I hate promiscuity.'

Giggle, wriggle, you'd think *he* had the skate wobbling round his belly. 'You'll have to explain that, Denis. Haha, you're a character.'

'Because one of my definitions of promiscuity is two people going to bed when less than two of them have their eyes open. I'll sing till I seize up about a willing girl being merrily laid, Hackett, but I've seen what your sort of society does to decent stupid married singers and innocent little kids that you could get the jail for. You've built the irresponsible fuck into the phoney modern folk-ethos, and that's the sort of promiscuity that scares me stiff! '

'To hell with your moralising. I'm asking you for the last time. Will you sing for me on April the fourth?'

Horses' limbs thrashing in the white clouds. Long

black moustaches in the Crimean battlemurk, brogues sliding on the slippery red turf. It's in the history books. 93rd, take the bayonet!

'You dirty weasel, I wouldn't piss on your offer.'

Quiet. Hackett's head went down, a bald patch glistening deadwhite as the dying faces of the Don's heroes. The tartans. Thanks, boys. Quiet.

'I've done all I possibly can to be decent,' he said without emotion. 'I'll break you, Sellars.'

'And me you, Judas.'

'You crazy goon!' Easy, Hackett, the neighbours, this is Heriot Gardens. My God, where has all that suffusion come from, specs whipped off and eyes sparking fury: 'Do you realise the sort of madman you're supporting? Do you know that he attends looney psychical meetings in London? Have you heard that he was wanted by the French police at one time in connection with some illegal society? D'you know that he put some sort of hypnosis on me in the Black Friar? He's a criminal lunatic—*you'd think he was in league with the devil!*' Hackett lurched back to his decanter, half-sob- and-tittering with fury.

'Your spies have been busy, Hackett, but I know all the myths already. Maybe you've got things the wrong way round.'

Hackett swallowing rapidly turned and threw his dregs over my feet. 'Get out, you poor bloody bumpkin. You're not worth half your brother. You're like a Congolese savage under the spell of a witch doctor.'

'Listen,' I cocked a Shakespearean ear. 'The bell. Somebody there. I could swear it.'

He crept through after a disbelieving glance; he's asked for this little present. Whipping the skate from out my grateful midriff, I took five light soundless strides and toppled the ugly monster behind the Thin Red Line. Stuck beautifully.

I was sipping like a teetotal cherub when he returned with a suspicious snarl and there's nobody there don't get funny with me you crazy village idiot. Sorry, Hackett.

'Get out, Sellars.'

'I must thank you for a delightfully informal evening.'

His suede feet slithering, bloodshot eyeballs swelling. 'Go on, Sellars, go back to your stupi' blonde bang and that big hairy grandad of a hack-writer. Go on, kiss 'is arse, yo' yella rat. Buddon't come back crying to me when I've broken you all in pieces! '

An allblinding lightning from my temper's equator answered the vicious storm of his insults: my arm extended with the righteous anger of a Crusader's lance, pushing him flat across the couch. Here's for what you'll never destroy, for the filth you stand for, for what Rob might have been, for insulting a kind heart that never—but no, the left hook is not the answer. I picked up my coat, left him limp.

'Why didn' yi' hid me? I'm too drunk to stop you.'

'I must be growing up, or something. And I washed my hands this morning.'

His shell went back to the Waterford crystal. 'Get out.' Hate rippling along his cheeks, the cobra-lamps Church of Scotland grass snakes by comparison. Courage, Denis.

A Parthian shot, for I espied the black Sobranie in his ashtray. I picked it up, smelling ashes of roses. 'Did you manage to buy *her*?'

'*Get out.*'

I bowed and withdrew, my last impression a dishevelled thirty-year-old, overdressed, wiping his brow with a blue handkerchief and drinking with the other shaking hand. Muddy eyes willing me dead before the door. No contempt nor hatred in me, only a little regret. We all touch each other somewhere, good Christ redeem my fellowneeding weakness.

I marched up the Mound, along George IV Bridge. Drenched again by the waves of dark sky. For once I'm proud of myself. Woods Street soughing in homage to the night, but right now I would not bend the knee to all the fine delicacy of France's last and tragic queen.

The Scala. Thick clouds of someday cancer, medical students and their nurses and typists. Twelve horse-boxes of pre-coital reflection, sometimes only one pair of eyes open per table. But by the door the aggressive unshaven face of my squat Connor's blood-brother, muttering bigoted sentiments about Maria the owner around his crumpled fag-end.

'Two coffees, Maria.'

'O.K. Denis. And-a take him away after that. He's-a sayin' bad things to all-a them girls that goes past him.'

The Rat shook a dirty fist. 'Nae cheek from *you*, ma beauty, or Ah'll take ye ootside an' show ye the scars Ah got on the beaches of Anzio! '

Maria made a very Italian gesture behind the counter. 'You never got-a them scars at Anzio. You got them last New Year when you wass-a drunk an' set yer troosers on fire!'

The Rat rose to take off his jacket, and all the smart young men laughing at him, whispering to their girls, Connor's you know, madmen.

I pulled him down. 'You've impressed your audience, Joe. Now what about Rob and Lisa Kendall?'

He supped his coffee thirstily. 'Ah've done a good job for you the night. Damn near perished o' cauld.' His azure eyes dancing, merriment all over his neat face, circles of black hair wet on his forehead.

'Where did they go?'

'They went up to her flat by the Links. He was squeezin' 'ur a' the way, Denis, Ah was fair disgusted.'

'How long did they stay there?'

'They never came oot again. Ah hung on for aboot twenty minutes, then a whole loat o' youngsters started goin' in the same stair. Ah tumbled tae who they were after a bit—it was a' the folksong groups: the Miners, the Corncrakes, the Buchan Billies: every group in town was there except the Moonshiners. They were still there when Ah left.'

'Oh, powwow.'

Treachery in the heart of this land. Quiet, you giggling physiotherapist across the way, you're for a fright tonight if I can read a randy eye, and I need some smoky peace to think. I'd bet that nearly all the youngsters'll go with Hackett, and Lisa I can hardly blame for doing all this. Revenge is sweet as the Russians said in '45. Rich sourness pasta and Parmesan, I love this café. At least Ricky wasn't there, must tell Nichol.

I pulled a green note from my pocket. 'Well done, Joe. I've owed you ten bob for long enough, and keep the change.'

'You're gettin' a big man these days.' The Rat slapped his forehead and hissed through his thin nose, his inimitable manner of throwing the gauntlet. 'First ye're offerin' a lawyer for Ollie, an' now ye're payin' me like a message-boy. Are ye lookin' for trouble?' but the act capsized in a gale of laughter, I know ye didnae mean it, Denis.

'What d'you think Ollie'll get next month?'

'About three months, it's his ninth offence. Maybe the psychiatrist'll get him off. But the auld friendships are worth mair than cash, Sellars.'

'A platitude, Joe.'

'Maybe,' said the Rat, refusing to admit lack of education, 'but you'll never know just how much Ah think of auld Rasputin.'

'Why?'

'Look at me,' puffing out his green pullover. 'Ah'm a silly wee bugger that tries to stretch hissel' by drinkin' strong drink, and then Ah'll pick a fight tae prove that Ah'm really as big as Ah feel. Ah ken fine that ye a' laugh at me.'

'We love you, Joe.' Taking his hand.

'So ye should, ye arab. But ye ken somethin', Denis, Mr. Nichol Ross has always treated me like a king. Ah could name some students that wouldnae say good-mornin' from the day they pass their Finals. But see him—ye'd think ma talk was really interestin' the way he listens, ye'd think Joe the Rat was his intelleckshull equal. Nae money, Denis; I'd die fur yon man.'

We moved to the door; Joe scowled ferociously at a six foot Yank coming in. Please don't jostle him, Hiram, I want home to Kate.

Next week's mission outlined and good-nights said, I exchanged a few secular pleasantries with those hailing me as is their paralytic Saturday custom out of doorways and wynds from the soft-grey lighted Cathedral down to my darker Canongate. Mysterious movement and escapists' laughter deep in there, pray that they've drunk themselves able to love. Before tomorrow.

Steak and chips waiting for me, I chased Meg Crossan home at one o'clock. I want to make love to Kate, ye auld night-hawk. Her beefy fifteen stones shook with laughter, and her farewell backslap concussed most of my spine.

'Let your hair fall, Kate. I just want to look at you.'

She obeyed in the lamplight. Viking goddess patching my sports jacket. What a sight. I feel utterly inspired.

'Kate, is there a typist in the Royal you can trust?'

'Yes, I'm sure there is.'

And so I drafted a great human document to the Chief Sanitary Inspector, while R. J. Dobbie's coal sang us a madrigal and the flames leapt enviously before the greater glory fallen around her crooning white throat.

Heriot Gardens,
Sunday.

Dear Sir,

Please excuse the anonymity of this letter but my husband is a respectable professional person and I do not want any embarrassment as he is too much of a gentleman and I am writing this without his knowledge.

An individual by the name of Hackett has come to stay near us in number seven which is in itself not really your concern. He is from London and runs T.V. shows, and I am told he is divorced. But that in itself is not really not respectable, you must realise that I have an open mind.

At first he was very nice, and always passed the time of day in a cultured accent and he even offered my daughter aged thirteen some sweets if she would accompany him for a walk in the Gardens. We were at first delighted to have such a friendly neighbour although he seemed a little intoxicated on his late returns home and once woke up my aged mother at 2 a.m. through his loud singing of a folk-song about King Farouk which was full of strange Egyptian words.

Last week, however, my husband and I noticed a dreadful aroma around the entry to his house, which issued a considerable distance, it was so bad that as a lady I can hardly bring myself to write on paper what it reminded me of. After two days we were sure it was coming from Mr. Hackett's windows so at seven o'clock yesterday evening I went along not to complain but to give him some advice about his drains.

Imagine my horror when about to ring the bell I

happened to glance accidentally through his ill-drawn curtains. A poor naked girl of about twenty was being chased round the room by this strange man (who was also undressed but at least his back was to me) but worse than this he was striking at her buttocks with what was undoubtedly a huge rotten fish! Pieces of this horrible fish were flying off every time he struck at the poor girl who eventually collapsed sobbing on the floor. Just before I averted my horrified eyes I saw Mr. Hackett who was absolutely dribbling with passion (at the mouth) go over to the picture above his fireplace and replace the filthy fish behind it! I have been in a state of nervous breakdown ever since.

The smell today is quite unbearable as you will find if you come within 100 yards of the above address—none of my neighbours has ventured outside and I am writing during afternoon tea. Could you please come as soon as possible and remove the fish? I am also drafting a letter to the Professor of Surgery at the University who my aunt knows personally as I feel Mr. Hackett needs medical treatment—no sane adult would keep a fish behind a picture and I can assure you I would not be at all happy about him taking my daughter for another walk.

Please do not think I am narrow-minded but could you mention this to the Medical Officer of Health? In this day and age we must allow for freedom of self-expression but unsanitary behaviour is a danger to the community as a whole, and Mr. Hackett has brought it home to my heart as a Christian mother.

Yours faithfully.
Professional Man's Wife.

For once dear John I place a hand in thine
And use such words whereof the righteous dine
Glad were I should their sound dismay a swine.

CHAPTER TEN

Snow had come to rest on us for a while. The whole City lying under a heavy mantle that pressed its skylines gentler. Thick falls twice a day, soft flakes blotting out the panorama, lying sticky as breast feathers on the cursing natives. When the Crags appeared their steep glacial cruelty deflected thoughts to the fate of such as Captain Scott. Murderous black and white. But at other times the medieval garrets took on a sweet cold loveliness; you saw the flames leap on glass and wished that Christmas was in February.

Warm inside on a Canongate evening, Sellars seeking a little light relief from his novel. Playing on paper a favourite City game—I-am-the-Almighty as begun by you— know-who(m). A game also called paranoia in some quarters and sometimes literary criticism. So Denis Sellars thinks of the saints who preached the love-words he loves above all others, and Jehovah Sellars tells them why they're only saints and not Jehovah.

The four, the writers of the Gospel, but one excluded who should have made them five, because he was so absurdly Great that it will take my bumptious pen years to dare confront him. I'm sorry, Dublin Jimmy, but I daren't start with you—I must leave you to gentlemen learned enough to reduce your language to the level of communication it forever surpassed. Haha.

The Gospel of Love, and here I must have a chat with St. David Herbert, because this is very fashionable these days. You, great poet-in-prose, are one of *the* writers of communication, and yet you leave me strangely unsatisfied. Heresy? Not really, for my sexual experience lies in documentary reality and your writing on the astral plane of Art. But you in the end postulated the natural fuck as the panacea, and the more I enjoy the great natural thing the more I realise why you sound so unbearably repetitive at times because the great natural thing is unbearably repetitive at times. I confess I find you both occasionally boring and boredom must surely have nothing to do with Truth; if I am an honest man, St. David Herbert, you were a very lyrical saint, but a very limited prophet to suggest that we can fuck ourselves into loving. I bless you, but *I'm* beginning to dream that we can love ourselves out of fucking.

St. Lewis Grassic of Scotland, why have I chosen you? What poverty of erotic description beside *Lady Chatterley*, perhaps only one-fifth of the communication-cords that tolled the sounding brass of *Sons and Lovers*. But you belong, and not only because you are the most underrated novelist in Western Europe. It was you who first made me realise that the bed depends in part on the dialects that mutter in its fastnesses, on the ghosts in its room, the flavour of city reeks, the colour of com and the peewits wheeling outside its window. It was all there, I welcomed its authority with loving arms, and I knew Chris Guthrie better from ten lines than Lady Chatterley from ten layings. For you and I (pardon the proximity) are provincials and it strikes me that there will be no such thing as panglobal natural love until all the great provincial writers like yourself explain their differences to each other. Had you been of a nation that respects both the bed and the province (possibly the chauvinistic froggys) you would have been a European classic by now. But you died too soon; your life and your writing both bear witness to my own tragic philosophy, and if tragedy *is* the end of all things, you are the literary element of it that I cherish most.

St. Lawrence of the non-Arabian desert, the exquisite all-time writer of a paragraph, our modem genius of moving shapes and colours. And when they told me that you were hunting the Great Truths, how glad I was, for how could such a master of Beauty fail? Well. Whether you achieved what you wanted, driving planes through time and space and God-knows-what, I'll never know. But I do know that you used some of the corniest devices in the history of fiction to reach your resolution (notably that awful accident) and in the end you tell me few convincing things about what I call Love. What you *do* teach me, St. Larry, is that provincial writing *can* be a very bad thing. Not Alexandria. It's all right acting God and entering minds all round but when they all appear as tediously exotic as each other I begin to suspect that you're bluffing. Provincial characterisation in a way I never thought possible: in all modesty I declare you the most flawed genius I have ever read. Long may I sharpen my courage to attempt your lovely craft; the northern nights are short with southern *Justine* and *Clea*. But the rubbish I find in my diary the following morning: *The love of a pregnant witch is greater than that of a one-eyed negro*: or again: *Here I find myself sitting fearfully in a chair with four legs—the whole spiritual history of our civilisation from Pilate to Carl Chessman*. I'd still read you on erupting Vesuvius, St. Lawrence, but you promise just too much—let's hope posterity damns my reluctant reservations as impostors.

St. J.P.D., ould darlin'. Some tell me you're depressing; which is strange because I turn to you whenever I'm depressed. What's more I believe every word you write, and I don't just mean you're telling the truth. I recognise more than a few splinters of your hero's cross, especially when his guard's down leaving Dublin under storm with a twisted heart muscle. I recognise your dirty linen, man of ginger, the despair that seeks relief in the absurdest sensations this grey orb affords us. You hit or fuck them before they enslave or betray you, and I don't find your better self anything less than a loveable old shite. And your tender moments make me cry. The trouble is, J.P.D., I've neither the guts nor the psychopathy to laugh with you all the way, and I believe that goes for many of us. Pity. But City Protestantism's a tougher foe than Popery and you're not half the Protestant I am. They say you're not quite the greatest. Maybe not, but to me there's nothing like you. Bless your lonely and wicked old heart more than any. So deadly true, your bitterlaughing loving ...

Hard going again tonight. This last chapter a swine and I'm frightened of it. Excuse.

'Come on, darling, let's go to bed for a bit.'

She laid down her James Bond. 'Good idea, Denis,' smiling and a quick throb and flush to her throat.

I no longer ask for too much. Take what is soft, give what is living. At home in this fresh-changed laundry, take my friendship for what it's worth, Kate, but she moaned and caressed and moved me on and a warm sea surged from somewhere till I surfaced sweating and rolled over on my back, breathing the hot air-stream of her nostril, twining her damp hair in my fingers. Nice and simple, and apart from that what was it that I once imagined in Düsseldorf?

Three buckets of water and I was tingling all over; I combed my hair, donned a fresh pullover and picked up my pen.

The novel was finished by daylight.

The Ewan Hall dominated its surrounds, a round green dome built from beer so they said. Its snowy crest glancing in sunshine on the morning that the Earl of Lammermuir and Baillie John Hardie represented the Festival Arts Committee at Nichol's private preview of his April test preview of his proposed Festival performance. Thirty yards beyond the huge stone edifice the Queen's Theatre fitted snugly under smoke-scorched tenements, its billboards displaying long yellow resumés of Hackett's imminent *Stringtime*.

The Hall a huge ball of twilight inside; area, grand tier and gallery, bottomspace for two thousand souls, odour of stale upholstery. The stage normally used for solo pianists and political hair-splitters and therefore a trifle shallow, but our experts had already sorted our curtain and backstage difficulties, the caretaker arguing with Nichol and a joiner, Andrew and Margot testing the formidable acoustics. Murdo and I sat among our colleagues, all rather overawed by the scale of the place, Ricky and the Moonshiners sitting without Lisa behind us. God. Not another folksinger.

Nichol's cloak swirling by my elbow: 'May I present the Earl of Lammermuir and Baillie Hardie, who have kindly come to witness the rescue of their heritage. Murdo MacAuley and Denis Sellars, gentlemen, two of Scotland's brightest hopes.'

Lammermuir, six foot two, thinning fair hair and Eton tie, murmured how interested he was and how delighted to be here. Hardie, Medium and nondescript despite his *charcuterie* empire, recent courageous banning of *Fanny Hill* and fining of a small back-street bookseller, remarked with a good-natured smile that he hoped we wouldn't all finish up in front of him. Guard your paunch, mate, no brothel queues for me.

Nichol was scanning his troops: 'By God, where are the other folksingers?'

Ricky quietly from behind, 'There won't be any more coming, Nichol. I think you can guess why.'

'I see.' His fists clenched, temples throbbing, black eyes searching for an object to victimise. But he turned, doffed his bonnet with a courtier sweep, informed Lammermuir in a brittle voice: 'I've had a little trouble, you know, with this chap Hackett.' Then to Ricky: 'Don't worry, the groups were your idea, he can have them. Maisie! ' He roared past the suddenjerking Baillie, 'we'll get started! Get up there and show them what traditional singing is! '

Murdo, Ricky, Sellars found each others' unhappy eyes with simultaneous swivels. I fear my distrust of Nichol's brave resilience. Not funny. For I smell tension and trouble coming.

The *hors d'oeuvres* of singing was on. Maisie's adenoidal artistry rich to the high lamps, waves of the Battle of Harlaw flooding into the startled emptiness, the lang swords o' the Hielandmen clashing in her hard consonants, horses' hooves drumming deep in her large bosom. Beyond the fixed politeness of the Earl the local knight of the clean word was staring in bewilderment. Peter Douglas followed, agile and pawky, purple nose shining, but he delivered the *Weaver o' the North* with a corncrake jocosity that made the Earl's bum slither. Polite sympathy. Damn, and beyond him Hardie smirking between smiles, this man demands beautiful sounds, doesn't appreciate traditional birdlife. Come on, Ricky, please get enthusiasm on their necessary faces. The Moonshiners blaring the medieval valour of Otterburn's great battle, their guitars haven't got the steely edge of Maisie's reverberating penetration, but they laid waste the last line with an eye-misting harmony, thank God, made the Baillie's grizzled moustache twitch an admission of appreciation. Now Bonnie George Campbell, saga of the empty bloodstained saddle, the high purples and the Lowland greens happily mourning the death of a Campbell; better, boys, Lammermuir tilting towards me to opine it was very sweet, Hardie moved to offer thoughtful stupidity all round. Then the murder of

Yarrow, rare choice of a Border cruelty, harsh as their swords grating between his ribs. But, said Baillie Hardie, aren't they going to sing any of this new stuff about freeing people in South Africa and Alabama? Hesitations on the last heartgutted phrases, a string gone sharp with grief; she wrappit him in her hair three-quarters-lang and bore him hame to Yarrow. She's got sisters in Alabama, Hardie, more than I can say for you. Not bad, but the Earl's face doesn't think it's enough to draw them. And when Murdo's young Islay singer gave *Caristiona* an elegy fit for a princess, they were exchanging doubtful glances. Hell.

But now the drama. For his present inquisition Nichol had selected the first two acts of Carson's occult epic *The Seal Man* and the last of James McNeill's modern drama. The curtain withdrew on the Seal Man, narrator returned from the twentieth-century sea to tell us the end from the beginning. Then Andrew Maclennan took over, playing Roderick Monroe fresh from the Indian Wars God bless Victoria to find his Sutherland township threatened with clearance. Flames crackling in the night, babies clutching leather-bottle breasts in the wintry heather. And the fight begun by Roderick Monroe, stand together boys, defy the absentee Duke and his redhanded bastards. We were told the end already, sure enough, but dramatic irony wilted before the ravaged virtuosity of Andrew Maclennan. Maclennan the has-been actor, the forgotten Marxist whom Nichol raised from the dead to rewrite ten pages of *Das Kapital* as Karl now knows he should have. Sorrow, fortitude, pride and forlorn dignity: we burned under each through the flicker of a finger, the cast of a shoulder, the terrible presence that electrified his silences, the impossible hope that floated lyrical as a young swan to the deepest recesses of the Hall where even the inanimate awoke to cherish the possibility that the preforeknowledge of the Seal Man was a liar.

The Seal Man's prophecy neared fulfilment towards the end, however, and our regret at Monroe's reversion to Andrew Maclennan was almost greater than our identification with his grief as we left him weeping on his knees by the cradle, and the ruin of his gentle Seonag swinging like a pendulum across the backstage window. When Lammermuir echoed my own feelings aloud I resented their expression; Hardie was frowning at his knees, suffering remorse over the bookseller.

Poetry and prose readings. The youngsters excellent, Ronald Johnstone twisting a rowan leaf through ten planes in enchanted free verse, and when he was finished we had to find a rowan leaf and look at it again, for it had some universal connection with all of us. Margot's velvety voice purring the elegance of our centuries from the Makars to MacDiarmid, Murdo up and interpreting the Celtic fire of dead bards, spirit of a mutilated brother-civilisation expressed in words I cannot but love without understanding. Nichol squatting side-stage puffing less cantankerously, the company donning poise and self-possession under the Hall's looming mystique; very promising said the likeable young aristocrat, the Baillie nodding sleepy agreement beside him, aroused from puritan reverie when the little tinker fiddler began to skirl the paint from the walls.

Relax, Murdo, that crimson curtain is going up on

unprecedented success. The Earl's offering Gauloises to everybody, Rasputin has turned the winds of Scotland, Skid Row is about to blast the lights from Broadway. All this and Kate.

'Now for even greater drama,' rasped Nichol, towering in the centre of the stage. 'The last act of the *Fifth Horseman*, gentlemen, and I defy you to remain unmoved.'

He gave us the build-up. This time Andrew is translated to the world of Glasgow big business, where they no longer cut each other's throats because machine-guns are cleaner. But at fifty John Graham is different. Pillar o' the Kirk, yes, beautiful good-family wife, yes, son captain of a fashionable school, oh yes, but a man who believes in Socialist principles, haha, all for his workers, and an idealist who intends to expand his new plastic monopoly into rural and Highland light industry. They all love him, the company directors, Margot as Isobel his spotless wife, his clean-skinned son, even the minister.

The curtain went up on Margot, raven-headed hourglass in jersey wool, slim crossed nylon legs by the 'phone. The Baillie began to take an interest, sweet smile on his pouches. But the instrument rang, the denouement already upon us, wave upon wave of acid dialogue swamped our senses before we could draw breath from surviving the last. Malicious voice of a friend, a tiny symbol of indelible superstition had dropped from John's deepest pocket at last night's party. So what, said Isobel Graham, recrossing her legs too skilfully for the Baillie, but the little disc had said: *I am a Catholic—in case of emergency please send for a priest immediately*. Crash. And they tore the truth out of him shred by shred, for the minister was tolerant but after all, our faith, and the directors were honourable Brutuses but the Masons, you know, and young Burns loved his father, but oh this terrible unschoolboyish dishonesty that he wouldn't allow among his own prefects. Andrew raging from wing to wing, cajoling, charming, lying, losing, slurring into drunkenness as he drained the decanter of its cold tea, till finally he reeled from one slaughtered foot to the other, dribble of hysteria glistening at his mouthcorners, Margot leaving ship. Look at all I've given you, Isobel, we've loved each other for twenty years, you can't walk out on all that. No surrender in Margot's sexberg stance by the door on gorgeous sheer calves, that's why I'll never forgive you, John, that you impersonated a decent man so well when all the time I was sleeping with John O'Donnell, a filthy bog-arab from Parkhead. Graham's head sinking low and wildhaired, we recall the story hacked out of him during the last half-hour...

Wonderful mostly but the climax could be better, said the Earl, and I almost agreed. Your criticism has some blind spots, Nichol, but thank God you're beginning to impress them. Enough?

'Well,' shouted Rasputin, 'what did you think of that?' 'Very moving, Mr. Ross,' said the Earl sincerely.

'Very moving,' grunted Hardie. A round of applause for the two kind gentlemen from our nervous artists.

'And we're not finished yet,' boasted Nichol; the Baillie's face fell. 'Maisie, let's show them how our finale will delight the April audiences! '

Maisie Hay was a sloe-eyed sixty-two. She

commanded the hall for the first twelve verses of the *Gypsy Laddies*, her stillraven autumn foliage shining and high, and the lord's lady was stolen at a gallop. But slowly the spell seeped out of us, Maisie was tiring by the twentieth. Ragged timing, lazy soft passages, the chase retarded to embarrassment, and when they were caught and hanged we all breathed in relief. Awkward silence, Nichol waving his hat frantically, come on Ricky, keep it going. The Earl and the Baillie whispered uneasily to each other for the duration of the Moonshiners' struggling *Rovin' Ploughboy*; steady, Ricky, you're overtaut, lad, don't let this mounting anxiety poison your lungs. Struggle, jangle, asynchrony, tenor one tone flat, the Earl shuddered and grimaced.

'Enough!' Nichol slammed livid across the stage. 'You young idiots are disgracing your colleagues and this whole performance. What's gone wrong with you?'

Barb straight into the professional belly. Ricky wincing, but confessing responsibility, 'I'm sorry, Nichol, but this can happen to any singers. We're a bit off today—'

'Not to *my* singers!' Nichol's hair caught a shower of sparks from the lights, turning to apologise to the honoured: gentlemen I assure you that these careless young blackguards will be much improved before I allow them on my stage again.

Upper-and middle-class winks were exchanged behind his back. I ran forward to hear what was happening behind the microphone; Ricky's monk-face was its codthroat colour of temper, pride bristling against Nichol's superlative condemnations.

'I beg your pardon?' Rasputin's voice incredulous and slow, replying to the stocky little guitarist who had stepped before him.

'I said that finishes me, Mr. Ross,' the Moonshiner pulling nervously at his own red beard under Nichol's. 'If it hadn't been for Ricky I'd have been away with Lisa and Hackett before this. Ricky kept faith with you, and you thank him with insults. Are you comin', Jock?'

The other Moonshiner nodded, began to move away from Nichol and his leader.

'Ricky!' I shouted, pleading up at him through Nichol's legs, but the growl of a waking volcano erupted from the giant trunk: 'Soooh! You are artists of such calibre that a little criticism reduces you to the pampered schoolboy intelligences that you really are! All right, go! I don't need you, you debased imitations of your ancestors! Go on! Go!'

I was pulling unheeded at Nichol's frayed turn-up, and Ricky laid a last gentle handhold on his arm which was immediately thrown off. 'You go too. Slater! I don't need you! I'm the only man of genius this country has had in three hundred years, and you're all trying to get me down! '

Ricky gave a sad shrug, began to walk to the steps.

'Ricky! ' I sideswung up and on, ran and held his shoulders. 'Don't be put off by this, think of the work we've all put in. It's just one of his tantrums, honestly.'

Hurt in Ricky's quivering upset eyelids. 'No, Denis,' he said flatly. 'This has been coming for a long time. We don't belong here.'

'Don't be crazy, man.'

'I'm telling you, old pal, and you'll feel the same way soon enough. He belongs to the past, Denis, when people believed in Divine Right. Hackett's a bum, but he is looking ahead.' What you mean, Ricky, is that the arrogance of genius has had it and that whining pop-art is going to—but a thump on both our chests and Rasputin was addressing us again.

'Don't waste time with this doomed creature, Denis. We are losing no talent, only a fifth-rate entertainer.'

'Shut up. Nichol! ' I've had enough.

'I beg your pardon?'

'I said "shut up! " You've nearly ruined our chances with the Committee already!' But whispering, 'Please, Nichol, apologise, I know you didn't mean it.'

His face was swollen with a rush of blood so sudden that I was tempted to protect mine against the drenching explosion; his eyes scorching with a weird heat, immeasurable in units, their whites expanding bluish; one terrible fist trembled beneath my nose.

Ricky took the arm calmly. 'Don't bother, Nichol, I am a professional folksinger, and I'd have left you sooner or later. We understand Hackett's language, and we belong with him. Goodluck, Denis.' The Moonshiners quit the stage, spiteful back-glances from the other two. Silence below us, only Maisie muttering whit's goin' on, but the Committee representatives both hastily concluding thirty seconds of laughter. Oh, God.

Nichol spitting-furious over the shadowy pit. 'Now, don't worry, my friends, this will make no difference. Our sponsors have been impressed with your endeavours, and I assure you that such a disgraceful scene will never be associated with us again. Those impostors! But you *were* impressed, gentlemen, weren't you?'

Oh, yes, they nodded and sugarsmiled, they were impressed all right, but, ahem, if we had no young singers left, inquired the Baillie, would we still draw the crowds?

'Baillie Hardie, my tickets are selling already!'

'How many, Mr. Ross?'

'Carson?'

Well, grunt, there were two hundred sold for the area, Nichol, and a few dozen in the grand tier, but we're still canvassing like mad and if only this man Hackett hadn't muscled in—

'That's enough, Carson!'

The Earl came forward and offered his hand. 'Thank you very much for an intriguing morning, Mr. Ross.' He smiled brilliantly. 'I can't promise anything definite until I sec how you fill the hall, but I am most interested in your efforts, and I shall be keeping my fingers crossed for you.'

'Me too,' said Baillie Hardie. 'You've got a good clean show here, Ross.'

'Wait a minute!' Nichol's right arm performed an involuntary Bolshevik salute, dissatisfaction and contempt twisting his face. 'Before you go away convinced that I have lost my most powerful assets, I'll get young Sellars to show you that I have other tricks up my sleeve with which to enthral the young.' They shuffled reluctantly to their seats. 'Denis,' continued Nichol, 'it's your turn to distinguish yourself. No, not your guitar!—read them your last chapter, the dialogue between Elaine and the sea! This, gentlemen, is illumination of young love at its most heart-rending.'

Murdo handed up the script; I stared at the first line. Below me our adjudicators, half-bored, half-amused, around them my competitive, critical compatriots, Murdo giving hand-signs, go on boy, Nichol's smoke puffing encouragement across me.

Pearls and swine were print on paper till now. I stole this, my best passage ever from an artist whose only ambition was to be loved by something warmer than a pen. No, people, suddenly this isn't right. My everkiss from outhwit. Counterpoint of inwit's agenbite. From only her, but as yet I haven't done it the literary justice it demands. I hate this place, I hate bloody Art, I want home.

'I can't do it, Nichol.'

'You can't do it? Are you ill?'

'It's—it's too personal, I can't spout it out like this.'

His fist dunted my back like the snout of a charging rhinoceros. 'You will damn well do what you're told!' He was pacing again, weaving long white tendrils of ferocity with his fast-moving hands: 'What's happening to you all? I've led you this far, haven't I? Why are you all trying to get me down?'

Of course you have, Nichol, the shades below me were muttering, but Sellars shook his head: 'I'm sorry, Nichol. This chapter isn't ready for a theatre audience.' The hall hanging hostile silence all around me.

'You disobedient peasant!' He struck me aside, peered for the Committee, but they were already at the area sidedoor; 'Thank you, Mr. Ross,' floating vaguely from the Baillie's vanishing rump. 'And good luck, folks.'

A left hand turned me round, ripping my shirt: 'You're trying to ruin me! ' Shaking me like a nerveless scarecrow, 'I've taught you all I know, and yet you disobey me!' Up with the prophetic arm, fireflash in his locks: 'Get out of here, and bad luck to you!' Without effort he threw me eight feet.

Fury answering his. 'Listen to me, you oversized megalomaniac. You'll never know just how loyal I am—but I am a rational human being who deserves a little dignity, and my writing is *my* writing. You're trying to drag us back into a state of feudalism where the Great Lord Ross can command his every pleasure. Now if we're going to be successful, Nichol, you'd better develop a little restraint and tolerance, or nobody will stay with you!' My muscles losing their synergism, damned milksop tears in my eyes again.

Nichol made a bullsrush hellbent on my severe injury, but now the stage was a Bedlam of restraining people, Gulliver among the Lilliputians. Held by eleven arms he screamed across their heads: 'I've loved you, you dirty little swine, and you'd do this to me. How could you, Denis? Merciful Providence, is there no justice for the man of genius?' Inspired by the dramatic choke of his own windpipe, he drove against them all, five of them askew and howling under him.

Run, Denis. Out of my way, Murdo, two leaps for the steps and my rubber feet slapping the hollow corridor, no feeling in my legs. I'm vomiting in the sudden square sunlight, leaning against the Hall steps inside a film of sweat, tutting Saturday shoppers think I'm drunk. Human race utter misnomer. Most of them belong genera below leprous protozoa. And my everloved father too. To hell with Scotland, novels, Nichol. All filth. One clear star to guide my weary feet over the scree, through the swamp. Everkiss from outhwit, this is reality. From only her.

Sun blotted out. Darkness upon the face of the earth. Standing over me, his forehead pulsing fury, outsize hawkface hovering as if to pounce, hot breath peeling from his outthrust tongue.

'Go away, Nichol.' I staggered upright, tried to walk at speed into the blurred cine-film of coldstained hopeless faces.

But he was buffeting through the human traffic of Lothian Road, impervious to oaths and complaints. He tugged at my coat-tail. 'I said why have you of all people turned against me?'

I dodged into the lee of a fat perambulating policeman.

'You're mad, Nichol. I'm not against you, but your ego is destroying everything. Ricky's a pippin, and you've presented him to Hackett.' A swift chop of my right hand and I tore away, oops sorry madam, and step aside for your life, here's Frankenstein.

He caught me again by the cinema commissionaire, why should I apologise to a man who's ready to run to Hackett, clitherclip, it's not only that Nichol you're far too bigoted you go on about needing people when in fact you use them, slap on my head, you impudent excrement, slitherclip, heavier chop to his wrist, stumbling free again.

Morningside matron, Indian doctor, insurance clerk cheekstained with port wine, God bless your sheltering bodies. Nearly clear to the West End, I'll insinuate myself down into St. Cuthbert's graveyard, safe there among all the lucky ones, and the rockarsed ancient fortress waving its wee Union Jack hundreds of feet above me. I jumped the last four steps, people watching, slowed down for the sake of reverence. Settle and lean against a Norman arch of ageing stone, face bowed into shadow, I loved her you know, although on second thoughts her stone says COLIN NIMMO (1818-74). Peaceful here, no movement around to disturb the dead. Earthy quiet fresh smell. Listen. Bubble. Grass growing again, the dead never learn. Nitrogen feeding slender green blade and so to cowbelly to the filth that makes me sick. Colin Nimmo, I've a mind to dig you up. Good old Burke and Hare. Helio crocus tip slithering through a glace of old snow. Bless you, little lover. I'd like you for Kate.

Oh no. Sun blotted out. Filth crunching gravel. 'Denis!'

'Go away!'

'Denis, please. I'm terribly sorry.'

I looked up. He had aged ten years in lurching three-hundred yards. No menace left, a sad ageing man with unkempt beard and rheumy eyeballs in a faded cloak, shrunk and stooping against the background of basalt, hyperventilating like a dying consumptive. Those poor broken veins.

'Sit down, Nichol.'

We sat on a bench, bending to play with handfuls of gravel.

'I shouldn't have blown up, Denis. This damned

thorn in my psychological flesh—everybody's worked so hard, and I've ruined it.'

A robin was hopping on impossibly fragile legs above the crypts. Sweet morning birdsong moving into my left ear, could swear one was a swallow. Sweetness and a humble man. Who said filth? My feelings are so fluid.

'Forget it, Nichol. We're all getting irritable. But you must stop bludgeoning people. We all have an interest in this.'

A flare of the old temper in the hand that clamped my knee. 'I'm still the boss, Denis, I have the Knowledge.'

'Maybe, but you shouldn't show it so gracelessly.'

'Denis, nobody else could be as brutal with me as you. I think the world of you, boy.' Hoarse his voice, hardly louder than a farside heel on the church steps, the vagrant swallow, the upslithering green manured by Colin Nimmo.

'And you're the greatest man I know.'

A bus klaxon high behind our secluding wall. 'Then why did you turn on me?'

'I didn't! Look, Nichol—I've just realised—that last chapter of mine means something special to Kate and myself. You had no right to order me to read it; I'm sick of your playing God.'

Sudden transformation, all the old aggressive colours, and a footpad's nudge:. 'Look, young man, with the Knowledge that I have, I have the licence to take liberties. My God, when I think of all I've taught you—your impudence! '

'Nichol,' I said, writhing like a masochist under the vitriol of my own voice, 'I love you as I love no other man. But let's get one thing straight—part of you is fake.'

The robin turned round; tiny disbelief.

'I-beg-your-pardon.' Arched back straightening, tautening his slack muscles.

'You're supposed to be a prophet of communication, but nobody can get near your real self at all. You boast a ruddy great philosophy of life, but you won't share it in full. You've found the one and only Grail, but you won't tell its whereabouts. You've found the Fount of Love, so you say, but you mutilate anyone who disagrees with you. And there's one thing more—'

He stood up, shrinkage gone, laying down his cloak, his eyes black and wicked. 'I am afraid it is high time for me to administer physical chastisement to you, you young liar, albeit in love.' Shepherd's tartan tossed to bench. 'But before I ask you to put up your fists: firstly, I am about to share my Truths with yourself sooner than you realise; and secondly, *what is this one thing more?*'

My stomach turning by dint of cowardice and the weird novel ring of my question: 'What were you to my mother, you double-talking old coward?'

The right swing was poised to plummet: I ducked unnecessarily to one knee. For he tried to speak and failed; instead a ridiculous sound, a faint yet piercing squeak issued from his larynx, the ghost of the rich man's cry to Lazarus. His face seized in an ashen throe, lips twisting, his hands clutched at his breastbone and he toppled backwards across the bench, rigid as a dead tree.

My hand flew to his chest. Pulseless? No!

Ohgodnichol, ohgodnichol, and I pelted moaning

up the steps to the street, grey curious people, pleasesir, pleasecomedown, my father's had a heart attack. Oh God I did this I killed him come this way get an ambulance get the police for Christs sake get a doctor! World spinning tilting through crazy planes, nothing significant outside the last two minutes. I did it. Killed him.

The little cloth-capped man held my shuddering shoulders round the staircase corner. 'Easy now, laddie—let's see whit's happened.' Robin gone, swallow fled, crocus hiding. Iced whiteness melting, sudden slither down the side of COLIN NIMMO.

But damn me I've been conned again oh thank God. He was moving, just, but conscious, then leaning forwards, rubbing his breast in slow motion. Spitting a little froth into the rutted gravel.

'He doesnae look deid tae me.' The swallow, the grass, the fourfaced church clock, dumpy monuments. Returning focus.

Nichol settled back wearily, wiped his lips. 'Sorry I frightened you, Denis. That was a near thing. But the cord's not ready to go yet.'

The little man touched his cap, bade us a mystified good-morning for Nichol said by God he wasn't needing any help. He doesnae look deid tae me, never mind, Jock, many thanks. The little man moving off shaking his head.

'I'm getting you straight to hospital, Nichol.'

He caught my arm, not even breathless. 'You'll do no such thing. I've had this a long time, Denis. I know more about the workings of the so-called heart than any quack ever did. Get me a taxi.'

'But—'

'I'm all right!'

'How can you possibly be all right?'

'Shut up and get me a taxi! And Denis—' calling after me.

'Yes?'

'I'll tell you the whole story very soon. Just let me prepare myself. Believe me, I know how you feel.'

Looking the honest picture, and right now I'm so distorted with relief I couldn't care less. I support him to his taxi; Denis, it'll be very, very soon. Never mind, Nichol. He wheezes ever so slightly, lips dark. Purple exhaust rasping away and again I suspect myself of dream-walking. The cord not ready? The time-telescoping wonder of the drama. The crafty old actor, side-stepped me again. I'm alone in the world on the pavement.

He'll tell me soon. But I'm depressed now. I've heard angry voices again this morning. This busy efficient street. Look at them passing. Narrow and fat City faces, rouge and brick-dust. A man could have died in that graveyard who wants to save them. Mary of Guise for all her French faults strove to humanise the black soul of Mad John; just read his gloating sadism when he heard she was dying of dropsy. These are City people, Johnseed. Gloat at the lungpewked froth of the noble or just don't care. That's the world, no vision. Once I dreamed of an earth where the heavens were royal and merciful and every white star was a trilling acolyte, an atom of loving angelvoice. Would smile and sing to me romancing a lass deep in sweet hay. Where birds were uneaten treasures, iridescent as the golden peacock, gentle-lyricked as a heathcrcradled skylark. Where shapes of animals were strong and faithful and sharptoothless. Where each day's sun splashed burnless yellow warmjoy, sired squads of light-infantry who drilled on green lawns to the pure rhythm of my little-boy's heart. Where mankinds moved to each other as loving as the tender thrrum of a Mexican's fingers, or the swish of the Virgin's kirtle. I handled poetry of nevercrushed barleyhead, safe and smiling only because of its beauty. Saw kind hands pluck Himself from needless Calvary.

Look at them. Johnseed. Only you, Kate.

Their heads are proud their Christian faces gleam
Good honest folk more cruel than they seem
For only you my love survived the dream.

CHAPTER ELEVEN

Evening rolled darkness backwards over 6 o'clock and up the hill to 7. Snowdrops pearling the woodwalks of Midlothian; mild days of the week whispered promise-of-spring, mollifying and sap-filling our frostsick hearts. Pale greens edging the death-colours from the Crags, our hopes should be stretching with the expanding lifelight. But on this last day of the second month fortune is slow to exploit the night's retreat, and winter is striking back with another grey reminder that he is still king of his icelorn northern vassals.

A hum of journalism round the City.

Buccleuch: Did ye hear aboot it. Tolly?

Tollcross: Ah did an' God bless them. The bastards have asked for this for years.

Bruntsfield: They're a quaint old crowd of warriors down in the Canongate.

Barnton: If you esk me they should all have been imprisoned. Thet's what heppens if you try to give those people better conditions.

Dumbiedykes: Is that so, Jock? Have ye ever had a chunk o' iron fa'in on the tap o' yer bairns?

Liberton; Now, now, anyone can make a mistake.

The builders are nice people. I've hed them over here at the Golf Club.

Craiglockhart: Exectly. The whole thing was disgusting. If they lived in Russia, they'd all have finished up in Siberia.

Small Clerk in a Contractor's Office: I—I'm not so sure. Please don't quote me, friends, but there are times I get sick of the goings-on round here. I could tell you about a small business I used to know—

Canongate: Tae hell wi' yez a'! We showed ye! Let's hae a dram for Lily Drummond that's left us!

And this that climbed the lower slopes of glory, for Sellars ended in loss.

The Friday afternoon after Nichol's public display of vanity. Our sales were picking up, however, no more losses after the Moonshiners, we'll soldier on without guitar and bass.

At five o'clock Charlie Reid's window was gushing twelve vertical rivulets, and inside the old fishmonger was chuckling across his bony face, serving me half-a-crown's worth of fynnon, and saying excitedly: 'So Lily's just gone roond tae borrow Dobbie's cart, Denis. They're takin' the thing up tae the Chambers.' Cling!

Kate engaged by young Allan Crossan at the doorway, bearing the fiery cross: 'We've beat the cops tae it, Kate. Lily'll be here the noo,' and before he remounted they were round the corner of the Wynd, twelve unmistakable Canongate figures huddled round the flanks of the old roan; driven by Lily, and Jock coughing beside her. So. Another balcony fallen. This is it.

Meg Crossan hailing us, her red moonface alight for battle. 'Come oan, Denis, we're off to show them that we're no' as saft as they think! ' The Canongate is about to march.

'When did it come down?'

'Half-an-hoor ago, frae the second floor o' the Craigview block,' cried Lily, a scowling Boadicea on her perch. Beside her Jock shrugged in exasperation. Another balcony. This is it.

The cart screeched and stattered round the corner, groaning under the mass of its shattered exhibit, two riven prongs pointed like supplicating arms above the toothy outline of the sideboard. Charlie throwing off his apron, marching beside us.

Metal jangling on stone, tramptramp of angry leather, damn this hill and louder damns from a hastily-braking lorry. Lily's beret, the lookedto standard, come oan, come oan, there's no' enough folk yet, to the windows opening high above, come oan, this thing coulda killt yin o' yer ain folk! Tramptramp, Meg Crossan our right marker commencing the *Soldier's Dream* threw us all out of step, but the wynds and closes pouring people, slowly at first, clusters of young headscarved matrons, bauchle-shod, lynx-eyed, varicose-shanked, whit happened why the swine Ah'm comin' wi' ye dinnae be daft Mary ye'll get the bloody jeyel. You shouldn't be out, Jock, Dr. Christie thumbing his waistcoat outside his Surgery, but past the new boutique where they dropped their snazzy coffee-bowls the breweries were in among us, fissured boots and grimacing against their indigestion, the

Tolbooth dreuths reeling up the pavements, cornua of our concave front. In and out of stranded vehicles; a sea of hair and caps, bobbing above the growing thunderstorm of our feet and voices, the long sharp houses quaking. Seven thousand outsize hailstones on a hundred square feet of corrugated iron.

Take my arm, Kate, St. Mary's Cross and the lights against us. But Lily drove straight through, shrieking insolence to the oblong cloudsky; up the hill to our left came the Cowgate, louseheaded methylated veterans from the Salvation Army Hostel, then straggling columns of the new Flats Holyrood and the Fishmarket, hairy muscular hands, bairns squawking from shawls, longlocked boys in shining leather, Tam the Guardsman swinging like an acrobatic pendulum on his crutches. WHO BUILT THIS? WHO BUILT THIS ? and the North Bridge stood in wonder, late-week shoppers standing round their jam-packed cars, informed loudly by Meg Crossan our P.R.O. that this is the Bloody Revolution and we're gonnae hing the Lord Provist.

A brave bobby stretched out for the reins under the Tron; Lily gave a wristflick and the roan dragged taut leather from his blisters; down he went wrestling with the lodging house bully. Tramp, tramp, our front flattening, row upon row of searoaring determination. But the Crows gathering long black shadows of them flitting up the wide High Street pavements, a mounted rank of black-on-bay sclattering a perimeter round the Chambers pillars. Pavements lined deep and waiting for the impact, the High Street populace joining us in ones and twos and dozens.

Tramp, tramp, martial crescendo of three hundred rough voices, feet quickening, roan trotting nervous, sparks on the cobbles and faint answering whinnies. Whitegleaming ranks of sharp faces; fists brandished, clubs of indignation. Faster, faster, ten yards to the unwavering rightangle of well-drilled authority. Beside me a middle-aged Cowgate woman was testing the weight of her shopping bag, in front six brewery lads wrapped themselves in a phalanx, Sandy Black the tramp drew a brick from under his tattered trousers. A pretty gap-toothed woman carrying an infant stepped reluctantly aside to the pavement, shouting profanity at the tall Inspector who stepped between horses and held up his hand. Clackratteramp-at-at.

He exchanged a few heated words with Lily, impossible to hear above the clamour of angry people and frightened animals. But Lily rose to interpret for her dangerously swaying mob, it's big trouble if we dinnae go back, folks, another step an' they'll charge us wi' their batons.

Evening torn with bloodseeking howls, a sharp crash of baritone and the Crows drew polished wood, their young faces unhappy as our front bulged menacingly towards them. Clattershapes, a new squad of police-on-foot arcing round the mounted cordon, two ranks extra to breach.

Meg Crossan flung a high fist, and the growl behind our right wing spurred its assault troops two critical paces forward, but with a charioteer's adroitness Lily twisted the roan across them; get back, ye silly buggers, that's what he wants. Let's play it the clever way, like thae University ban-the-bombers.

'I said siddoon! '

The front rank descended in ragged order, then the whole army jerked unevenly to the square stones of the High Street. Not a minute too soon, Lily, dozens of Crows lining the gutters now, we're picketed off. The police loomed forward, cavalry and flatplates, horsefoot and Crow's probing for a yellowgut. Moan here, curse there, but the Canongate sustained the bruising, the half-hearted lawmen retreating.

And now the High Street was a black wedge of sitters, buzzing with hungry purpose like flies on a dungheap. WHO BUILT THIS? WHO BUILT THIS? A constable bent to lift Meg Crossan, finished it with a red face and the help of four; a small workman in the crowd threw down his cap and replaced the hole in the front line. Three more were lifted; the cordon was breached in three places, no gaps among the rebels, boys.

The Inspector now imploring Lily to move with despair written on his blunt features, but in the hush our warrior queen was adamant that immediate action be taken aboot this heap o' junk in the back. The mounties looking pathetically redundant.

A tall sad man in striped trousers emerged from the entrance. Clerk o' Works, said a wise man. Hush. He approached Lily.

'—But just what do you want?'

'Ah want a promise frae the Lord Provist *on paper* that he'll get men on thae flats right away.'

'He's not here, madam.'

'Then get 'im, ye glaikit eejit! '

Black Marias screaming up in fleet. Crowds converging from all trade winds. A few people picked up but sporting schoolboys replacing them. A Jacobin yell from the street and the pavement warned the two enterprising policemen who were all for making an example of Lily; the Inspector waved them back.

A nondescript face and plump figure came forward to stand beside Boadicea hunched intractably over the roan's rump. Baillie Hardie, by my troth. Hush. 'The Lord Provost is in Newcastle, madam, but you have my assurance—'

Lily flapped her beret in his face, led the jeers. 'Get it on paper, mister! '

More discussion centrestage. Baillie, I suspect, demanding more brutal action, but the Inspector and his plain-clothes colleagues shook their heads. Lily received a large bundle, handed over the crowd from the distant white figure of Peter Small, the Canongate painter. Secret Weapon X2A57. In ten seconds the banner was flying, three-foot black letters over the cart: THIS BALCONY WAS BUILT BY OUR GOOD FRIEND COUNCILLOR ADAMS: the Baillie scurried inside.

Rain reached us before dark, showers of strengthsapping wetness lashed the squatting army that spat back and stayed. Photographers flashing spooky lights on the stubborn singing faces, the aching flesh; flasks and coats were passed to us over the weary gutter-guards. Lily dancing a reel of fury all around the heap of masonry, cheer upon cheer, every square inch of Cathedral steps and Lawnmarket scraped by encouraging onlookers' feet. A tired policeman winked at Kate; by God, lass, the local tribes are coming together at last!

We're apprehensive now, for the oldest and youngest are dribbling away. Lily delayed the defection, Jock assisting her between his coughing paroxysms, hurling vituperative over our sodden heads: hing oan, hing oan, we've goat them! Suddenly Baillie Hardie walked to her with downcast Homburg; a piece of paper thrust at her breast like a knife.

'Wad ye believe it, folks?' Up with her skirt in a jig-kick and the *Evening News* photographed the seat of her black bloomers. 'The Lord Provist's signature!' The street was a lunatic skirl, friend clasped shamefaced foe in the downpour. 'The workmen'll be doon the morn!' Curtain falling, darkness finally had the grace to smother the chaos.

The Crows made a few belated reprisals on exuberant individuals, but let's shout the moral victory. The homeward procession was headed by Lily waving the document from her triumphal chariot; first time in thirty years there was dancing in the Canongate, and the Tolbooth siphoned dry of its heavy beer in one hour flat.

While the reporters still pestered us and the trellis of scaffolding climbed up Craigview flats, Jock Drummond succumbed to a vicious attack of acute bronchitis. After three agonising days the Royal informed Mrs. J. Drummond that he would pull through.

I came home from a rehearsal to find Lily and Kate both in tears by the fire. What's wrong, girls?

'Ah'm sellin' the hoose, Denis—leavin'.'

'No!'

'The doctors say that if Jock steys here, he'll no last

another winter. Ah've goat a sister in Sussex, better off, ye ken, an' she's gonnae take us.'

The red rug looks so peaceful. Our square wall mirror so serene. But sorrows never rest.

'Let's face it, Lily—wouldn't he rather die here?'

'Nane o' that, Sellars, if it wasnae for ma daft scheme this widnae uv happened.' Her face pale, but her voice hot brass. 'Ah've suddenly realised Ah widnae change him fur forty balconies; Ah'm finished wi' fightin' for causes.'

'I never thought I'd hear you say that, Lily.'

'Think whit ye like. But when ye're ma age, ye realise just how few folk really mean a damn.' She rose red-eyed, took my hand. 'God bless ye both.' Kissed me, kissed Kate. 'Be guid tae her, Denis, fur Goad's sake.'

Aye, a touch of early crucifixion ahead of spring this year. Lily and Jock and the other thing.

They tried Ollie the Bull on a bright salty morning when the earth was as hard as iron. The gallery was packed; Ollie's finest audience ever at his fifth Sheriff Court appearance. Murdo and I had begged him to solicit the aid of a psychiatrist, but he became so violent in argument that we desisted for safety's sake. I shall defend myself, boys, with nothing but my blazing genius.

The commodore, a snowy dapper sixty, recounted with emotion the tale of Ollie the Bull's anti-social activities. Ollie, clad in an old dinner-jacket and corduroy shorts, sat in the dock shaking his kinky head sympathetically and acknowledging with a gracious smile the leering attention of the public. No questions your Majesty.

The procurator-fiscal called a succession of nervous secondhand-shopowners and their assistants; the whining evidence mounted up and between the rallies of laughter that appreciated Ollie's incredible cross-examinations, the varnished air warmed putrid with quiet legal inhumanity. The laconic Sheriff, the destructive competence of the florid procurator, the expressionless policemen, we grinning gallery-louts; brothers we are the progeny of the vilest race in European history, who invented the myth of justice and the reality of the cross and the Colosseum. Even the ponderous silences prophesy the downswept thumb.

Notable passages:

OLLIE THE BULL: (marching before the witness box, shoeless in tartan hose) 'I take it you regard yourself as a man of reasonable memory.' (Picking his nose in accurate imitation of the procurator.)

ASSISTANT: 'Yes!'

OLLIE THE BULL: (crafty sideglance, crouching and pointing) 'And you are sure that I am he who sold you these volumes of Scott?'

ASSISTANT: 'I am. Definitely.'

OLLIE THE BULL: (arms folded, smiling to Stan and Connie in the gallery) 'Did you notice anything about my breath when I was talking to you that day?'

ASSISTANT: 'I certainly did. You were stinking of whisky!'

OLLIE THE BULL: (wheeling like a black herring-gull on the Sheriff) 'You see, your Majesty! I never drink whisky! How can you accept the evidence of an idiot who can't tell the smell of whisky from rum?'

Screechlaughter—order! Ollie doing a Cassius Clay samba to thunderous acclamation.

Or again:

OLLIE THE BULL: 'Are you in the habit of dealing with publicans and dishonest men?'

BOOKSELLER: 'I am not.'

OLLIE THE BULL: 'Are you a Christian?'

PROCURATOR: 'Your Lordship, I object! '

Awballsgrowl! Bang! Order! Ohgodstan! Hahooahuhauhoo! Watch your language, please, Mr. The Bull! Obeovrruled.

OLLIE THE BULL: 'Are you a believer in my ancestor, the carpenter of Nazareth?'

BOOKSELLER: 'I am a Deacon of the Church of Scotland.'

OLLIE THE BULL: 'Nevertheless you are an honest man, and you wouldn't consider dealing with unsavoury vagabonds?'

BOOKSELLER: 'Certainly not.'

OLLIE THE BULL: 'Look at me.' (posing in stance of She Who Guards New York, eye-whites innocent as golf balls) 'Do I look like an honest man? Do I look savoury?'

BOOKSELLER: 'Well, to be perfectly frank—'

OLLIE THE BULL: 'Exactly.'

BOOKSELLER: 'Right now I would say you don't.'

OLLIE THE BULL: 'Exactly. Your Majesty, now this man says I don't look honest, but a month ago he thought I did. I put it to you, citizens, this man's evidence is worthless, and anyway his shop is so dark you couldn't recognise your mother!'

Huha, gallery exploding. Murdo and I between prodigal laughter and tears. Sheriff ordering Ollie to stand down from his seat and stop shouting *Sieg heil* at the procurator.

Ollie called several witnesses including Joe the Rat, whose attestation of Ollie's character was somewhat disturbed by his recognition of an old uniformed adversary standing opposite. His heated plea for compassion was stopped by the Bench's languid white hand; Ollie then called for the parrot and directed a semi-slanderous statement against his late benefactor when the court was informed that the bird was too ill to attend; Ollie was warned by the narrow caustic voice that he had enough charges to answer already.

The Bench closed his case while Ollie was still admonishing his last witness, one of the arresting policemen, for being ignorant of his reputation as the City's greatest concrete poet; he scowled, danced a quick cha-cha, and subsided in the dock with all the heroic exhaustion of a marathon champion.

Now the final choice presented, Mr. The Bull you may be put on oath by the Clerk of the Court, or if you wish to make a statement from the dock, you may do so. This, of course, means that you cannot be cross-examined.

'I will speak from the dock.' Titters running wild, drum of cold feet, rustling inquisition glaring resignedly at him below our birds'-eyes. Please, Ollie, get it over with quickly, you're making me detest my sense of humour. And please don't mention the money you gave me.

'In my cultured travels I have never loved nor painted nor written about a place as I have this City. It is obvious that a versatile maestro like myself, at present widely imitated by French writers and painters, would never stoop to such a crime as this. The commodore has built up a false impression of honesty: I have been too full of compassion up to now to mention that he possesses a large collection of the works of Turgenev and Korolenko.' Ollie paused for dramatic effect and was honoured by a puzzled silence, involuntary tap of the Bench's offguard finger. 'This,' continued the intense ebony face, 'considered alongside the mysterious fate that has befallen my feathered brother who was to have testified for me, leads us to only one conclusion, remembering the corruption in high places that has recently been uncovered in London. Fellow-countrymen,' Ollie jerking his thick arms high in holy exhortation, 'this man is obviously a Russian agent!' Hear, hear, they were screaming, ignoring the hammer and threats, and when silence was regained it was broken by the commodore's angry voice hidden below us: 'You lying brute! He's bluffing, your Lordship, he's not all that daft. And another thing, you thief, those are my shorts you're wearing!'

At the seventh attempt the Sheriff silenced him, but Ollie's eyes were closed, a serene pity glossing his flat expression, his hands clasped in prayer. The Sheriff's open mouth seized in mid-sentence; for the first time our silence was painful.

'Dear Lord,' Ollie prayed softly, 'soften the heart of this spreader of falsehoods. What is more,' he declared, furiously fumbling at his belt, 'you can have the stinking rags back right now! '

Last screechhowl, final hardening of the dyspeptic clefts by the Sheriff's mouth, and Ollie's voluminous record the final entertaining tit-bit. Three months, Mr. The Bull, but sentence to be deferred over a probationary period, pending a psychiatrist's report.

We heard later through Dr. Pat Leitch that this was fair and detailed and worthless. Schizoid tendencies, sporadic delusional patterns, suggestions of inadequate psychopathic traits, but not enough grounds to warrant a life-saving name-tag. Thanks again, you old black sweetheart.

I brooded moodily over my lunch, suffering visions of Ollie the Bull condemned to another phase of time-chewing. Could I have saved him?

'Try to forget it, darling. We'll just have to take him under our wing when he comes out.'

'It's not just that, Kate. But Providence seems to have gone round the twist.'

'Come again?'

Sullen hands in pockets, I went over to confront my favourite Crags, uncomforting though greening. 'Kate, the night I met you, one of my chief enemies was sheer boredom. But now there's far too much pace to life—all our own struggles, Nichol, trouble with Hackett, Lily and Jock leaving, and now Ollie. I have a nasty feeling, love, that there's too much bloody excitement round me now for one man to cope with.'

Another soul committed to the snare
For Rome and John are everloved and rare
So black my face and do I really care.

CHAPTER TWELVE

March still gave us mornings of bitter recalcitrance, but the tide of battle was turning in the parks and gardens. Snow became a memory, frost a luxury; waiting for Kate by the hospital's East Gate I watched for the random multiplication of little miracles that would soon be gracing the ashes and elms. The streets dry and cool and bearable, an old song reviving under privets and laurels. Rehearsals daily now, the whole thing unbelievably greased and polished, but the tickets still slowish. Hackett's photograph appearing quite often in the *Scotsman*, but we don't see much of him; under softer skies Nichol and the troupe are more relaxed and confident. It's good to laugh with Rasputin again, but I don't altogether like this loss of tension. Some cliches I respect. Lulls and storms.

March 26th. A brilliant Wednesday morning, cobalt-and-lemon on loan from Elysium. Sellars glowing from the fire and recent cold water, Kate cracking eggs in among the Ayrshire and tomatoes.

A little flesh shed this month. I've never seen her so printworthy. Her waist barely full, skirted hips and jutting breastline clean as the City's profiles. The hairdresser used his craft with skill yesterday, slendered her face in a bit, and her neck looks smooth enough for skating. Apron and high black heels do wonderful mystical things to her. I'm utterly provoked by the flirting of red lip and protruding tongue, the spark of blue mirth in her eye lighting her pink face to elegance.

About to pounce, but forestalled when she spoke: 'What are you going to write next, Denis?'

'Dunno, Kate, I intend to read some oriental philosophy this summer. Maybe that'll give me some fresh ideas.'

'And what about your own philosophy of tragedy? Is that not still your Bible of Life?'

'It's still there, Kate.'

'But it's not enough, is it?'

'No, sweetheart. For good or bad, it just isn't enough.' In six months I have grown old enough to hope.

She winked, covered the serving plate on the range. Collapsing on my knee she said: 'I suppose we'd better make love before breakfast?'

'Why d'you suppose that?'

'Come off it. I saw you looking at me.' I pulled her into the bedroom, chest breathless and bounding.

We stripped each other white, sounds of slithering tenderness then a ray of sunlight turned a corner and we were locked gold on the coverlet. Soft voice amoan telling me she loves me, first-best springsong this year. Quietness gone, second excitatory plane of anaesthesia, the lashing reflexes, oh Denis oh Denis Kate sweet Kate mouths and teeth and fleshtips roaming faster over shivering abandon, bone and skin simmering on bone and skin, her Colgate breath and tart perfumed thrapple. Danger danger something disappearing and the light among it all roads of feeling lead to the moist clamp creepy thigh and back forgotten Denis my love Kate darling third plane the scarlet greenness of our friction should be getting hotter in fact I confess something's happening I've no words for or do I imagine during vinegar-strokes of infinite absurd delight cool groves of birch and hazel swim in profuse cascade of blackthorn see the Himalayas stretch to China beyond this snowfire Everest sunset must be imagination but my God glory of glories here I smell the role of Cross and sage and scientist faster faster bleed me Kate ring out the bells of eureka God this is absurd but now I suspect Kate that the formula for absolute absurdity is part of what we really need there's a constant πer than π here Kate faster faster drown me it's coming I think I feel it birch hazel diaphanous green spring-youth Everest Jesus Confucius we've got a bit of your formula down here the same wild energyscreeching Truth-Electrons! GONE! Only a faint sliver of blossom in the nostril, last lingering memory of flawless sun, two vowels of a parable. But I felt it. And that is enough: from now on you and I can play hell with Time. I think I recognised the strange voice, saw the ancient mysteries of Gizeh and Chichen Itza; hold my happy hand, Kate. They'll come again, and even if not your hair is richer than sunlight and no hazel leaf stroked a morning more tenderly than your fingers touch the greyness of my temples. I think I saw them of Einstein and the Aleph. Einstein and the Aleph.

But wait a minute, Sellars, a crucialest minute. I see. Do you hell. I see, don't kid yourself, of course I see. I SEE. I've just been seen into myself by myself and this is even more fantastic. For you've just caught yourself telling a pack of truthful lies. The line between invention and imagination, here is where I lie and stand. All that I've just been inside spouting is honest enough but these are images that I knew already and were easily summoned by this oblivion of perfect sensation and it's all a bit willed and straining and incomplete. For I saw something MORE. Beyond membranebellybrainandmindthrill. This was really realler.

As I was finishing it seemed to be all womaneyes. Greek-eyes, Hawaiianeyes, everywomaneyes. Then your eyes. Then you complete. Not as I have seen you but as I know you are to-morrow. Wonderful. Because you looked different tomorrow and my limpness is no longer sad because it knows you looked so much more and precious to-morrow because we've been Here to-day. And so it will go on, Sellarskate, until one to-morrow I believe we willseesaw ourselves outside all clock-qualifications. This beyond the outraged fidelity of faithful penis or love-purse. Even if I do fall which I doubt. For we have seen ourSELF. A lover of all that is, hurt, needing, willing. But still utterly ourSELF. Now infidelity irrelevant as conceived by wise and silly men. Irrelevant to I saw you to-morrow. Not absurd enough. No emotion here. I am cool and wise but these are poor shades of the words that will rise in the heart that recognises this.

For my destiny is the tale of an endless chain, and I nearly wore myself out pulling on one single link. You taught me so many others with willtosmile and othercheek- turning. Giving everkiss. Now we're tautening into action. Here, a kindness to-morrow, then where? What wonders beyond through all our brave learning.

Quiveriver. Aaah. Sigh. 'Kate, love, just for a minute

there I thought I knew the End from the Beginning. The queerest feeling I have ever had.'

'There's a mystic hiding in you, Denis. You've more in common with Nichol than you realise.'

'You're right, love... you're right.' Snuggling with her under the quilt. 'Kate, I would hardly change this contentment for the literary reputation of Shakespeare.' The excitement that waits outside the window, on the calendar.

Dozing euphoric, I hear plates and steel. Breakfast, Denis. Coming, honey. Airnip on my trunk, quick into my slacks, and she's singing something new through in the kitchen. Quite like it, some modern-type composition about the '45 Rebellion. Tune a wee bit boring, but there's an authentic bite about the words:

> Tangled ringlets I left tawny-spread on the pillow
> In the green twisting vale of the Cree
> Since I set my face west to that sail on the billow
> We had known what the ending must be.
> And my song of despair from a dungeon leaping
> Begs no pardon but bears through a dark land's
> weeping
> The poor ghost of my honour to thee—
> Had I loved thee more well on thy breast I'd be
> sleeping.
> But my dearest on earth it was he.

Food and happy no-talk. Wiping the yellow from my plate, 'That's an interesting song you were singing. Where did you hear it?'

She hid in a huge blush, quicklooked shyly. 'Will you promise not to laugh?'

Of course.'

'I made it up.'

'You're kidding.'

'No, Denis, I'm not. I was lying in bed one night, after we'd been loving; you were snoring, but I just couldn't get to sleep. Murdo had been talking about that TV Culloden programme, and all of a sudden I knew I had to try and write a song. It took me a week, but there it is.'

I wouldn't have believed it, but oh my God I do. Magic. I never guessed from my own ten thousand suddenly-better words, I know it because of an incredible quite-good song. Farewell fucking.

'Kate, lass, sing the rest of it.' Picking up my guitar, 'I think I can improve the tune a bit.'

She was kissing me: 'I was so worried you'd laugh at me, Denis. But I couldn't sleep for thinking about one of those men lying in prison dreaming about his family, and knowing the hideous things that would be done to him in the morning. Come on, pet. G Major, I think—'

Plucking and picking, seeking the notes and cadences that blend best with the care in her voice; the language of love that can fill a room, a grain of sand, seven galaxies. The subtlety's coming, sparing with your modal changes, Denis, contrast them with the pretty harmonies of her line-middles :

Little ripe-wheaten locklets that bounced to my
    wither

By the sweet Christ your father disown—
There's a heart turning stone, there is blood on the
river
Nor a love left to call you its own.
For the scream of a face in the grey smoke dying

Or one red broken heap of the tartan lying
Were a price far too great for a throne;
Like a fatherless babe and its silly crying.
Or the wail of a woman alone.

Shining head golder far than the sun's pale replying
Supple author of darkness and pain
Ere the sprit of your bark set the white sand flying
Your sweet tongue had licked sense from our
brain . . .

Together we plunged through the chords, the words, deep to the soul of the song. Sang it seven times till the lump in my throat dissolved on the victory in the last line, and I laid down my instrument to caress her by our morning window.

'Kate. I... I love you.' Tick, tick.

'Denis.'

'I think I knew it subconsciously already... since I realised that we're both discontented with apparent reality . . . we're compulsive beyond-lookers.'

And the Crags reared giant, sounding out a green symphony that flew across the roofs and monuments, striking chords of redeeming artistry into the awakening heart of my City, orchestrations unheard before by ears waxed-up with selfishness and cynicism, music that had long awaited the opening of my third eye before it could be seen.

Incredible that three days later the Dark had counter-attacked. For we briefly forgot. There was a special Hackett morning session in the Crown; over breakfast I suggested that we go.

'Are you sure it's a good idea, Denis? Hackett'll have all his *Stringtime* people there, and it's a bit near to the show-down.'

'Never mind. I want to show off your song.'

We walked to the Crown in twenty minutes of sunshine, birds twittering in rone pipes. The streets roaring with motors. Cars gleaming long starry splinters. Cheerful clanks and swearwords through the bar, blue clouds in the back room. Kate slipped into the back row, too quickly to notice who she was plonking down beside. Hell.

Hackett leaned across her wreathed in smoke: 'Just a few more days, Sellars, and you haven't a chance. By the way, I've got a decorator's bill for you—your fish left quite a mess.'

'Don't know what you're talkin' about, Hitler.'

Hackett preparing to utter further malice, but Rob appeared beside me and took my hand: 'How are you, Denis?'

'What do *you* care?'

'I'm your flesh and blood, mate. I worry about you.' Hand on my shoulder.

'Obviously. Thanks for stealing our singers.'

'We didn't steal them. They just moved our way. The same way as you will.'

'Fuck off.'

He was called up to sing. A few requesting cries from the front seven rows, just watch him give the barefoot lassies the shivers. Very smooth, Rob, your confident presentation of ripe voice and whining steel, but to my smiling surprise it sounds a bit tired and spiritless. Hackett's guiding genius seems to have gutted your style; your brainless young admirers aren't clapping you like they used to.

He was followed by the Moonshiners, soon ahem to be singing in Len Hackett's wonderful new televised show which we know is at long last going to put this City ahem properly on the folksong map. They nasalled *Lord Lovat*, reasonable copy of the authentic, followed by Lisa droning us all towards tender nostalgia with *The Water is Wide*, she caught sight of me before the last verse was finished, and smiled. Jeez.

'Rob, I want to sing.'

My brother's voice obsequious, 'Can Denis sing, Len?'

'I think so, Rob, the kids need a laugh. We must show some Christian forgiveness, mustn't we?' He had me trapped in his sinister smile, mouse-under-catspaw, with even more relish he added: 'But one condition, Sellars: if you dare to advertise your old nutter and his Ewan Hall circus, I'll have you bounced out of here in ten pieces! '

Kate's tight lips saying should you let the animal

abuse you like this, but I desperately want to get our gem across. These kids know where I'll be singing next week.

I knew I was right after ten seconds on the platform. The first line riveted them, apostle-behind-guitar I sang them the lay of Man crucified; a slender dark lassie dabbing her eyes surreptitiously for the ripe-wheaten locklets, a current of excitement racing across the clouded faces as thundery air vibrates through an orchard of blossom. Glancing to the back during the last verse I saw Rob's rapid questions being answered by Kate's proud explanations, his arm round her shoulders, kissing her congrats on the cheek to make her redden again. A new ice-claw of terror has me by the short hairs so that I blast out the in-spite-of-it-all braggart climax with more fire than necessary:

—for the quick craven speech through a young
  mouth flowing
May we never give sons to be slain.
Yet if such should return and a north wind blowing
I would rise to draw steel yet again!

Quickly back through their huzzas and encores I waited for Rob to give me my seat back. He sat ignoring me, and I wish I'd never started this. Denis, this girl is a revelation. Kissing her cheek again, and the bitch doesn't stop him. Strings whimpering under my tautening hand. I was sitting there, Rob. If you don't erase that knowing slyness, Hackett, I'll twist your balls off slowly with my E-string. Of course, Denis, Rob rising smiling at Kate.

'Darling,' she said, 'Rob thinks our song's terrific.

Don't you think you two could shake hands now?'

'We're going, Kate. Get on your feet.'

'But I'd like the words.' Rob asking softly with an injured frown.

'They're not for the like of you. Kate, you want your head looked, consorting with these guttersnipes. Remember whose side you're on.'

'I'm as much for Nichol as you are. I haven't said a word to *him*,' pointing to Hackett. 'But it hurts me to think that you and Rob aren't friends.'

Lisa making some final remarks on the platform; I pulled Kate from her seat, felt the plump flesh of her forearm wince: 'Come on. We shouldn't have come.'

Leading the rush to the door I heard Hackett's smarm behind me: 'Well, well, Rob. I think the man's jealous! ' Swearing and pushing at her back, I thrust her through the long public bar, the backslapping Legion, good for you, Denis, out into that rectangle of sunlight where we've been before. What's wrong darling I can't understand, oh shut up! Shouting angry, straight into Nichol who stepped massively out of a shop doorway.

'What's going on here, Denis? That's no way to speak to Kate.'

His censure unwound me; I squeezed her hand. 'You caught me in the act, Nichol. I was about to start a stupid fight.'

'Not really.' She took both our arms, squeezed mine secretly.

Nichol bent forward, addressed me suspiciously: 'What were you doing here?'

The truth's too fantastic, he'd never understand. 'I

just looked into the Crown for old times' sake. But it was a mistake.'

He swung us into a marching pace, talking ceaselessly. '—Then I had an uncomfortable aura of your whereabouts about an hour ago. I came up to investigate, and to invite myself for lunch! '

Haha, our quarrel vanished in the hubbub of the North Bridge, I feel so much better turning arm-in-arm down this familiar slope. Clattering carts and pretty girls suddenly bareheaded and coatless. One day, Nichol, I'll tell you what I saw three mornings ago that surpasses all your boasts.

He left us for a rummage in a second-hand bookshop in St. Mary's Street, give me five minutes, folks. I'll follow you down.

Into the Canongate, and my arm to Kate's waist, 'mornin', Meg,' the walls of our passage washed in healthy light and smelling of April already.

'I'm sorry I started that fight.'

Clipclip, slitherinkle. 'That's all right, Denis, I understand.'

Dodging a downandout and handcart, 'You know why I got annoyed in there?'

'Of course I do, sweetheart, you thought I was flirting with Rob.' She loosed a thick chuckle. Bloody smug.

'So you think I was jealous?'

Of course. When you first said you loved me I could hardly believe it. But you should have seen your face when Rob kissed me—that proved it, Denis, and I nearly screamed with delight.' Another fat peal of laughter, and this is too much of a good thing.

'So you did it deliberately? To make me jealous?'

'Did what?' Slitherstop by the close-entry, question drowned in busroar.

'Let him kiss you?'

Of course not, there was nothing in it.' She punched me on the breast-bone with rare indignation. 'What right do you have to grill me?'

Seizing a handful of her warm coat-front, 'What do you mean? I'm in love with you! '

A spasm of pain seized her face. Unshed tears hanging. 'I'm sorry. Please forget I said that. This memory of mine is too long.'

Guilt, premonition, guilt. I don't like that hurt tone. Guiding her into the entry, 'Tell me what you mean, Kate. *What do you mean?*'

'Denis, your face is awful. You're frightening me.' She backed against a patch of red brick.

I shook her by the lapels. 'I asked you, Kate.'

Suddenly she nailslashed my bunched knuckles, held my own lapels, crying: 'I've been in love with you for months. How d'you think I feel about the way you betrayed me with Lisa Kendall?'

Her lower lip's crumpling, so is this lovely dream I've cherished for three dawns. Oh no. Have mercy, Lisa, it's too late for revenge. How could you burrow into such perfection and prise it apart? For when a Scot feels guilt he can feel nothing else. Kate's harsh sobs pouring in my ears and gravitating through me like paralytic poison. Guilt I deserved. Denial of everkiss I didn't. It meant nothing, and it's going to ruin everything.

Her throat soft in my desperate palm, here goes.

'Forget her, Kate!' I'm banging her head in temper. 'Don't dare mention her name! She doesn't mean a bloody thing!'

'Do you deny that you slept with her?'

Who told her? The pig. I'll have his foreskin for a plectrum. 'Who told you? *Who told you, Kate?*' I'm lost. Thump, thump your head, I love you to the kernel of my ideals, how dare you ruin what we found?

Her face drained of its intense colour, God I've gone too far, hands about to loosen and caress when pain stunned my nape, spinning me down on one knee by her hem. Nichol's ash struck again, flattening me against the wall: 'You brutal scum: how dare you?' The stick cracking across my cheeks like a dragon's tail, whiplash shocks of bloody pain, again and on and again.

I struggled to rise on one elbow but he cut it skilfully from under me. 'I'm going to thrash some humanity into you! You've nearly strangled her, you animal!' Whipwood slicing through the protection of my tweed jacket.

This flogging, I can't bear it. Sick inside, try to rise, but he slashed skin from my straining handback. Kate recovering now, the blessed girl has smothered the flaying arm.

What a swine I certainly was, I need her. I was so wrong, still crackle with unquenchable remorse. But that reptile Nichol, I'll settle him. He's panting, resting against the wall, slowly I rise, throbbing with castrated pride.

'I'm terribly sorry, Denis, I lost my temper. But I couldn't believe my eyes. I just can't bear to see a woman abused. What got into you, for Christ's sake?'

I wiped a gobbet of blood from my numb and thickened lip. 'You arrogant old cur. You've shown us how strong you are. Are you happy?'

'Look, Denis,' extending his palm. 'You asked for it, laddie, but I'm sorry. Take my hand.' Old Testament savage, primitive big sadist.

I slapped his wrist wide. 'You dirty hypocrite,' my ripped mouth curling down. 'I had no right to get wild with Kate, but compared to you I'm a bloody seraph. What sort of a man would desert a woman like my mother, or could pretend that he loves his own sons when he denies what they really are?'

'Denis,' Kate bent over me, shaking her head. 'Denis, stop it!'

Nichol's face was grey only for an indrawn breath, then a horrified bewilderment seeped crimson all over it. He started towards me. 'But, Denis—I'm not your father, laddie. Oh, God, why didn't I tell you sooner?' Swivelling back to thwack his forehead on the rough stone: 'I'm not your father, Denis—I wish to God I were!' Thwack, thwack, crunk.

And the world suddenly spun into a mist that blotted out the bloom of noon and the girl hugging me: through the blurred disintegrating outlines of the close I tried to croak a dearloved fantasy back to life. 'You're not my father? But you must be! ' The dream-well suddenly run dry, I never knew how precious this water was. Croaking again through earthhard fissured lips: 'But you must be. YOU MUST BE!' I sprang forward to squeeze the admission from him, but he buffeted me sideways, his face more fearful than angry. I ran again, head down, yowling: 'You are my father. I *know* you are!' This time he let me shake him, wagging his mane helplessly. Kate screaming let go till I found myself vicing the tendons of his neck and he had to batter me over again. I staggered upright, rose on my toes to plunge at him.

'Denis,' he pleaded, 'please listen.'

I'd love to kill you, Nichol, you've made me forget who I thought I was. You festering heap of pigshit, your evil hairy mug and that barrel-chest heaving your ringlets on and off your ragged collar. Breathless and bloody I have never hated as I hate now. I love you, Kate, but I find it easy to forget for this molten hatred is as near to another world as the splendid absurdity I saw with you.

'Denis,' she grabbed me against her quivering trunk. 'Please, it's all my fault. He's telling the truth! What does it matter?' Her voice tailing off when I thrust her aside, stood face-on to him, scarfaced Sellars the rootless son of nothing.

'I hate you, Nichol Ross,' and I spat a slimy curse at the turgid eyes, the cyanosed lips, the sagging jowl. 'I curse your filthy soul—you hellspawned *liar*! '

'Denis! ' she screamed again, her thick hair tumbling wild, but I dodged off the wall, jumped my guitar-case, and ran out on to the cold loveless brae.

Canongate, who am I? Liar! Liar! LIAR!

Four bars, five, six, reeling in stages to the brow of the Lawnmarket. Jostling elbows, sour swirling beer, stomach acid powdering my throat to hot ashes. He's not my father. You're the worst kind of bastard, Sellars. Brow dripping with nausea, I need some food. But I'm not going back yet. Only Kate's worth a curse, but I must die for a wee while. Or maybe a big.

My feet slapping down a narrow wynd, cheekbone split as I shattered a wall lamp. A thousand fat yellow fireflies hanging in moisture. Then darkness. Smell those cats. Only twenty yards from the plush flats above the Gardens that form the synthetic period skyline of the picture-cards. Pitching in slime on the bevelled steps, but they've heard me. A post of white light fattening, the Rat's voice: 'Quick, Starkey, it's Denis! ' Merciful unconsciousness.

Behind the drum of a tom-tom they were laying me on the rickety bed, rolled newspapers for a pillow. Stench of iodine, wonder where they stole it. What happened, Denis? I told them, so I'm finished with the whole crazy business, boys, and if anyone comes knocking you say you've got the plague here, O.K.? Five pounds in my wallet, Starkey, we'll booze the lot. God, he's not my father! He's not, Joe! Easy, Denis, ye nearly took ma heid off. Quietly, quietly ... Connorslove never dies till we do ...

Night turned day turned long dusk veiling the chatter of lovers through the dirty window, smacking kiss-sounds of stone flags sliding under eager feet. You poor darlings. Inevitable postulation, no hope there, you tragic young blind. Nichol. Gie 'im another dram, Starkey, he's ravin' again. Once I dreamed of a luminous earth lit by my father's face.

Wind rising. I'm shattered with rattling glass. A DRINK, STARKEY, GET ME A DRINK! I love you,

Kate, but I can't come back yet. Dank seas to swim first, a blackness thicker than damnation, all the pins of witchcraft are transfixing this gibbering clay. Help me to the sink, Starkey. Fag-ash and cold beans on the naked table.

Nights swimming into dawns where strange beasts lurk and mock me from the greasy fireplace. Roll and turn, twitching as they dress my cuts again. Bless you, lads, reach me my amber friend in that tumbler. Fire of ancient sorcery searing my screwed-up middle, dull me, dull me, shut the sounds away. The lie of love is whispering outside my little hell. Quietly, quietly ... hammer on the door but no answer out of the faithful silence ... time an endless circle, on and on and on ...

My head. My stomach. And shaking limbs, icy needles probing every nerve. I lurched to the cold-water tap, Joe and Starkey crouching over mugs of tea in the half-light that filtered through the dust.

'What time is it?'

'Half-past-ten, Denis. A fine mornin', if Starkey wad only wash the windaes.'

In the broken mirror a battered yellow corpse is scowling. 'How long have I been on the batter?'

'Four days. It's Wednesday.'

Slipping my coat on in this world of shades, pockets empty, some broken matches, 'Have you any money?'

Starkey handed me two notes. 'Get going back to Kate, Denis. D'you want to finish up like us?'

I looked round the room. Peeling walls, cracked grey ceiling. No, I couldn't stand it.

My hand on the dryrotten door. 'I'll never be half

the gent you both are. God bless you, boys.' Good luck, Denis. They know.

I fell twice when the light struck me in the wynd, staggered into the street-cries that spiced the Lawnmarket air. Weak and sick. This faraway world is almost soundless, maybe I really snuffed it, pasty women moving like wraiths. But this is real City April I'm whiffing from the direction of that menacing Cathedral; far Dutch tulips and near damp stone, last souvenir of March adding a breath of chill. The prodigal's coming, Kate, but first a drink; courage required to beg forgiveness.

At three o'clock I reeled into the shop below the heavy brass balls, three quid for my watch. More booze needed, I just can't lose this homicidal compulsion, I still want to kill him. Little hunchback smirking behind the counter, no sympathy for my own scars of kinship.

Fifteen zigzag paces and I clutched the pillar-box safely. Street very peculiar, only a few people, sky scowling orange and fawn. Funny, as they say in the pictures, it's too quiet.

I'm frightened, shimmering City, why this waiting in the air?

He's coming for you, Sellars—hark! The Word, the Word is there!

Oh no. Icy perspiration, legs trembling crazy, I shouldn't have had so much. Standing on the far side of the High Street, forefinger accusing me. I ran as well as able towards St. Giles', hid behind the fountain, glanced round it with furtive eyes. Twenty yards away he was straddling the crown of the High Street, ignoring its few shadowy pedestrians. The flat blue bonnet, black cloak, beard hanging to the huge book held on his breast. Those heroic Satanic eyes. John!

I fled again, loose mouth spittling, three schoolboys staggering apart with frankest astonishment. I rocked off the High Street, down the Mound, tripped in the gutter, sank exhausted against the upper Gardens railings. Save me, wide valley of Princes Street, my ears are still full of craziness. I looked up past the round plot of awakening green shoots to see him glaring down from the slopes. I banged my head on the iron, eyes shut, but no deliverance. Sweet living Lord, what have I done?

'What do you want? Leave me alone, I'm ill!' People giving me the whole pavement to myself. Slaves of his already, no fight left.

His long finger arrowed forward; '*You have sinned, Sellars. You have followed an evil man! Now you must destroy him!*' The black cloak unruffled by the racing wind.

'I hate him, John, he's completely denied me. But I can't—I worshipped him! '

A crowd gathering behind me, scattering downhill when I snarled at them, rattling the railings. The black figure expanded, telescoped till its bonnet obscured the ragged outline of the Castle; 'Listen, Sellars, he serves false gods: *let not thine eye spare him, show him no indulgence or favour, hide him not, but utterly kill him: let thy hand be the first upon him, that he may be slain*—there is your only redemption! '

'I disown him, isn't that enough?' A sudden hailstorm filled the valley from a ponderous black cloud, John unmoved and hellfire-eyed as the white particles bulleted through him, wind screaming across the high red gables.

'—destroy him, Sellars,' gunfire out of the bowels of the storm. John was stretching out of sight into the black beyond, but still rasping his sermon. 'There is a way, the sword of the elect is in your hand.' Lightning lifted a spew of earth from under his feet and his last words were a broadside of thunder: '*I have offered unto you the verity of Christ Jesus!*'

The thin sun slid through again, hung on the City glistening under its new fresh film. Sporadic figures walking, slowing, walking on by. No imprint where the Prophet stood. I'm surfacing from the pool of horror, it's all simple again. I must destroy my enemy. The Anti-Christ who has used and rejected me. Or I'm as damned as he is. Last dream-question : how can I do it, City, are you still John's spokeswoman? How? How?

Your way is downhill from here, Denis. You know. Heriot Gardens. A whisper on the wind.

Of course. The way is downhill. Mechanically I lurched through the Hanover Street crowds. Hills of Fife in the distance. My wet palm tilting the iron fist. Clam! Bam!

'You're drunk, Sellars. Shove off before I call the police.'

'Please, Hackett, I must speak t' you a minute.'

'Well, well. Very humble now, aren't we?' He hitched his dressing-gown, made a gesture of the lordly host.

I sat down opposite the empty wall that had once held Balaclava. 'I—I've had a terr'ble time, Hackett. Been seein' things. But'm finished with Nichol Ross.'

He drew jerkily on his cheroot. 'You've what? Why?'

'Never mind; 's too personal. Jus' let's say I've seen 'im for th' fake he ish. Give me a drink, f'r God's sake.'

Stiff whisky handed, gratefully single-gulped. Hackett's neat slim figure beginning to agitate with incredulous excitement. 'Is this a trick, Sellars?'

I began to cry. 'Does't look like it?' Fall, ceiling, fall on me.

Into the bedroom, back wearing his specs and carrying white foolscap. 'I'll start you on Friday in the Queen's Theatre. Will you be fit for it?'

I scrawled the two empty words. 'Yes. If it kills me.' Hackett's hands were shaking, he gave a long sigh when he lifted the documents: 'Remember, you bastard, if you double-cross me. I'll put you all the road.'

'Give me another drink.'

'Sure, Sellars.' He filled me up, moving round the room with a new, confident grace. 'This is wonderful. I told you he was a heap of trouble.' Clapping his hands: 'I'll tell you what I'll do. I'll put you on in Rob's place. He can run the Clydebank club this weekend.'

'Rob's place?'

'He's getting a bit too smooth, Denis—a bit off-form. I'll put you in as a deliberate contrast—what a build-up I can give you! "Dramatic last-minute appearance of Denis Sellars on the side of progress" . . . "Rob Sellars' brother" . . . Rob's reputation will help here . . . "but with that touch of earthiness that TV audiences have never seen before." This is ruddy marvellous. On you go and get some sleep. I'll get on to the papers right away.' He clapped my shoulder at the door, rather a nice smile: 'You can see I'm not a bad chap. I'm glad we're working together.'

Frankly I do not know what I think I mean when I think I don't care. 'Sure, it's great. Thanks, Hackett.'

In seven hours I walked the disease from my body and the daylight from the City. Strange streets I've never seen before, sunny Leith, salty Portobello, lines of Duddingston bungalows. Answering with the same voice everywhere:

You're right, Denis. He's evil. Destroy him before he kills us all. He's mad—doesn't belong in this space of Time.

My Canongate was chilly around ten o'clock when I finally turned off the Wynd and made for home. Youngsters eating golden morsels off sodden paper, hi there, Denis. Clip, clip, pray God he's not there. How dare you, Nichol? How dare you not be the fountain that spouted me into being? *This was my fulcrum of meaning.*

Clip, clip, clipclipclip, clang clang, clam-bam.

'Denis! Oh, Denis, my darling, where have you been?' Her hair glimmered in the shadows, profuse as her Jacobite heroine's, her strong arms round me, sweeping my bruised cheeks into the welcome of her softmoulded breast. This I can never betray.

'Please forgive me, Kate. I love you.'

'Where have you been? We've been looking all over for you.'

'Never mind. Is anyone in?'

Murdo rose from the fire. Only me, Denis. We've all been worried stiff, you silly bugger. You'd better get some sleep—the final dress rehearsal's tomorrow.'

'Murdo,' I sat down in my favourite spotless armchair. 'I don't know what Kate's told you, but Nichol and I are finished.'

'Don't be an imbecile. You've no right to blame him. I can explain it—'

'You hairy-arsed Lewisman, you had the father you wanted, didn't you? Why shouldn't I? The old liar! Damn him to hell! '

Kate rubbing my sagging head, Murdo's coat swung elegantly to his shoulder. 'He'll be all right when he's dried out. I'll see you to-morrow.'

I stared hard into a yellow lick of flame. 'I've signed a contract with Hackett. I'm singing in the Queen's on Friday.'

Kate's gasp must have stretched her bra, Murdo hissing a Gaelic gasp out of his ashen disbelief. '*Dhia!* You would do this—you, his favourite? You're joking, it would kill him. Of course you're joking!' He babbled on, shut him up for Christ's sake.

I showed him the white copy. 'Think what you like, but you don't understand. Nobody could . . . I'm finished.'

A hideous silence, then Murdo's murderous whisper. 'You, my friend . . . My friend no bloody more.' He threw the contract viciously in my face, leaned forward. 'You've thrown him to the wolves, you Lowland bastard! God!' He turned in the open doorway. 'Get your things, Kate. You can't stay with this dirty Judas.'

I looked up fearfully, saw her still struggling under the blow, tempted to follow him. But a fractured voice said:

'Maybe I shouldn't. But... he's my whole world, Murdo.'

Doorslam. Kate on her knees, Denis, please, you can't, things are bad enough already, the tickets are still only half-sold and Andrew's down with a quinsy throat. He was saying that Providence is turning against him, this will kill him, he really loves you, please, Denis. No Kate, no Kate, nokate, NO! !

She went to the sink. 'I'll get you some supper.'

'Are you going to leave me?'

'I could no more leave you than I could stop nagging you for a baby.'

Kate. Everkiss again. I'll fill my life with ambition to love you and nothing else just as soon as vengeance is mine. Saith the Lord Sellars.

Nichol. Father. Rasputin. *Why*?

More hail stoning the window. As in a fit of fright she ran across the room, wrapped herself against my body draining out its last grief. 'It's this damned country, Denis. It makes maniacs of us all. Why do we do these things to each other? Why?

Dear God in Heaven there is no right nor wrong
No father-hand to make my weakness strong
And but for she no safety and no song.

CHAPTER THIRTEEN

This Spring is mistress of irony. For April the Fourth and its evening are the mildest kindest hours of the so-far year. No smell of crisis in the Old Town, people breathing deep and upturning their slackening happy faces to the incense on the breeze. They say the pines round Belsen were once perfumed as any in Lower Saxony. And now you'll not hear a bird for miles. In this morning's Evening News I saw Nichol's last desperate advertisement, and this afternoon I saw the Legion marching in Woods Street, their final attempt to instil literary conscience into my City, but they're old novelties now and shopkeepers laughed at their doors without listening. Nichol's kept away from me. Must know. I'm a neutromaniac now, Kate, there's no point in wasting your breath. Just don't feel a thing about him, my hate-love tissue has been excised. I only know I never want to see him again. Do I?

We walked to Castle Terrace in quiet cool, hand-in-hand through modest scenes, her wavespilling scalp interrupting old men's talk on benches, her stilettos clicking echoes off the backside of the Castle rock. Picking up people as we neared the Ewan Hall, car parks filling, brighter cigarette-ends suggesting the insidious approach of the lonely hours. Clip, clip, not a word, small knots of people tied outside the Ewan, columns converging from the bus-stops, a solid mass seething on the Queen's Theatre pavement. Twenty-five minutes to curtain up for both. D-Day, for delight or disaster.

We stopped outside the Galloway Arms, garish neon lights opposite the disappearing green dome. The Gardens windborne to us. Smell the living stuff sighing all around,

Kate. This is no night for neutromaniacs. But this is no City for anybody.

'Well.' Her hand over my guitar-carrying. 'Good-luck, darling... you don't mind me not coming with you? I must pay Nichol this last respect, Denis.'

'On you go. And Kate—'

'Yes?' Answering halfway across.

I was going to say wish them luck, but the thought has released guilt-hormone. 'Nothing, honey. I love you.'

She vanished into the lighted square, fumbling at her white bag. The little clumps outside the Ewan slightly pathetic. After all I went through with him and them. Stop it. He's no blood of yours.

He came out, flanked by Lammermuir and Baillie Hardie, a weaker stoop to his shoulders, every movement that iota slower, just too controlled. Slide into this gloomy doorway, he mustn't see you. He removed his bonnet, walked to the pavement's edge, scanning the street, appearing to shrivel each time his head turned. The Baillie and Earl finding great interest in their feet, none in the trickle of connoisseurs moving past them into the Ewan. Strange, how many of those look upwards of fifty. Nichol's arms spread horizontal then flapped slowly to his thighs like a dying eagle's wings. He shuffled to the Committee, Hardie cheering him up with some fatuous bluff, the big head rebuking it with a hairy shudder, Lammermuir mediating with the polished skill of Eton, Nichol's voice rising over the thoroughfare, unsweetened. Bickering and division already. Lump in my throat. Time I was off.

It was no easy fight into the Queen's. Backstage Hackett had a flower in his buttonhole, quick Denis you're late. Contemptuous glances from old friends, Ricky and the Moonshiners turning their backs in the corner, mutter of I-wouldn't-trust-him-one-inch. Sorry, boys, life is so personal you'll never understand.

Now look, Hackett was saying, we are nationwide for two sessions to-night and I want good strong singing. Good strong singing is the important thing, kids, and remember girls, watch how you place your ankles. Those old boys in the orchestra stalls, giggliggle. Hackett, after such an inspired address my voice feels capable of charming Saul into the Queen of Sheba. Good strong singing, kids, and leave the hairy old stuff to Denis, he knows how to put it across.

I changed quickly. White shirt, fawn slacks, Murdo's old mess boots, yellow cravat. Tuning my guitar, treble-E one semitone sharp to get the hairy old edge. This evening could make me for life. You're on at the end of the first half, Denis, same as the run-through this afternoon.

The side-stage door was twenty yards from our packed dressing-room. Behind the green-and-gold curtain the props awaiting the urban voices of our rural soil, real folksy, a cardboard cellar, barrels of ale and a genuine oaken stool for Hackett's scrawny seat. On the other side a squat Edwardian auditorium filling steadily from pillar to pillar, T.V. cameras and technicians right left and distant, scaffolding covering Adonis and what's-her-name beside the gilded boxes. Wonderful sight, but hell take this nauseating anxiety, I need a drink.

Castle Terrace was dusking, noisy with expectant faces pouring into the Queen's. That's Denis Sellars, little chap whispering to his fur-hatted mummy. Jolt from body to body. Thank God for the Galloway Arms, I daren't look across the road.

The lounge was full: fathers reluctantly downing their last before the songfeast. Double, please. Aaah. Fine evening to-night, sir, if you ask me the Queen's is doin' much better than the Ewan. Nobody asked you, and I said another double. Long hurt face, white-coated trog. If he'd any self-respect he wouldn't pretend that I'm worth talking to.

The red leather chairs were emptying around the glass-topped tables. All moving off to see the settling of destinies; Knights of the Grand Philistine Order, they'll never know the power of life and death they carry in their palms and pockets.

Over my shoulder, against the wall, a feverish noble face was brooding into the bar-mirror, shapely hand swirling a whisky and green ginger. 'Why, hullo, Andrew. MacLennan.

His eyes acknowledged me in the glass. 'Hullo yourself. Two pink diamonds burning on his fluted cheeks, Roderick Monroe is going to sound hoarse tonight.

'Are you feeling better?'

'Keep your smarm to yourself, Sellars. We've got a new name for you across the way, also beginning with "S".' Throw down that whisky. 'Can I get you a drink?'

'Shut your mouth, and don't talk to me.'

'I see,' averting my eyes from his red-streaked whites. 'O.K., I'm not asking you to understand. How is he?'

'How d'you expect?' He coughed, held his throat against a thrust of pain. 'The Hall's barely half-full, some of the bastards have changed their minds at the last minute. Margot's had an argument with Carson, and you can see the state I'm in; yet funnily enough he can hardly talk about anything except you. Murdo didn't dare tell him the whole story till this afternoon.'

No. Jesus spew me sour and dying. No end to suffering and causing it. 'Another double, please, quick! '

Andrew MacLennan grimaced at his last swallow, lurched past me; the heat of him carried five feet. 'We'll make it yet, in spite of you. I can't understand why you've shattered him so much—I don't consider you all that good. But you should see him.'

I followed him out. Twenty-three past, seven minutes and he'll have Maisie up to start the renaissance. *And me not there.*

Andrew vanished into the hurrying throng, not looking back, shoulder-blades shuddering together. I began to walk with the stream, stopped after five paces and climbed a dentist's steps. In the sparsely-peopled doorway Margot and Murdo were smoking listlessly, her hair showering tiny flames under the silver light, her hand leaning gently on his shoulder. Sad and noble young specimens; these were my kin, and now their eyes keep dropping away from this passing rejection they never deserved. Dinner-suited Carson Hall shaking a fist to James McNeill flushing wrath behind them, plenty fight left and they're too big to realise it's too late. To hell with Hackett, I belong on that God-forsaken far pavement!

I was two steps down when Nichol charged out of the glare, bonnet in hand and hair pulled seven ways by fiendish invisible hands. Murdo made a restraining tug at his cloak, but a straight-arm push sent him reeling back into the foyer. Nichol's mouth opened and a sharp bellow incised the silent anticipation of the pleasurebent mob. He was in among them, his round voice carrying clear to me across their rising complaints.

Two jumps to the pavement, and fighting through to him wasn't easy. I apologised to three elderly ladies, exchanged short words with a large fat student and bounced backwards off the deliberate shoulder of his ruthless friend; I was wriggling between two angry little Cameronians when Nichol's second shout turned all heads from ten feet away: 'You fools! You fools! Come in here—here is where you belong!' Mouths opened, faces turned, feet decelerating, faltering, some stopping. A solid ring three deep had formed round him, worsteds rubbing, whispering, what's happened why it's Nichol Ross. Vainly I charged against the dyke of flesh, caught sight of him between two balding heads.

'Listen to me!' Messiah's head was backflung to the descending darkness, his Balmoral flapping in the gloom above the yellowlit faces. 'Listen to me! You have been deceived by the propaganda of a man who cares only for money. Come in to the Ewan Hall, my people, that is where you will see the real talent of your country—I, Nichol Ross, swear it! If you care for Scotland's future, come in and support us! Come in! '

He was defying the momentum of the crowd, his hands performing uncanny miracles of explanation, but his body and legs fixed immobile to his stance, a colossal combination of madman and prophet. He was holding them, slowly the next rank wavered and listened, excited schoolgirls, frightened workmen with anaemic faces, white-collared suburbanites frowning beside their overdressed wives, professional mens' ladies with deb-imitation hair hanging lank as pruned seaweed, booked for the dress circle in the Queen's. Heavy respirations seemed to swoosh in a weird mass-rhythm; Rasputin's eyes never blacker, searing his spellbound audience like the organs of some superhuman hypnotic power, charring their distaste, mocking their innocent faith in the norm. The big head turned, twisted and reared, the fiery nape-locks writhing, the two mighty legs still rigid below the sweep of his cloak. God. Steel trunks platinum-riveted into granite.

Twin furies below the unkempt line of his eyebrows. Sweeping us all with disdain and magic. Here beginneth the call again: 'Come in! Come in!': the compound of fire and thunder that men have always honoured too late—Churchill on Hitler, Himself in the Temple, Lot foretelling the nuclear blitz of Sodom. 'Come in! Come in!' An energy that might topple evil thrones and untomb the just. What richness in his voice. Fly with me, citizens,

Sellars hears between the majestic syllables, fly into the Ewan and flee the wrath that will surely come upon the vulgarisers. People are no longer breathing in this street. He's got them.

Then low to my right a swot-faced little college lass threw a giggle. Nichol lunged round towards her irreverence, but he turned too sharply on his wide base and overbalanced in a splutter of sparks. He was on one knee when a red-faced club-tied fifty-year-old began to shake, followed by his wife; in five seconds the bulk of Rasputin's immediate audience were contaminated, hooting laughter at his irate disbelief; in rising he did the splits and nearly capsized, and they were completely free of him—hahahahahoohoo did you see that? Hahahoo.

'Shut up, you fools! I'm not finished! ' But the spell was fading amid their chattering amusement; inexorably as stormtide overwhelming a bar of sand their family groups gathered, pushed, stopped, then drove on again with no intention of staying.

'Nichol!' I was through to him by virtue of disgusting un-Queensberry flailing, but he appeared not to recognise me; he gave my face the blank appraisal of a blind man, then he was back into the mass: 'Stop! Please, you must listen to me!' They grinned, nodded, paled when he seized at them—a small grey woman offered him a shilling. 'Stop! You must come in—we've done this for *you*! but he's drunk said Liberton, insane said Portobello, we should get the police said a New Town Lady in black silk. 'Nichol!' I tried to bearhug him and was thrown five yards when he stretched his shoulders irritably.

In the near-darkness the crowd's relentless surge and

derisive commentary created an atmosphere of cold-blooded cruelty: I pulled at a large woman's hem and came up terrified. The last packs of curtain-racers were on him; his voice lost discipline: 'Stop! Stop! You brainless sheep, stop!' He clutched at four lads wearing Varsity scarves, imprisoning three in a wide pincer-hook, but the taller fourth neck-locked him from behind with a sportsman's savage grace. They moved on, and the wondering tail-enders with them; the street was suddenly spacious again, and in its gutter Nichol Ross was raving on his knees, his hair trailing between the bars of a gurgling drain: 'This can't be true. No! Merciful Providence, what has happened to my people?'

The trampled Balmoral lying at my feet. I deserve every hellspang of my misery as I bend wearily to retrieve it.

Ronald Johnstone was helping Nichol to his feet: 'Come on, now. It'll be all right, we've got to get started.' His other allies moving out to sympathise.

'Nichol.' I ran after his slow, painful progress. 'Here's your bonnet.'

The same blank stare. Oh, yes. Thank you, Denis. Thank you very much.' A crooked cut over his left eye. He turned away, limping on Carson Hall.

'Where are *you* going?' Murdo's palm slammed flat on my throat.

'I'm coming in. I know I made a hellish mistake, but—'

'Get out of here, Sellars.' A young poet had me by the collar, the Legion and others forming an angry circle on the pavement. 'Get away, before there's murder done.'

My voice a metallic jangle, my fist preparing to right-cross him: 'I'm his best friend. Stand back, you bastards, or I'll—'

Ronald Johnstone's cane cut the air in front of their concerted rush: 'That's enough! Go on, take Nichol in!' Sure, Ronald, Murdo spitting at my feet and ushering the others away. You're just rubbish, Sellars, from St. Peter.

'I must come in, Ronald. Please! '

The white hair shimmered in the foyer's light: polite refusal. Honest grey eyes. 'You made a mistake, I know,' he drawled. 'In time we'll sort it out. But to-night we don't want you, Denis, and you can't blame us; you're too late to help.' He turned abruptly; beyond his upright carriage I heard a spasmodic burst of clapping.

God help them and me. Two unreal feet clacking footfalls on the deserted roadway. The sensitive night spreading a last thick blanket over a shameful nightmare. Somewhere in this hideous universe of curving space and contracting time there must be a junction called Atonement.

Twenty minutes more in the Galloway Arms and I was drugged enough to return to the Queen's Theatre; I slipped unobtrusively behind the barrel reserved for me at the stage-cellar's back. Smiling faces all around, sipping at cokes and fortified fruit drinks, howling the choruses with vocal lust and thumping feet. Hackett and his flower on centre-stage both looking very scholarly, all manner of read-up comments flowing with admirable nonchalance from our folk-lord's lips: this, ladies and gentlemen, is a good example of how a court-song can permeate all the social strata after a breakdown of feudal society. Very good, Hackie, poor Rob's a good script writer, with what saintly courage you've shouldered the burden of his experience.

The strange noisy kaleidoscope heaving and tilting, faces singing out of focus, strange elongated young men and desirable young women. And the great noise beyond the footlights that never failed to shatter the poignancy of the final silence; crash-crash-crash, we love you, successessessess.

And no wonder. Blossom of our land, these young folk, but they don't realise their routes of nourishment have just been cut.

Hackett the magnificent. Not a square inch of stage wasted, not one gag: a thick accent, an unfortunate dress, a pot-belly—every jokeworthy feature was shaped into spontaneous satire, and the audience set rocking with laughter at the expense of a grateful blushing singer. He pranced in and around the barrels, personality among puppets, don't forget, folks, I am the lord of this dance. A natural.

Ricky and the Moonshiners provided me with the early evening's rarest memory. What an improvement. The crash of their high-strung steel struck terror in among us, I felt the arrow-shafts of armoured men splitting my own sodden flesh, Ricky's knuckles rapping his soundboard between lines—oh, the madness of those burnraping days when the hills of home ran scarlet. And the terror of our own time, just a little rain falling and what have they done to it? A different cold-blooded chill that seeped through the skin, the bursting atom and this drink and Hackett and me are all made of the same nuclear stuff. Disgusting thought, but those unearthly, plangent banjo-runs of Ricky's were the song of a Hiroshima child-ghost once un-ionised and beautiful and they were mature tragedy before the last line tinkled out on a sixth. This is the future's pop-song all right.

Lisa I remember. Tall and elegant and clean. *The Yellow Bittern* again, and as a drunkard this night I know how that poor yellow throat felt. The barrels stopped creaking, the far white face-blobs were paralysed, the world was clean tragedy, clean voice, clean notes, clean heartfelt words. But this sort of cleanliness just doesn't wash out the soul, Lisa. You should ask Kate, it just isn't enough. The cameras shuddered from the applause as she stood in her final wilting lily-stance: wonderful, and maybe one day we can be friends again. Maybe not, for I don't apologise for asking too much the night you failed.

Talented young men and women passing before me, and I listened and felt nothing. Not even Hackett. I'm drunk. Not even Nichol. For the moment life is pentathol. Not even Kate. I sit listen and clap and this cellar and the olde worlde props are neither vulgar nor cosy. All this nothought doesn't worry me. I suspect I am enjoying a secret mystical communion with Malcolm Muggeridge.

Hackett was saying something about the hairy old grizzly you all saw dancing in the street and the people were laughing. And something about here is this young chap nevertheless he's got some sense now though you wouldn't think it to hear him sing. Hahahaha, those people out there have a truly sophisticated sense of humour. Well done, Hackie.

One of the Cavaliers leaned over my barrel. 'It's you, Denis. Hackett's introducing *you*, you drunken oaf!'

Suddenly I am feeling an awful lot of things, and catastrophic despondency is not their half. Hackett taking my arm as if I were a bairn at a party. Go on, he whispers, give them the contrast. I shake loose, smile into the dazzling giant eyes of science, and we're off with Kate's song. Hackett clumping with surprise on his perch behind me, thought I was going to sing the ploo'man. But this is what you're getting, faceless ones, a shining creation forged in the furnace where despair and love fought for the soul of Denis Sellars, and the winner was a girl with plaintive blue eyes. Tangled ringlets I left... listen, you decent fickle people, this is how the best of past and present should be fused. Little ripe-wheaten locklets... this was the vision of a June morning in the paddock that he treasured in his chains the night before they took him and half-hanged him and ripped his goolies from him and flung his withering intestines on to the fire before the decent laughing English people ... Shining head, golder far... can't you see it, decent folk? I'm trying to show that I'm still fighting for Nichol, can't you see it in my sour face, hear it in my hissing breath, I don't belong here! Wrists and hands dancing again, best ovation I never earned. Hackett announcing the interval, but don't go away, folks, we'll be back and don't forget they're televising our last twenty minutes as well. Give your hair a comb. Haha.

In the corridor he was furious: 'Sellars, you'll sing what I tell you, and don't forget it. If that song hadn't come off, I'd have sacked you. Have you been drinking?'

'I'm all right, Hackett, leave me alone.' Not time yet. 'You're nearly as unstable as your bleeding brother.' A cruel eyegleam. 'Is there a streak of insanity in your family, or something?'

I turned quickly on my heel. The dressingroom full of high spirits and free beer, kisses for Hackett from the T.V.-baptised maidens. We can relax for most of the second half, kids, but remember I want good strong singing for the last twenty minutes when we're nationwide again. A can for everybody, Ricky, but not old Sellars, he's going to sing 'the ploo'man lad' if it kills him. Look at him brooding in the corner there. You hear that, Sellars? Yes. You've just answered a rusty Christian prayer, Hackie.

'Lisa.' Hackett fingercrooked peremptorily. She came slowly, and to my utterest astonishment dropped a sympathetic hand on my shoulder while she listened, first sincere contact since I left Kate. 'Lisa, run up to the Ewan and see how Buffalo Bill and his Red Indians are doing.' Lisa hesitating, undiluted loathing on her face. 'Go on, Lisa, we all want to hear how our friends and rivals are performing. We're idealists, aren't we?' Bringing the house down, what a comedian. I feel sick.

Lisa's pony-tail swung through the door, but not before her look registered in my corner. Wait two minutes... they're tiring of the baiting, leaving me alone. Hackett out to the toilet, and I pretend to follow suit, then turn left downstairs on to the street. Ruuuuun.

I found her by the Ewan's gallery entrance. 'What is it, Lisa?'

'Denis—is there nothing we can do for Nichol now?'

'What sort of a line is this? I've heard enough jokes for one night.'

'Look.' That wide swing of hair, memories floating from last year. But no vamp left in the lethargic eyes, she took my arm gently up the narrow steps. 'It's taken me a long time to see what Hackett really is.'

'I don't understand.'

Clattatter, uh-uh-uh. 'You won't believe this, but in the last few weeks Rob and I have grown terribly fond of each other. Hackett's sucked him dry, Denis, that's why you're singing in the Queen's to-night. You've no idea how much I regret what we've done.'

I pulled her down beside me on the top step. 'That makes three of us. But it's too late now.'

'Is there nothing we can do?'

'Not for Nichol. He's been betrayed by more than you and me. It was a forlorn hope from the start. You know, Lisa, you and Rob—I just can't—'

'You thought he was just a philanderer, didn't you? Don't you realise that inside him there's a little boy needing a mother just as much as you? I've grown up a lot since I met him, Denis. The old selfishness is going.'

I gripped her hand. 'I'll be damned, but I'm glad. No hard feelings?'

She shook her head. 'That was mostly my fault. It was the old story of the square peg.'

'Are you going to get married?'

She thrust her face deep into her hands and cried like an orphan. Jerkily she sobbed: 'He asked me to marry him last week. But Hackett's threatened to blackleg him everywhere if we try it. You know why?' Her tearstained face was ugly with venom. 'I'm enjoying great popularity at the moment, and the bastard's terrified of losing another meal-ticket to the kitchen sink. I turned Rob down. I just couldn't see any future in it. You've never seen him so despondent as he was this morning—going off to Glasgow to run a piddling little club! '

No compassion left. My inside contains a cold pillar of steel and to-night somebody will suffer. I'm suddenly nursing a new vision of vengeance. And this one is going to be constructive.

'Come on, Lisa, you'd better get your reporting done. And we're not finished yet.'

I was taking her hand past the sleeping box-office when two young men burst out of the gallery, swearing violently to each other.

'What's it like inside, lads?' My heart began to hammer. The red-faced City boy was buttoning his raincoat with hasty rough temper. 'It's shite! Ye cannae hear what the leadin' actor's sayin', an' yon auld fishwife is enough tae drive ye tae drink. There's no' a real singer there.'

'Aye,' said his smaller companion. 'An' yon poatry's goin' oan and oan, and yon daft bugger Ross is startin' tae swear at the audience because they're no' clappin'. The folk are startin' tae leave.'

'The worst show Ah've ever seen,' affirmed the red face. 'We should uv goan tae the Queen's.'

Lisa and I exchanging sceptical glances, but as if in deliberate confirmation of our most sinister fears a pale ghost of Nichol's berating voice struggled through the double door, answered by a resentful rattle of feet.

'Do you want to go in, Denis?'

'No. You go on back to Hackett. I've got something to do first.'

I followed her down, watched her dissolve into the darkness. That glorious Galloway Arms, give me a last bit of comfort, old friend. Three more drams. And outside the mellow night blazed a crescent of silver and a promise of wallflower suspired from the Gardens. Walk on, ghostie-man, and pray for a shower of murder. Hackett scowling when I stumbled behind my barrel. A meek bow to him, and a reassuring nod to Lisa before I'm lost in the music.

The pride of the City, the finewoven harmonies of the Moonshiners, the keeeeeening melodeons, the banjos and guitars, the cilinkilinkiling mandolin awakening gentler emotions that never existed till now. The Cavaliers, cocky pitstock, evoking laughter with their droll sagas, sobering the imagination with the Blantyre disaster. Three raw-boned colts of Northumberland, declaring Lord Percy's side of it, ballads are equally dramatic on both sides of the Border. This is magnificent, Sellars. Now a Carribean sun-dance on tin shacks in that muscular Jamaican's nailtips. Then hands flicked the word round, the wicked yellow peepers swept our cokes and cloisters, and all our producer's reserves went into the energising of the televised finale. The buttocks wagged, the pop-songs appeared, suddenly sanctified, the thirds and fifths sweetened and thickened to a syrupy consistency, a pretty brunette contrived to sing a jazzed-up spiritual and copulate simultaneously with the microphone. Oh, God, but I'm waiting. I'm past hearing the mindless clapping, or wishing that Nichol and Maisie were here to add style and nobility to all this vivacity and freshness that's being debased. Nearly ready. Ten to nine, nine to nine, eight to, five, four—the Border Reivers finished with a Hackett-backed halloo and St. Leonard cut the uproar with his graceful hand.

'Ladies and gentlemen, finally we have our surprise packet, Denis Sellars, brother of my own prodigy. When I think of all the trouble I've had to convince people up here' (he leered knowingly into the stalls and was rewarded with a mirthful roar) 'that I can give them good folk-entertainment, I still consider that one of my greatest achievements has been to wrench this talented young man out of the parochial morass in which he was suffocating.' Stroking his chin suggestively and clawing his arms wide like Dracula— another guffaw, the City quick to get the message. 'He's a bit rough and ready, ladies and gentlemen, but I'm going to teach him to be a folksinger. Here he is, with a song he got from the tinkie folk'—he lapsed into an atrocious stage-Scottish—'Denis Sellarrrrs and "the ploo'man lad"!'

People have poured blood for this country's soul. And in the end those smirking chimps sit down there showing off their sensitive ignorance in comfort. Wallace disembowelled, Montrose on the scaffold without a quiver, hungry men scrawling their courage till the cramp in their fingers banished the pain in their bellies. MacDiarmid an' a'. Nichol in the gutter, his hair in the drain. I'm whacked. This is the best I can do, boys.

I put my hand fondly on Hackett's shoulder. 'Let me say one quick word, folks, in—in gratitude.' Straight into the circular tunnels that led to Great Britain, a testimony. 'People can say what they like about old Len here, but in the last few months I've learned one thing and you ought to know it too.' Patting Hackett's grease above the widening smile, 'Ladies and gentlemen, the greatest man in this city to-night is called Nichol Ross, and Len Hackett is a filthy little—'

Most of the misinterpreting audience were laughing, but the front ten rows squeezed some horrified gas out, for they could see details on our faces. Hackett made frantic manual commands to the technicians; in Bermondsey and Lancaster astonished viewers were asking why the credits had come up minutes early, in the Queen's Theatre they saw Hackett drag the wildcackling madman backwards behind the closing curtains. From the other side we heard a short curious applause, feet thudding into the plush aisles.

Hackett was yabbering obscenities at me, his sallow face twisted beyond recognition. Two of them had me from behind, you sod you've ruined it; I crushed my eyes shut as one of them backswung the glittering coke-bottle, but Lisa had already vaulted a stool, kicked at the cable and was wrenching the switches; I ducked into the darkness and heard a clunk and squeal from behind.

'Where is he? Get him, Jimmy, get him!' I went limp from the waist up, but scissor-kicked at the moving shadows and toppled the wrong target. Jimmy and I were grappling blindly when a scream of unbearable pain pierced the floor-smelling scuffle. My right hand free, I bit gouging fingers, rolled from a boot on the forehead, drove my stiff straight hand karate-wise into rebounding flab. I scrambled through the scrummage, came panting on my feet and fleeing when the lights flashed back on to the chaos.

Lisa pulling me to safety behind two big policemen. The Cavaliers, Moonshiners *et alia* releasing each other tipsily like junkies coming out of an opium-dream.

The screams were coming from D. Leonard Hackett, pinned under the largest genuine ale barrel on the stage, his soft white hands groping for the fracture in his pelvis.

Too late for Roman hill redeeming pain
Could never win the Garden back again
But this enough to wipe the mark of Cain.

CHAPTER FOURTEEN

I'm safe with you for a small while, Kate, thanks to our new friend Lisa Kendall. The guts of her, and but for that they'd have had mine. But she engaged my spluttering evening-dressed accusers so sweetly, after Hackett was carted off to the Casualty Department and the professional care of Dr. Pat Leitch and his superiors. I'm warning you, gentlemen, she said, all this evidence seems a bit fragmentary, nobody really knows what happened when the lights went out, and you can take it further if you like, but if you do all these sentimental journalists outside are going to get the gory details of what Hackett has done to Rob Sellars and a few others I could mention, and we'll see how well *Stringtime* stands up to that. They used disgusting swears containing metaphors reminiscent of de Sade, but they were good men at heart and their soft eyes said she means it, boys, officially it was an accident, and the Black Crows were consulted briefly and dismissed, satisfied that justice was out of their hands as usual.

The reporters were not so easily blindfolded, but apart from calling me a hooligan and a few unfashionable fourlegged things, they stuck to their usual Saturday cliches and devoted screeds to Leonard's gallant fight against his injuries and the skill of the Royal surgeons. But remember, folks, this thug Sellars should never be allowed on a folksong platform again. *Stringtime* received some elegant notices, we've been waiting for this for years, come in the flesh if you can but if not get yourself a telly.

Here and there a few half-columns deplored the abysmal performance in the Ewan Hall and the rude remarks addressed to the audience by Mr. Ross, a once-distinguished novelist. Only the *Scottish Times* possessed an editor gallant enough to allow a full critique: moderate praise for the struggles of Andrew MacLennan, the readings of Ronald Johnstone and the shorter songs of Maisie Hay. But the whole too disjointed, and Mr. Ross's choleric diatribes a disgrace: although the concept was good, the execution was disappointing, and it was obvious that despite the promises of the winter the programme had been criminally under-rehearsed. And the flat little footnote on Sunday morning: 'The Festival Arts Committee have intimated that owing to the poor response to *The Heart of Scotland* staged in the Ewan Hall on April 4th and 5th, they have decided not to grant the Hall to Mr. Ross's company for this year's Festival.' Light the fire with it, sweetheart.

Shopping in the High Street for Sunday lunch Kate met the Legion who informed her sorrowfully that Nichol was disbanding his organisation for good. Among other things, they themselves were preparing for a disillusioned walk down the A1.

She had bought a ticket for the second Ewan Hall performance, but couldn't bear to watch the massacre all over again. You should have seen it, Denis, everything went wrong. But I'm proud of what you did in the Queen's. Whatever you've done, darling, you're my own and nothing will ever change that. I love you, Kate.

We spent Sunday by the fire, neither admitting the bow-strung tenseness summoned by every footstep in the stair. Alternate bursts of nervous smoking and self-recrimination, but after lunch I gave my battered head to her hands and the softness of her cardigan. So much to forget, and tomorrow I start trying.

Whenever I use the word Scotland again, it'll have to be associated with the past tense. Whatever it means, the thing I loved is dead. That's what causes arguments, people using big loose words when they're only seeing one wee bit of one dimension. People dying and being born all the time. And the same stupid symbol used for the babies. Ridiculous. Thank God for new wonders to ponder. That despite it all I fear nothing inside this warm woollen fastness. That I can associate tenderness with present and almost future. That when you circle your arms round my neck you do it with the impetuous dedication of a sixteen-year-old, that the gesture has a flavour as moving and tasteful as a newlyread love-poem. This only reality fighting for my life.

Sunday evening, and I began to walk the floor. There are enemies outside that door, probably gathering strength to come at me from some other direction. No sign of Nichol. I think I'd let them take me away quite happily if I could only have one warm handshake, it's all right, Denis, you're still my son.

Kate preparing a light supper, haddock stewed in

milk. I took my script through to the bedroom, reading it on our old walnut dresser. Sunlight came dodging between the rooftops, gave sparkle to the head of a nine-year-old sergeant marshalling his soldiers outside ANTIQUES. Nice sight. Better. Quietly I began to edit the tragedy of Elaine and Jacques,

Clump. Clump, clump, clang! Heavy feet, carrying about fourteen stone. Him? Please God. Clamambam.

'Oh?' It's not a kent face, and it's frightened her. They droned at each other, then she cried. Oh, no!' A whisper, come in, officer. Horror icing through me, I've no feet left. They've come for me, Lisa's valiant counter-attack wasn't enough.

'Denis, it's a policeman.' Muted, a choke in her voice. Fifth attempt, I managed to stand. He must have snuffed it. I'll demand a silken hemp.

'Mr. Sellars? Denis Sellars?' The young constable clean and ruddy-faced, rising politely. Trying to tempt me into thinking he's not unkind. The panic in Kate's face. For some stupid reason I'm thinking of Absalom, his long hair caught in the tree.

'Get it over with, Kate, what's happened?'

The young fellow shaking his head, definitely not unkind.

'I'm afraid we've got bad news for you, Mr. Sellars. I'm sorry we've taken so long to find you.'

'What is it, man, for God's sake?' The room reeling, thunder of my coward chest. Nichol!

'We had a message from Glasgow, Mr. Sellars. Your brother's very ill. They want you to go through as soon as possible.'

'My brother—Rob? What's wrong?'

Twiddling his cap miserably, flashing spirals of black and white. 'From what I gather he's taken an overdose of aspirin. I'm sorry to bring such bad news, Mr. Sellars.'

For half-a-second my wanton relief sang thank heaven it's not you, it's not even Nichol. Then the inevitable rushed in. Memories. Long before that dreadful night when he began to act like a member of competitive society. They laughed at us in Dunfreckie, at first we used to walk about hand-in-hand. He lost his front baby-teeth early when the fat boy called us bastards. The evening I stole the jam, he crawled in behind me, rubbing my bruised back: never mind, Denis, when I get big I'll kill him with a big axe. I'm your flesh-and-blood, Denis. Five skirts to raise in six days, mother-of-pearl toilet seat. But Lisa told me why. He knew my darkness. My wee brother.

'I'm sorry, officer, give me a minute to pull myself together. He's my twin, you know.'

'Of course, sir, I understand.' He smiled with shy sympathy.

Kate reached for me, separated my wringing fingers. 'Buck up, sweetie. They can do lots of things for aspirin poisoning.'

Brushing my eyes, 'Sure.'

'There's a train at twenty to eight, Mr. Sellars. And I forgot. We traced you through Miss Kendall; he had her address on him.' Handing me the torn back page of Friday's *Stringtime* programme: *Please excuse the writing, Denis, but the world has just opened under me. Can you make the 7.40?—I'll meet you at the station. If he dies I promise to finish what you started. Lisa.*

'Thank you, officer. Would you like a cup of tea?' Tactfully declined. I'll keep my fingers crossed, Mr. Sellars. Thanks very much. Blam.

'Oh, Kate. God knows, I don't want him to die.'

'There, there.' The round arms clothing me again. 'We'll just have to pray, Denis. My own love, just how much more can you stand?'

An echo of despair from my everkiss, and I wonder how much more. Who was the author of the camel and the straw? Oh godgodgodgodgod. You bugger.

'You'd better start changing, Denis.'

I was admiring the seven April greens of the Crags. At least I've been loved. They can't take that away says an old song. But this is it.

'Kate, dear, would you mind nipping down to the station and booking me a ticket?'

'On a Sunday night? There should be plenty seats, honey.' 'Kate, I'm taking no chances! Please, I haven't the bloody strength to argue.'

'All right, then.' Her eyes were questioning and unhappy during the coat-buttoning. 'Are you sure you're all right?' Breathy, trying to read my face.

Stupid life. You spend six months fashioning happiness out of disillusionment then you tell it to walk out the door. Just like that. Out of cold mornings when you lay awake early and sick with apprehension, and stuffy evenings when boredom whined between the clockticks. You fight for friendship, suddenly find its better, dream then live a miracle. The sun falls and you usher her out when you should be singing her beyond forever. I'm letting her go. Just like that. And our last time should be full of gentle regrets, remember all those phases of light and darkness that we shared with only ourselves. A last critique of our living Art. But at least I've been loved. Triumph somewhere.

'On you go. I'm going to get ready.' I swung her full against me, kissed her a long tribute with tender moving lips. 'I love you more than anything in the world.' Just hold her, soft strength and magic, treasure this into infinity. This finest silence.

'Oh, Denis,' anxiety in her throat. 'Let me stay just a minute, I'd love to talk to you. Please let me—please!'

This wide generous face God made for loving. A pearl among souls, my life's one privilege. 'Go on, sweetie. Go on!'

She couldn't face the stubborn cast of my eyes and mouth. Faint sobs striking me from the door's otherside, reluctant dying of her faithful feet.

Farewell love.

My hands lingering on brass and polished wooden things, little trinkets bought for each other, each signifying another successful weave added to the love-cloth that was to warm our dreams. Paring-knife in the sink. I often wondered how large hands could slice onions so finely. But then I liked the flavour of onions and her hands knew it. And I could narrate little incidents and fondnesses on quarto till the characterisation of my princess burned optimism into the hearts of lonely old cripples in garrets. But I knew, watching him spin his cap, why I wasn't so veiy surprised. The wisest family tradition in the Sellars-

Laidlaw line. You just can't win. Too bad, and they're right. It's in the blood.

I unlocked the top drawer of my writing-desk, lifted the small white box that rattled. Thirty yellow pellets. Kate once said she'd seen twenty do it easily. I ran a full measure of cold water into the tumbler, walked through to the bedroom, wishing I felt as full of *savoir-faire* as is classical in high-class fiction. Before I had sat down in front of Elaine and Jacques, the bells had started, thirty hard metal voices jolting the boots of the dwindling faithful to where you'd better come or else. The red flames. Courage, Denis, your vast intellect says there's nothing beyond. Top off the box again. Better do it quickly, fill the mouth then slosh down the water before you panic and gag them back. Courage.

I tilted the box to my left hand.

Clump, clump, clump. Clambambam. Can't be Kate already. Oh, no. Can a poor man not poison himself in peace. Sit tight. Clambambam. Go away, for suffering Christ's sake, you're an excuse for delay. CLAMBAMBAM. Give me a chance, you bastard! Hold on a minute, those steps were heavy. Maybe the policeman with more news, maybe Rob's all right, or maybe—

I ran back into the kitchen, desk-drawer opened and barbiturate hidden away. Turn that lock. Stealthily I went to the door, a furtive creeping loonie. Turn sloooowly.

'Can I come in, Denis?'

'Nichol!

He swayed in the dim light, ten years older than my last memory of him. The blunt stoop hunchbacked and sharp now, what was red is grey, and what was grey is white. His skin flour-pale, wisps of beard drooping and stuck to his clammy neck. A faint tremble to his swollen hands, the eyes robbed of their jet dazzle, still clinging to a spark of defiance. Without forgetting the last ten minutes I clasped him in a fierce embrace. 'Nichol. For Jesus' sake, thank God. I never meant to do it. Forgive me, can you, Nichol?'

'I already have.' We both stepped back, two-way perplexity. 'And I think we have something more important to discuss.' No decay in that firm tone, he followed me in, sat in my own chair with a poor gasp of effort.

Somehow his presence seemed completely unconnected with anything I had recently experienced; momently the kitchen assumed a soft unreal atmosphere that was as real and tangible as cotton-wool.

'You *have* forgiven me! But what I did, Nichol—how can you?'

'Because as you well know the whole thing was doomed from the start. There was too much personal pride in it, Denis—my old failing. And I treated you shamefully. No—' He waved still my opening lips, 'there isn't much time, so let's get down to priorities. I promised you the truth, and you'll have it very soon.'

There isn't much time. Coincidence. I slithered weakly into Kate's chair. 'I don't understand.'

He glowered into the spreading pink shades outside the window; the last rind of setting sun disappeared, and we listened to Kate's clock in the gloaming. 'Denis,' he said, 'let me start it this way; about half-an-hour ago I had an uncomfortable aura concerning you and Rob. You're both in some kind of trouble, aren't you?'

Lord. He can't stop even now. 'I suppose you heard it from Lisa? Be honest with me, Nichol, it's too late for crazy pretences. If you start this spooky stuff again I'm going to roar the house down.'

His stick falling with a hollow snick. Both hands pressing his temples, and the withered physique began to shake till the shelves faintly rattled.

He spoke as if he hadn't heard me. 'We must be honest now, Denis, yes, we must be. Sorry, I can't quite get it, but he's in trouble, isn't he? Near the shadows ...' The tremulous voice beginning to frighten me, sounding like the unearthly memory of his once-eyes: 'Sorry, Denis. I just can't see him as clearly as I saw you.' Ooooh, shivers.

I ran to the standard lamp, but its soft light made him look even more mysterious: 'Why must you indulge in your phoney perceptions now? Rob's dying, Nichol'—I began a hysterical giggle—'he's dying of aspirin in Clydebank! How can you start the act again at a time like this?' He stared at me hard through his new terrible colour. 'I am not acting. And Rob is not going to die any more than you are.'

'What? What d'you mean?' My hands clenched on the sides of my chair.

'Just a minute.' He pressed inwards, hard on the pure white coat of his temples; I waited for the skullsplit. 'Yes, yes,' moving crabwise across the floor, he stopped before the writing-desk, rapped the top drawer with his knuckles. 'They're in there, aren't they?'

I stared wildly round every cranny of the room; no escape. 'What are you talking about?'

'No pretences, now, it's too late. The tablets you were going to take are in there.'

A noise beyond the breweries. After nine ages of crouching lordliness, the Crags have probably fallen. They say the Firth is made of marzipan and that Ollie the Bull is the reincarnation of Elijah. For three minutes I sit and gape, Nichol, while you rattle on. Staring, staring, listening, staring. My mouth open.

I came to my feet looking dumbly through him, shuddering and cold. 'You knew? How the hell did you know, Nichol?' I sound like Snow White. '*You knew?*'

One of his flawless radiant smiles moved his face back six months to apparent health, and its unaffected kindness quelled the rigor in my muscles. 'I knew, Denis. I've often known, or half-known, things that affect those who are close to me. Sitting in my Morningside sitting-room half-an-hour ago, I knew you were contemplating self-destruction.' We both sat down, watched the scarlet tongues, on he went and my mouth hanging like a moron's.

'Nichol... all those other times, when we thought you were acting a part. Your auras, and all your other claims. They were all genuine?'

'Look at me, laddie.' Tick, tick. 'What do *you* think?'

'I think I believe you. But I can't take it all in. God, how lonely you must have been. Didn't you know the Ewan Hall was going to be a mess, or that I—?'

Head wagging. 'I'm not God, Denis. It's only now and then that I break the barriers. There's so much of the self in me that it isn't easy. But what I've told you is true, I swear it.'

'You don't need to. I'm speechless... utterly.' I lit cigarettes, Nichol coughing violently between drags.

The white cheeks settled again. 'Now, listen. You already suspect that I was your mother's lover. I was. She was a wonderful woman, Denis.' How can that statement sound so natural and guiltless? Go on, Nichol. 'By this time next week you'll know an awful lot more, but certain things will have happened first.'

'Why don't you tell me now? Maybe it's later than you think for me.'

He laughed shortly, a faint echo of the old boom. 'If I thought you were going to use those filthy things I'd heave that desk out of the window. But you won't, there's far too much for you still to do.' Another laugh, stifled by a sudden gulping sigh.

Exhausted, drunk with conflict, I closed my eyes and listened. My mother's lover. So what. Concentrate. You haven't heard a word for a minute.

'—I have compiled my life's work in manuscript, Denis, and in a few days you will be in a fit condition to read and learn. I have long known that you were the natural successor to continue my quest, but right at the beginning I want to save you from the pitfalls that have shattered me. Kate, Denis. You've found something really special with her, haven't you?'

There are no more surprises under the stars. 'You'll never know how right you are.'

'I knew it. The first time I saw her. You must treasure her, laddie, she's at least half the key to your understanding. Treasure each other, Denis. Don't make the mistake that I made.'

'Wait a minute.' But I was cut off by the flow of an oft-heard typical sermon. Concentrate. Till a word rings a bell.

"—And finally, Denis, don't worry about Rob. As I said before, he's not for death any more than you are to-night. I know.'

But this time I'm not convinced. Mechanically, 'Yes, Nichol.' Wicked subterranean doubts surfacing again. Please don't go. There's so much I should be saying. I'm not having much luck with the talking. So many clever words I need for such a sense-defying situation.

He rose laboriously, cocked his bonnet, and gave me one of his irresistible rakish looks; it flicked deadly serious as I knew it would, conveying a dramatic effect as sudden as a scream. The moment possessed an absolute indefinable beauty, and all I knew was that I wanted to harness it, fondle it, never relinquish it. He looked at me. Long and waiting. Seems to need just a sentence. Awful strange.

'Nichol, there's so much I'd like to say, but I no longer trust words. Look at what we've done to each other, and here we are—me contemplating suicide, you knowing it, and both of us blethering as if we were going to a football match. And Rob, too. What *is* reality, Nichol?'

'We only see slivers of it this side. Keep looking for the word within the word that sounds like "love". There's an exciting journey ahead of you, Denis.'

I wonder. 'Oh, God.' I pressed my head into the mantelpiece.

He handed me a small photograph. 'Rob sent me this several months ago.'

I looked at my own face under a service cap. Captain Melville Sellars. Casually I placed it behind the blue china box marked TEA.

'Aye. So what?'

'You must apologise to Rob for me, Denis. If I'd only made more of an effort, I might have dragged him out of the wilderness. But I know you'll be brothers from now on.' Hearing him faintly I looked down at my numb hands. Still there. 'Denis.' He placed his palms on my shoulders. A flame scattered spears of light up to us; I looked for an age and an instant into his sorcering eyes of yesterday, and the air between us seemed to harden into a gleam of binding steel. Tick, tick, fading. Two men breathholding. Forever amen.

'Forgive me for not being your father, Denis.'

My first smile of the day. 'You *are* my father, Nichol. My only father.'

Emotion rippling along his lower lids and a hoarse whisper: 'And you're still my son, laddie. You do love me like a father, don't you?'

I nodded. 'A dozen photographs couldn't change it.'

He took my cheeks gently, stooped and kissed my forehead. 'Good-bye Denis.'

'See you, Nichol.' Ushering him on to the iron balcony. He chuckled on the stair. 'You will, probably early in the week. And you'll have all the arguments your own way for once.'

'Come again?' But he doffed his bonnet, thrust up his long right arm: 'God bless what I might have made of

Scotland, laddie!' Echoes bouncing down the close. 'But there are greater dreams, my son, far greater dreams!' He was gone, cloak swallowed in the first full darkness.

Ten minutes later I was sitting by the fire, still turning the sounds and memories over and over and over . . .

It sounds so true. Does it? And we used to laugh. My father's become my God. Has handpicked me to tread the narrow path the greatest Gospel prescribes for those who worship the fire of the pen. And the like of Kate Fraser. Revelation, bloody fantastic, but one thing wrong. He said he has his limits and so have I. And if you've got limits you need faith and then you're liable to get hurt. Neurotic me handpicked by Nichol to carry the Torch, the Light-Counterpoint of dogmatic heathen darkness. But it's a merciless fight and I've no guts left to buy faith with. To love and strive, and all that, it's a hellish gamble, I couldn't bear the past winter over again. Responsibility's a bastard. And it's always snooping around things like love and faith. Much easier to fabricate nice big abstracts and live by them. Inevitable postulations and eternal procrastinations. Death-wishes. I once looked in a mother's eyes when her wee chap ran across a busy street. Not for me, Nichol. One of your limits, you overestimated your young Denis. He'll remember that he found outhwit's everkiss. But to hell with Truth. A soldier can't fight when he's tired. And I feel the darkness closing in again.

This is the nonchalance the books yap about. Hurry before herself comes back. I re-opened the drawer, took my box back to the bedroom and my tumbler. I sat down slowly, gazed through the window into the space where the night and the rifts of April easterly were fighting a running battle with the muttering lamps of the Canongate.

I must scribble some sort of note to her... Last loving salute, inadequate as everything else of me . . . Feeling frightened again . . . Maybe there is a fundamentalist yon-place . . . Stop it. . .

Somebody, please listen . . .

Before me a window, and the night beyond it, haunted by swimming shapes of stone . . .

Courage, Denis. Damn that adrenaline and do it. . .

Salvation or perdition is yellow and now, for the flames I feared are less than those I have ignited in my present wreckage . . .

> Sweet God of John Thy gracious hands into—
> Gurgle, gurgle . . .
> The flames, hellflames, flames, hellflames ...
> FLAMES . . .?

AND BEYOND—

A POSTSCRIPT

Red demons flitting across shapes that writhe and twist out of their earthly forms and never escape the all-pervading firebath. Sharp talons spark and clutch at the liquid darkness, cool and tantalising and beyond reach. Deep in the pit the bloody rivulets trickle and gather and flow and gather and pound and gather and run from the eye's half-blinded confusion, curling long tentacles round the wretched creations whose one-day destruction was inevitably ordained before the foundation of the world. Heat! heat! heat! screams the wild, vivid scene; shapeless monsters roar from the gloom, their lightning tongues flick across all the colours of roasting flesh like dazzling silver lashes. The holocaust scorches the eye but there is no warmth for the tortured bodies that shudder, battered and soaked by exposure to the hours of vengeance that have crackled on through endless space to wreak havoc on the souls of other men.

As the redness fades the wonder and power of it all, its cruelty and majesty, sear the spirit like a shaft of purest light; mortals bow their heads, stony fingers fashioned for the glory of the Eternal slide into the outer darkness, quailing under a last fork of flame. And for a space there is nothing.

Then the blackness drives another pack of screaming fiends upon the ears, the screw and the worm and the unseen unquenchable are abroad no less: howl,

howl, howlon, how long? Never to end, scream the voices, we are the law of this chasm of night, we have sung our hellish song since the First Sin, and aha! we sing for ever. This is our domain. Here we reign. With John.

—I don't need to describe it to you, Murdo, it's the sort of storm you've seen yourself, one of those rare thundery days you get here, when the sunset is too dramatic for words, and the wind turns round and comes in off the sea at night. You'd think we were back in winter; I've got the fire blazing, and the old grate is howling like a banshee. May, did you say!

You went off so quickly after the funeral that we never had a chance to compare all the things that Nichol had told us separately. Maybe I'm getting hard or something, but despite the utter hell of the past few weeks I still find myself quaking with excitement as I put the pieces together. Just let me have a wee greet, then I'll continue!

Firstly, I'd better mention that I was right in my suspicions about Denis the night we got the news about Rob— remember what I said over the 'phone? In all the fuss I forgot to tell you, but when I came back from the station he was crying in front of the fire. All he could say was 'I can't leave you, I haven't got the guts. You matter more than even my despair.' Then he took me on his knee, quite gently, and we sat like that for an hour without saying a word.

By the time he and Lisa got to Glasgow Rob was already coming out of his coma, and when they came back that night Denis was like a new man—full of the reconciliation, full of new plans—that's why I rang you on Sunday morning, and you should have come no matter how you felt. Anyway, when I was cleaning the bedroom on Sunday afternoon I found a small box of Nembutal hidden in the fireplace; my premonition had been right after all. How can you continue to blame him? We'll never know what he's been through.

I burned the box when he was out 'phoning—there was no answer, of course, for Nichol had already gone for his walk on the Pentlands. And was I glad I had destroyed the pills when that Black Monday arrived? I've often thought what a mercy it was that the Connor's boys got wind of the terrible thing so quickly—I don't think I could have stood another policeman. I couldn't believe my eyes at first: they stood there, the two of them looking like waifs, then wee Joe began to sob, and Starkey said: 'It's Nichol, Kate. They found him out on the hills this morning'. . .

... I shouldn't bother you with all the agony over again. Judging by your face at the reading of the will you were hearing as little as Denis. From the time the boys left till we got to the lawyer's office he moved like a zombie; he just ate, drank and dressed without saying a word, and I gave up trying to comfort him because it was like talking to a dead man.

But now to the strange bits. Did you ever wonder why Nichol had asked for the will to be read before the funeral? You probably didn't notice when they finished with the poor old estate that the lawyer called me back. Nichol had made two secret bequests: a letter for me to be opened there and then, and a big bulky package for Denis not to be handed over till after the burial. The sight of the familiar writing made me howl like an idiot all over again and poor Mr. Sims had a terrible job getting me to quieten down.

Well.. . I've decided to write out the letter verbatim for you; I'm praying it will help to bring you back to us—He needs your friendship more than ever.

Here it is:

A Cheit, a gràidh.

When you read this, my sweetest daughter, I shall be— but no, Rasputin of Argyll was never one for the cliché! Never mind where I'll be, for there will be time enough for geography at our next meeting.

What is not me, however, will be on show at my erstwhile residence—God help the good name of Morningside if any of my spare parts decide to haunt it!—Nichol Ross's decomposing flesh will be there for his privileged friend, Denis Sellars, to see on the day of the interring. I want you, Kate, to make sure he gets a good look at the body. I do not care how many of the others find it too much, and want to remember me as I was etc. etc. (in better times Denis would add 'and all that emotional flatulence') but make sure that Denis stands and damn well stares.

In case you think these are the ravings of egregious conceit or terminal anoxia let me explain. Your young lover is about to set out on a great adventure, and you with him, for I know that the exquisite telepathy of true love (and I use these last two novelette-murdered words with conviction and precision) is already speeding faster than light between you, as I predicted one dark night when you stood beneath my hands on the memory of Montrose. The sandals of devotion will certainly speed you both in the right direction but as long as your mission lies this side of the Great Impostor Denis will require the armour of honesty which you already possess.

Yes, Kate, you have it. Have you ever watched the self-deceiving faces of younger people? Sixteen, twenty-five, thirty-four, what matter? They read and absorb and experience and debate and never for a minute gain the invaluable conception of their own mortality: 'Of course we'll all go sometime,' they say, but hardly a one is ever enlightened enough to know it. But you know it, Kate, you know what you are really seeing behind the first grey hairs and the swelling abdomens, and in my present incomplete state of illumination I am human enough to speculate on the details I have never asked of you. Was it a father, a mother —or someone even closer? But this at least I know—you have looked on something precious and seen that its true reality had fled; and from this experience you have truly realised the passing significance of your present status.

Hence the honesty I saw in you, and so to Denis. No matter what he has done, Denis Sellars has loved me with a deep filial love, and if I know him rightly, he will retreat into a state of shock when they tell you all that the cord is finally parted. Be sure he looks at me, and well: this last trust I place in your hands. For if he sees he will be changed, and his endeavours to expand the vision of the work which I bequeath to him will be all the more impassioned.

God bless you, and may you soon be workers of

sorcery, practitioners of the blessed Art I enjoyed in too small part because of my dark inhibiting self. But there are pieces of the Knowledge in my script; I leave the understanding of it to your love and open-minded honesty, the great interpreters.

Again God bless you, my rare queen: you are of the same fine Scottish womanstock as Jean Laidlaw, and to you I leave the keeping of our spiritual offspring.

Till we meet again, exhilarated by something even better than Connor's delectable amber.

I salute your womanhood and remain

Your Eternal Friend

Nichol Ross

. . . I often wondered why he had insisted that only the three of us plus Ronald, Carson, James and the Connor's lads should attend the funeral, and when that strange old scholar turned up at the house to take the service I didn't know what to think. Have you ever heard a funeral address like that, Murdo? Most of it was above my head, although it left me with a queer optimism that seemed both tranquil and exciting.

But before the service, while you were all having a drink downstairs, I managed to get Denis into the bedroom where Nichol was lying. We just stood there—the fine head looked so serene and relaxed in the sunshine—then I gave him a nudge and he walked over to the coffin. He placed his hand on Nichol's brow the way that the north-east folk often do, and my heart sank for a minute when he stepped back. Then he stood looking until I couldn't bear the quiet; I was almost waiting for Rasputin to rise up out of his cloak and give us one of his old sherrackings. Denis came back, walking with his eyes closed as if he was trying to write something on his mind, then he gave me a funny smile and we went downstairs.

At the cemetery I was so spellbound by our mysterious preacher that by the time it was all over and you had slipped away I had forgotten all about Nichol's letter. Then Mr. Sims walked across and gave Denis the package and it all came back.

He said nothing, but as we walked slowly back to the Canongate he started to whistle—after hardly speaking for three days. D'you remember what a magnificent evening it was? We've had some April warmth for once, but the town still has a spice far too exhilarating to be sweet, and you know that special feeling that the air has on your cheeks, and that golden skin on all the slates and stones. Just before we got home Denis gave a funny wee laugh: 'Kate,' he said. 'All of a sudden I don't feel so lost.' He banged the parcel with his hand and said, 'I've a feeling he's not finished with us yet.' He was into it as soon as we were inside the door. .. . for the past month we have been poring over it together. It's difficult to put any known literary label to it. It's about 250,000 words, in various prose styles and some free verse. In some passages which relate to his 'supernatural experiences' he uses obscure symbolic word-patterns which make me yearn for the simplicity of Finnegans Wake. In parts it is incredible autobiography, in others it's written as a novel in the third person, in others it's like a Platonic dialogue mixed with a glut of Oriental metaphysics. I've never seen anything like this in European literature before, and yet so much of it is difficult to grasp that I sometimes wonder if the old rascal is having us all on.

But Denis is convinced that there is a key to every passage, and much as I distrust my own critical faculties, I must confess that some of the simpler bits are already beginning to look like the plain sky-pieces of a fantastic jigsaw. I'm struggling daily with all my doubts and cynicism—it would be such a marvel if this work of Nichol Ross could vindicate his memory and enrich the letters of the world. Pray that we're not dreaming.

Now. I think we have one of the most important keys already, and you are about to read it. Denis is too proud to sanction the pleas that I've already written above, but he knows that I'm writing to you, and he gave his blessing to my including several passages of the letter that was enclosed with the manuscript, as a matter of fact he said you had a right to read them because of your own closeness to Nichol.

I'll go straight into it without boring you further. Here, then, is what we read that night of the funeral: the last written words, I believe, of our beloved father-figure.

Sunday morning
5 a.m.

Denis, a mhacan,

I have already written Kate and you have both seen me dropped into the moist spring soil, so to hell with pleasantries, and let us sit down to business. I still have a fierce undying belief in you, my son, and curse myself roundly for lacking the courage to tell you earlier the things I put on paper here and which I began in part in the Canongate last night.

. . . as a boy and youth I knew that I was different; my clairvoyant experiences had begun even then. Sometimes part of me appeared to move outside time and communicate with the departed, and once in a vivid dream I seemed to be carried on a moving cloud to a township further up Loch Fyne, where I hammered on the door of a friend. Later he told me that he had heard a sudden knocking that night, but had found nobody at the door. Somehow I never came to terms with these unusual faculties, and by the time I left school, like many Highland people I was tending to consider them an affliction.

Your mother and I met at our first University dance. She was a creature whose face and flesh would have set Michelangelo's hand trembling, whose subtle wit and transparent soul would have defied the combined descriptive talents of Proust and Tolstoy. For a year her presence banished every bleak feature of the North from my love-drunk eyes, for where she walked the gutters smelled of Persian summer, and around her bewitching laughter the very wind and sleet became heralds of infallible promise. And in her I found something even more wonderful; at times we could read each others' minds.

Then disaster. As you will see in this beautifully-written passage (pp 95-124) I was already creating, and receiving some considerable praise from our better critics. In a moment of thoughtless conceit I left Scotland on an utterly selfish quest, seeking greater experience and knowledge for my maturing talent, unaware that I was turning my back on the most precious catalyst that ever inspired the ingredients of word-alchemy into vital association. I set off for Europe with the usual glib bittersweet phrases, leaving Jean Laidlaw so broken-hearted that my eyes still smart as I write the cliché.

I realised my dreadful error soon enough, but my guilt and misery were partly recompensed by the fortunate and exciting new contacts I had made with some of the most avant-garde intelligences in Europe. The list of addresses is appended, ranging from Cracow to Salonika; use it well, for these minds are mentors without equal. Jean Laidlaw's letters stopped after months, but again my wounds of loss were soothed by the balm of self-knowledge which I was acquiring under my new tutors. At this stage of our century a new race of thinking Europeans had risen in revolt against the tyranny of materialistic philosophy, and a strange new society was forming behind all the horrors of Hitler. I listened to fantastic interpretations of the cosmic unity of mind and matter, of the traditions of reincarnation (which, some claimed, had actually been taught by Christ) on the revelatory statements which link Einstein, mystic poet and prophet—in Luxembourg I actually came across a psychiatrist who claimed to have developed a para-psychological time machine which had given him access to prehistoric civilisations more sophisticated than ours.

Like all truly great men, I am no sceptic, Denis: no matter how ridiculous a theory or personality seemed, I listened patiently, then the night's talk was recorded in my notebook. I described my experiences, and heard them explained in various ways by brilliant and liberal intelligences. One thing seemed crystal-clear: to the Truth-seeking saint all descriptions are incomplete metaphors, irrespective of his denomination, thus the true scientist, artist or philosopher and the truly religious man are all brothers under the different colours of their visionary skins. They are all men who know that the vilest weeds inhibiting growth in the Garden of Light are definitions and dogmas.

One word of warning. As often happens, when a wave of fresh knowledge washes the shore of human consciousness, it attracts wills intent on harnessing its energy for evil purposes. And so the Crusaders of Darkness, with all their foul Nietzschean and Wagnerian heritage, were studying the same terrain of knowledge as my friends, but out of the very opposite motives. Never forget their example, Denis: it is a terrible demonstration of how psychic energy can be so easily abused, in this case through the mediumistic power of a demoniac like Hitler. (I discuss this at length in pp. 165-174).

One night in Florence I fell into conversation with a delightful old Italian nobleman, a life-long psychical researcher. I had been in a rather bitter mood, describing the valiant struggles of the Scottish Renaissance in the knowledge that he had a strong current of Jacobite blood running in his own veins, when suddenly he said: 'You don't know how lucky you are, Nichol. I believe there are traditions left in your Highlands second-to-none in Europe.'

I asked him to explain. His knowledge of Celtic history and myth was as vast as his theory was incredible. The latter postulated that in terms of sensory awareness modern man was an angel fallen from a Golden Age when his psychic powers were completely uninhibited. One of the last functioning outposts of this era was situated in Central Asia; the religious insight it possessed was the superior antecedent of what are now oriental philosophies. This civilisation was devastated by some mysterious cataclysm, and some of the immediate descendants of its survivors became the Celts, who moved west in the first Aryan wave, their priests and people still retaining an inkling of their fathers' spiritual wisdom. Hence his conclusion: although sensitivity to natural phenomena is the heritage of all men, it has remained more fully-developed in pockets of the Celtic hinterland than anywhere else in Europe.

This all seemed ridiculous, and I said so, quoting for example our notable lack of mystics. But he was not to be deterred: although priest and church had been the enemies of man's true religious aspiration in Scotland and Ireland as much as anywhere else, there was not another corner of our sub-continent where a more natural and unbiased attitude still existed towards the unexplained mysteries of men and Nature, and where the materialistic standards of neo-Cartesian thinking had penetrated less. He then talked scathingly of the Celtic Romantic Revivalists whose facile and sentimental comments on pan-Gaelic mysticism had so thoroughly discredited the genuine stream of sensitivity flowing through these peoples.

We went on to discuss the clairvoyant in Barra who described the battle of Sherriffmuir blow-by-blow; the people of Boreray who had a dramatic vision of Culloden; Coinneach Odhar the wizard, the secrets of the fridh, *and that fascinating bardic class in the old clan system, the filidh, a class of seers who were considered superior even to poets and musicians. Listening to him, I felt as if a flame of intuition were bursting into light inside me, illuminating the shadowy reasons for my pride in my heritage, which had been far too long obscured from my natural eye through clouds of doubt and timorous logic.*

I stayed on in Italy for a year studying under this gentle soul, reading everything from the Bardo Thodol to the descriptions of modern 'Psi phenomena'. ..

... and yet something was still lacking. I had gained a wealth of knowledge but the steel of my resolve seemed to demand the fire of some personal experience in which it might be tempered to perfect conviction. When I returned to Scotland to find Jean Laidlaw married I realised too late what I had lost. Her twins were now eighteen months old, she was seeking solace from her rebound marriage in the bottle, and driving your respectable insensitive father mad. I was still arrogant enough to believe that I could redeem my betrayal of her; reluctantly she agreed to a clandestine meeting at Neidpath; yes, the very spot where you were infected by the invisible ghost of her despair. It was only too plain that this lovely, delicate creature still loved me, but she adored her children and felt honour-bound to her husband; when she finally refused to leave them I drove her to her car with a stream of filthy vituperative. The conflicts aroused by our meeting must have driven her over the verge of mental breakdown—the physical consequences of this are now tragic history.

For months I was mad. Dearly wishing to kill myself but somehow lacking the courage. I roamed the roads and cities of Europe, wood to ditch, tavern to police cell, a stricken murderer haunted by the brutal aphorism of Oscar Wilde which burned through my conscience like a sirocco: 'Yet all men kill the things they love' . . . and in this pit of darkness my precious learning fled from me.

The summer that Melville Sellars joined the army and abandoned his children I found myself half-alive on a small island in the Outer Hebrides, where a kind woman gave me board and shelter. Her face still haunts the sweetest corner of my memory: fissured, stained walnut with toil and time, yet as serene as a singing angel's. Fighting with her against the cruelty of the windswept island tundra I grew to love her, and often when her compassionate eyes looked into me I was near confessing the agony of my guilty soul.

She was visited one black night in September by two women of the township. Their husbands had been out fishing when the storm blew up and they were beginning to fear the worst. She bade them sit quite calmly, and I watched with them while she sat looking into the hearth in complete silence. Then in a few quiet sentences she reassured them: their men were safe in harbour further down the coast. They left her radiant, confident and hardly surprised; by morning her words were proved true. And so the following evening I poured out my own sorrow to this marvellous old witch, remembering with fresh understanding the conversation I had once had in Florence—here, sure enough, in this secluded backwater of "civilisation" ruled by the iron rod of the Mad Churches, I had stumbled on a simple woman whose powers of perception mocked the most modern techniques of science.

She described all manner of local cults and beliefs

which bore reference to my wider reading. Slowly and patiently her counsel healed my sickness; slowly and painfully my dead spirit revived, and my yearning for the Beyond returned. One night she was explaining to me how communication with the dead must be spontaneous and unforced, as the departed themselves are not mere slaves to be summoned at will. During this tranquil session by the fire I felt the undeniable presence of Jean Sellars, and slept peacefully for the first night since Neidpath...

... but by now Britain was involved in the Fascist bloodbath. Thanks to my linguistic talents I was granted a commission in the Intelligence Corps, and I spent several years commanding a schooner behind enemy lines in the Aegean. Here I found time and peace to write the lesser novels on which my reputation now stands, but at the same time I was fashioning out of my experience the draft of my life's work which rests now in your hands.

When I returned home in 1946 I was horrified to find that Mairi Iain Bhain was dead. Desperately though I tried I could find nobody of her calibre anywhere; the remote North seemed more bitter and defeated and cloth-ridden than ever. I still endeavoured to honour the example of my Continental masters, but while my experiences and learning continued, I was denied a real sense of fulfilment by two regrets: the loss of a lifetime with Jean Laidlaw, and my country's non-participation in the re-awakening of the great religious awareness which links Heisenberg, Brain and Einstein with Blake and Newton and all the great teachers of antiquity.

But at this stage I still didn't realise how universal are the seeds of this awareness. Don't listen for it in the mindless chants of congregations, Denis, or look for it in the crushed eyelids of the Pharisee. Try to observe your brothers and sisters with an almost unconscious fondness, then you will suddenly see flashes of magic: the modest face stroked to beauty by a boy's finger, the arthritic revived to supple youth under the wand of Mozart, the shepherd whose head becomes a royal thing as he watches his mountain under sunset. When you recognise such visions which brush and pen would only diminish, congratulate yourself and them: these are prophets who are wondering into and through and beyond the objects of their attention, and the love of God is being born and wooed and won. And through them our pathways will still lead Home when surplice and steeple have become the playthings of scholars' children . . .

. . . when I first met you and Rob I knew in a flash who you were, and some of the old pain returned. I saw so many of my own flaws in you, Denis: the religious warping, your distrust of affection, the bitter arrogance, the tragic philosophy that was once mine. I decided there and then to make amends, to father the fatherless, and how extraordinary was my delight to find that you were an imaginative writer, an applicant for initiation into the great brotherhood. Here in you my quest might be fulfilled. But let us not dwell again on failure, on Rob's prodigal wanderings, on all the selfishness and pride of the past winter through which you and I so nearly lost sight of each other. Courage, my true son, victory can still be yours and Mankind's! Scotland's and Europe's and the world's!

. . . Kate, Denis. Your finest secret, whose marvellous soul I sensed at the beginning. In our great spiritual revolution two Voices, in my opinion, have still to play

their part. I have dealt admirably with the role of the creative writer in pp. 217-240, but it is my contention that the Voice which should be harmonised with the artist's is that of Real Discovered Love, including the sexual, despite the bigots who deny its relevance. (The physical shape of the love-act is but a symbol of the movement between opposite and complementary poles which is the dynamic poem of the entire Universe).

We need love and the inspired pen desperately: they are two of our greatest tacticians in the war against (a) the pitiless materialism of modern society, where science is so often betrayed to the enemies of progress, and (b) the forces which threaten to debase and distort man's recovering Godhead—the new sectarian-isms including Spiritualism itself, hallucinogenic drugs, the purposeless modishness of pop-yoga. I often feel that if only the atomic scientists who rule our world could be taught the arts of loving, we would fear Bomb, Kremlin and Pentagon no longer. The communicating-centres of emotion are capable of releasing a greater finer energy than that of our very sun.

Seek this paradox, son, wherein fleshly and spiritual elements of man and woman so overwhelm each other that their personalities are drowned in a sea of greater sensation, wider existence, plunged in a fathomless light where all opposites like themselves are made One. This indeed, is another route... I know. Seek it, then write it and write it. Your early terms will be crude, but ignore the jeers; take heart from the verbal sorcery of Joyce, the terrible communications of Dostoyevsky. Love Kate truly, and take your place beside her in the shining Crusade whose mission includes the reunification of East and West and the transmutation of the human soul! Look at the great lovers of print —what is the great constant binding them? Troilus and Cressida, Deirdre and Naoise, Daphnis and Chloe, Abelard and Heloise. Happiness? Not always. Tragedy? Not necessarily. Romance? Perish the evil word! THEY INSPIRED SOMEBODY TO SIT DOWN AND WRITE ABOUT THEM. Few things are greater than that.

Soldier on, Denis. God knows you are headstrong and foolish, but you are privileged, and between Kate and your hand there lurks a tongue of fire that the darkness cannot quench. Pick up your pen, remember Thornton Wilder's Bridge, and spit in the nihilist's face. ..

I think that's enough, Murdo. We have talked this manuscript over so often: sometimes in despair we write it off as the ravings of Nichol's overdeveloped imagination, but we always come back to it. What was, or is he? This incredible genius, who still seems a part of our love as surely as he writes the word so often. Crank or prophet, we need your help if we are to give his vision a hearing (how's that for a mixed metaphor?).

Denis is a bit sick of Scotland for the moment, and we're off to Europe next month. He intends to follow up some of Nichol's addresses, and he's managed to land a job teaching English in Trier—up the Mosel valley, on the border of Luxembourg. This suits us very well for there's a philosopher in Bastogne whom we are strongly recommended to see. Is this really me writing all this?

Anyway, just supposing the Celtic part of Nichol's dream is still valid how about taking over that aspect of the research? Just think, Mairi Iain Bhain lived only 20 miles from where you are now . . .

. . . Lisa and Rob have landed good cabaret jobs in Brussels, so it looks as if we will be seeing a good bit of them over the water. They're coming for supper to-morrow. Hackett is slowly recovering, but Stringtime has a very able new producer who's putting it over very well, pop an' a'. It all seems very far away now, but what the hell!—they're providing pleasant entertainment and that's what people seem to want. Nichol's actors and singers are all dispersed to the winds, poor loyal souls. Roll up your sleeves, boyo, maybe we can give them some greater ammunition some day!

. . . been writing for hours. I'd better stop. I know you'll come, so I'll plead no more. Let's all look to the great day when the full testament of Nichol Ross bursts into print. Stop laughing, MacAuley!

And think of the special clause he had for me. I'll bet you're wondering how that's coming on. Let me tell you a strange thing, Murdo. That's the one part of Nichol's letter I never doubted. I loved Denis honestly from the first night I saw him, and it's just grown and grown and grown. And now that he feels something similar we are getting closer in a way I describe all too clumsily, but it's there—you know, there are times I shudder with happy ignorance and pray that it won't change. God bless Nichol Ross. There are times like just now when I look at Denis sitting by the fire, and I almost feel as if I can get right inside his mind. . .

*

Bless you, Kate. Bless the chuckling bravado of the demondancing fireplace. Bless my City I'm leaving. Bless the last men of Connor's who are dying. Bless everybody.

Hellflames I no longer fear. Real or not. What a seven months, one day I'll write it. Was he mad or Christ? I'm sure he wasn't all mad. Sure of it. Again I am a man who means, but differently. Bye-bye, John, no more dialogues with you. Because all of a sudden you're dead. Dead under the shining bayonets of light-infantry that wait to drill on green lawns to the pure rhythm of littleboy's heart.

Aaah. Slippers and cool muscles. Again I mean. Not necessarily because of Nichol, though I'm intrigued by so many of his ideas. This theory of oriental-Celtic enlightenment could contain elements of truth: but I've heard of remarkable psychic developments among certain African citizens who would have had old Buddha and his succulent belly in the pot long before nirvana was properly discussed. I don't know it all yet. Much to do.

But everkiss from outhwit. Yes.

This I know. Nichol's script may achieve in the end little more than a few mad critics. Murdo may not come back. Scotland may putrefy, the North sea may curdle. But this I know. That when I thought of you I just couldn't do it. That you are mine and mine and mine. That you are sitting there as meaningful and as precious and as moving as the first bush that ever blossomed. That where the fire strays lecherous and slow on your high crown, where it flicks a finger over your blushing skin, where it showers glory along the hang of your kirtle, there is love and there is confident peace, there is not a little mercy.

Stuart MacGregor died in a car crash in Jamaica in 1973, aged thirty-seven. Following his death, a Stuart MacGregor Memorial Prize was established by Edinburgh's Department of Community Health.

In 1958, with Hamish Henderson, MacGregor co-founded the Edinburgh University Folk Society and was its first President.

He wrote a number of widely recorded folk songs about Edinburgh life including the humorous "Sandy Bell's Man" about dating medical students, and the romantic "Coshieville."

MacGregor's poetry appeared in an anthology published by Reprographia in 1970, *Four Points of a Saltire.*

This highly recommended volume featured the work of four Scottish poets, the others being Sorley MacLean, George Campbell Hay and William Neill.

MacGregor's two novels were *The Myrtle and Ivy* (1967) and *The Sinner* (1973), both set in the Edinburgh folk scene.

A radio play, *The Month of Mary Paterson*, was broadcast by BBC Scotland in 1968.